THE REUNION

At school Hannah and her three best friends, Laura, Jenny and Annabel, were known as The Inseparables. So when Laura calls out of the blue with the idea of holding a reunion, Hannah is excited at the prospect of seeing how the years have treated her contemporaries. But things soon turn sour when one of them is found dead, drowned in her own swimming pool...

Janet Tanner titles available from
Severn House Large Print

The Dark Side of Yesterday
Dangerous Deception
Porthminster Hall
The Penrose Treasure
No Hiding Place
Forgotten Destiny

THE REUNION

Janet Tanner

Severn House Large Print
London & New York

This first large print edition published 2009
in Great Britain and the USA by
SEVERN HOUSE PUBLISHERS LTD of
9-15 High Street, Sutton, Surrey, SM1 1DF.
First world regular print edition published 2007 by
Severn House Publishers Ltd., London and New York.

British Library Cataloguing in Publication Data

Tanner, Janet.
  The reunion
  1. Female friendship--Fiction. 2. Best friends--Fiction.
  3. Class reunions--Fiction. 4. Murder--Investigation--
  Fiction. 5. Detective and mystery stories. 6. Large type
  books.
  I. Title
  823.9'14-dc22

  ISBN-13: 978-0-7278-7794-9

Printed and bound in Great Britain by
MPG Books Ltd, Bodmin, Cornwall.

One

The Inseparables, they used to call us. And later, when we were in our final years at Mowbury Comprehensive, and *Charlie's Angels* was all the rage on television and the gorgeous Mr Golding was our Year Head and coach of the swimming squad – Martin's Mermaids. Martin was Mr Golding's first name, and the four of us were his relay team: Laura, backstroke; Jenny, breaststroke; Annabel, butterfly; and me, Hannah, front crawl. Annabel was the best individual swimmer amongst us, which was why she got to swim the fly leg – the rest of us struggled with it and floundered along like beached whales. But as a team we were pretty good and we won our fair share of medals at galas. We trained two evenings a week after school, and sometimes in the early mornings too, which meant being at the council pool by six a.m. But it was no hardship. We'd have done anything for Mr Golding – we all had the most massive crush on him.

That's almost twenty years ago now, but when I think of it, I can see it all as clearly as if it were just yesterday. The four of us ploughing up and down the twenty-five metre pool and Mr Golding in tracksuit and Speedo flip-flops standing on the side at the deep end, checking his stopwatch and yelling encouragement. By the time we finished we'd be breathless and glowing. I remember laughing with the others in the showers and emerging into shiny summer mornings, dressed in uniform ready for school, and bitterly cold nights when the frosty air turned our wet hair into icicles. Our parents would be waiting for us in the car park, heaters blasting to warm us through and I don't think I ever caught a single cold from that icy wet hair, even though it was long enough to tuck inside the collar of my parka. And after morning sessions we'd all pile into Mr Golding's big old estate car and he'd take us straight to school, stopping at the Greasy Spoon trailer that was parked in a lay-by on the main road back to town to buy us bacon sandwiches and sweet steaming coffee in polystyrene mugs.

In my memory they are still great days, happy days. I suppose there were the down times, but I remember only a few. There was the time when Mark and I broke up – we'd been dating for three whole weeks – and my dog Scooby died, both in the same weekend. I went into school with a cloud like Vesuvius erupting hanging over me, and Mr Golding said: 'This isn't at all like you, Hannah,' and I burst into tears, and he gave me his handkerchief and a hug. This was, after all, in the days when teachers were allowed to touch pupils without being branded perverts.

Then there was the blazing row Laura and Annabel had because Laura asked Annabel to give her an alibi so that she could go for a walk with a boy she'd met at the fair and whom her parents had forbidden her to see. When Laura's mother caught her redhanded coming back along the old railway line with the boy, she was as angry with Annabel for lying to her as she was with Laura for defying her. Annabel demanded that Laura own up to the fact that Annabel had lied at her request, but Laura, who was terrified of her mother, couldn't bring herself to. Things were very awkward for a few weeks; that incident came very close to breaking up our little gang.

Most crises seemed to centre around Annabel actually. She was the one who talked the rest of us into taking it in turns to slide down the banisters at school one afternoon. We thought all the teachers were in a staff meeting, but we were wrong. As each of us came hurtling down we were each greeted in the lower hall by a furious Miss Day. She was very strict; an English mistress from the days when our comprehensive was a grammar school, who still wore a chalk-stained black gown which billowed out around her so that she looked like a bat. She was hiding behind the stair well in the lower hall and none of us had the slightest inkling she was there until she stepped out, beckoned to each of us in turn to join her in hiding and wait for the next culprit. We all ended up with a detention on the hottest day of the year.

And once, not long before we left school, Annabel got in a terrible strop with Mr Golding. He'd taken her aside to have a go at her about something – they were sitting in his car for ages talking, and afterwards Annabel tossed her head and flounced off whenever she saw him coming in her direction. We assumed her recent attitude to training was behind it – she'd been missing sessions and we'd come only third in a race we should have won easily – but Annabel was too proud to admit that she'd been torn off a strip. Laura, Jenny and I were really worried that she'd be kicked off the team and one of us would have to swim the fly leg. But it all blew over eventually.

Mostly, though, when I look back, I remember only the good times. The carefree, happy days, when the worst that could happen was that we'd get an unexpected maths test, or one of our swim team would go down with a bug just before an important gala, or Becky Westbrook would tag along and try to butt into our private discussions – we all felt sorry for Becky, because her mother had died, but she just wasn't one of us. Perhaps I was naïve, but I honestly never realized what tensions were fomenting beneath the surface, and I had no idea of the secrets that friends I'd have sworn I knew almost as well as I knew myself were keeping. Certainly I had no premonition that twenty years into the future those tensions and secrets would be resurrected and not only destroy illusions but also result in violence and tragedy.

But I'm going too fast. If I am to make any sense of what happened and come to terms with it, I have to start at the beginning.

And that, of course, was the reunion.

When I got the phone call from Laura, I was surprised – and pleased. We'd always kept in touch, exchanging Christmas cards every year without fail, and at one time, when I went home, we'd meet up for a coffee. Laura had married Mark – the boy who had briefly broken my heart – and they still lived a few miles outside Mowbury, where we'd all gone to school. But after my parents retired to Devon I had no reason to go to Mowbury any more, and it was a good five years since I'd last seen Laura. I recognized her voice at once, though – vibrant, bubbly, as full of life and laughter as it had been when we were Martin's Mermaids.

'Laura! What a surprise!'

'I know. It's been ages. How are you, Hannah?'

'Fine.' That wasn't quite true. I was going through a bit of a bad patch. I'd recently been made Head of Department at the school where I taught Geography and I was finding it more stressful than I'd ever imagined it would be, trying to balance my new responsibilities with doing my best for the pupils in my classes and sorting out problems with disgruntled staff. Added to that I was having to put my house on the market and find somewhere else to live.

It was two years now since David and I had broken up – a fairly amicable split when we'd both agreed that we really didn't want to be married any more, though it had undermined my confidence more than I cared to admit. At the time David had been working in the States – a secondment from the British end of the aero-engineering firm he worked for – and he'd been content to let me stay on in the marital home. Now, though, he was not only back in England, but he also had a new lady in his life whom he wanted to set up home with, so the time had come for dividing up the spoils. I knew I'd been fortunate that I'd been able to stay on so long in the pleasant, four-bedroom detached that we'd bought with such high hopes of making it a family home, and I had no wish to make for unpleasantness now by digging my heels in. It wasn't easy finding something to replace it at a price I could afford, and sorting out our shared belongings was pretty stressful too.

I wasn't about to unload all my worries on to Laura over the phone, though, especially when I hadn't seen her in so long, so I simply said, 'Fine. And you...?'

'Yes. Fine.' Laura's bright tone could have been concealing anything too. She'd always been the cheery optimist, but also a bit secretive and slow to confide problems even when we were close. Now we were virtual strangers, our shared past the only thing we had in common.

'The reason I'm ringing, Hannah, is it's eighteen years this summer since we left school. And we're trying to arrange a reunion. Just our year and some of the staff. I've already talked to Jenny – she's moved back to Mowbury, would you believe – and she's going to help me track down the girls. And Mark and Ian Crane are trying to get in touch with the boys. It's going to be a huge job – so many people have moved away – scattered to the four corners of the earth, really – but we're going to do our best to find as many as we can. What do you think? Are you up for it?'

'Yes, of course. It would be fun to see everyone again – find out how things turned

11

out for them. When are you planning it?'

'We thought July, to coincide with the last time we were all together. Do you remember all the parties we had that summer, because we'd all be going our separate ways come autumn?'

'As if I could forget!'

Endless sunny days going for long bicycle rides through leafy country lanes; congregating at one another's houses to laze on someone's lawn, laughing and chatting the hours away; even a grown-up dinner party when Annabel's mother cooked us beef bourguignon and lemon meringue pie and we all dressed up; the girls in their prettiest frocks and the boys in suits and ties instead of our usual casual uniform of shorts and tee-shirts. Not the whole class, of course – just Laura and Jenny and Annabel and me, and the boys who made up our circle – Mark, Ian, Sean (known for some reason as Stan) and Peter. Occasionally we included Becky – the girl whose mother had died – and Tristan Forrester, who'd been badly bullied and seemed to have no friends of his own, because we felt sorry for them. But mostly it was just our close-knit little group. Alliances sometimes changing, pairings happening and breaking up, but basically Martin's Mermaids and the gang of boys we became friendly with when we graduated to the sixth form. Already I was rather wishing

12

the reunion would be confined to our own special crowd, but clearly what Laura was planning was on a much grander scale, and I supposed that was only right. A reunion of our year had to be open to everyone.

'We thought we'd make a whole day of it – maybe even a weekend,' Laura said. 'A tour of the old school in the afternoon, perhaps. There have been so many alterations since we were there. And then a gala gathering at The Beeches.'

The Beeches was the best local hotel, a lovely old house set in extensive grounds with the sort of facilities that allowed them to cater for weddings, corporate Christmas dinners and Masonic Lodge Ladies' Nights. They'd expanded recently, too, Laura explained, increasing their capacity for residents by converting what had once been a stable block into a dozen luxury rooms.

'I'd imagine a lot of people coming from far away will stay there,' Laura said. 'So the merry-making will probably go on till the Sunday too.'

'I'd better make a booking right away then,' I said.

'Oh, there's no need for that! You can stay with us, Hannah. We've got absolutely bags of room.'

They did, I knew. Mark had done extremely well for himself by going into, and revitalizing, the family haulage business, and he

13

and Laura had bought the Old Vicarage, a rambling, ivy-covered house that had been built in the days when the vicar had dozens of children and standing in the community and was expected to host garden parties on the lawns. They'd modernized it; put in damp courses, under-floor heating and en suite bathrooms; bought a ride-on mower for the lawns, laid ornamental gravel on the old cracked drive and even installed a swimming pool. When I'd last visited there'd been floor-length curtains at the big bay windows, deep shagpile carpet in a dangerously pale neutral shade in the living room and polished solid oak flooring in the hall. And no children to mess it up. No dogs to leave muddy paw-prints or make the carpets smell, no cats to deposit spent fur on the brocaded sofas or hide the remains of small rodents and birds beneath the granite island in the fitted kitchen. Luxury, pure unadulterated luxury. But I didn't think I'd feel comfortable staying there. Laura would be the perfect hostess, I felt sure, but we weren't that close any more.

'That's really kind, but I couldn't put you to that trouble, Laura,' I said hastily. 'You'll have more than enough on your plate with all the organization for the reunion. I'll book myself in at The Beeches. For the week, probably. I might as well make a proper break while I'm there and look up old haunts.'

'Well, it's up to you – but the offer's there.'

'I know. And thanks again. Now – is there anybody I can help you with? I ran into Tristan – at Bristol Airport of all places! He's living in Germany now. Working for some multinational drug company.'

'*Tristan* is? Good lord!'

'I know. Who'd have thought it? You'd have expected him to be an accountant or a local government officer, wouldn't you? But no. Deutschland. I've got his card somewhere. He insisted on giving it to me.'

Laura laughed. 'Tristan would! He was always trying to worm his way into our crowd, do you remember?'

'I know. He didn't seem to have any friends of his own. I felt sorry for him actually.'

'I know you did, but he gave me the creeps.'

I knew what she meant. There had been something slimy about Tristan. Lanky, too thin by half for his height, with owlish glasses and acne, he was probably the brightest boy in the class. But he'd been too eager to make friends, always trying too hard to be nice. Turn around and there, right behind you, would be Tristan, smiling his sickly smile and making remarks that he thought were clever and the rest of us thought were stupid.

I'd been surprised at the change in him, though, when I'd bumped into him at the airport. He'd grown into himself somehow, the glasses now made him look distinguished rather than nerdy and he'd filled out so that he looked trim and athletic instead of a skinny beanpole. In his expensively cut suit and carrying a briefcase that probably contained a laptop, he'd been every inch the successful businessman. But the over-eagerness hadn't changed. He'd kissed me on both cheeks in the Continental manner and pressed his business card on me with a plea to keep in touch. I'd said I would, but actually I'd been rather relieved when his flight was called and I was able to escape him. It was ever thus!

'Well, we can't really leave him out,' I said.

'No, of course not.' Laura sighed. 'You'd better let me have his contact details.'

We went on chatting about arrangements for a few minutes and as we did so I was searching the myriad pockets of my bag until I found Tristan's card, tucked in between my little mirror and some old duty-free receipts. I relayed his telephone number and e-mail address to Laura, relieved that it was she, not me, who had taken on the mammoth task of getting our old classmates together.

She rang off, promising to be in touch soon, and I went back to sorting out the problems that were complicating my life. And apart from booking myself a room at The Beeches for the week in question I more or less forgot about the reunion for the time being.

Laura, however, had no intention of letting me get off so lightly. Over the coming months cyberspace hummed as she e-mailed me, keeping me up to date with the former classmates and the teachers she had managed to track down.

'Found Miss Day. She's in a Residential Home. Bet she's giving them hell!'

'Mr Golding is definitely coming. He's still teaching at the old school. Married with three children!'

That set me thinking, and remembering how we'd hero-worshipped him. Martin Golding had seemed totally out of reach in those days; now I realized the age difference between us wasn't as great as it had seemed then, when he'd been a teacher and we were his pupils. But he had probably only been in his early twenties – Mowbury Comprehensive had been his first teaching post after he'd finished college – and in the intervening years we'd gone some way to catching him up. David, my ex, had his fortieth birthday just before we split up; it was entirely possible Martin Golding and he were much about the same age. Bizarre!

The next e-mail I got from Laura was a plea.

'Any idea what happened to Aaron Flynn?

Nobody seems to know where he is. We can't have a reunion without Aaron!'

I knew exactly what she meant. Aaron, strangely enough, had been the one I'd been really looking forward to seeing again. Strangely, because he'd been the bad boy, a law unto himself, the one we'd all have liked to be like if we'd dared. And perhaps not strange at all, because he'd been the most interesting ... let's face it, the most exciting.

The rest of us came from dull, respectable backgrounds; Aaron had a mother with a racy reputation that was whispered about, and no father in evidence. Some people said he was in prison, others that he'd walked out on Aaron's mother before he was born – that they'd never been married even. Unlikely as it sounds today, that was quite a cause for gossip in a small town like ours twenty years ago. Aaron was very dark and swarthy, like a gypsy or someone with Mediterranean blood, and since his mother was small and fair we assumed he got it from the father none of us had ever seen.

Aaron was a rebel. He skipped classes and got into fights and spent a great deal of time outside the head's study waiting to be disciplined for something or other. Teachers predicted he'd come to a bad end. But there was another side to him too. One of the fights he'd got into had been on my account. Some boys from the year above ours had cornered me and one of them was, not to put too fine a point on it, molesting me. Aaron happened to come past, saw what was happening, and laid into him. I escaped and Aaron got yet another detention although I spoke up for him. Authority figures always chose to believe the worst of Aaron, but I thought he was a hero; a sort of Robin Hood figure. A little bit dangerous, a little bit romantic, and a whole lot of fun. Out of bounds, but very attractive.

No, I'd definitely been looking forward to seeing Aaron and discovering how he'd turned out, but I wasn't altogether surprised no one knew what had become of him. I wasn't even sure that reunions would be his style, or if he'd want to come, even if someone did manage to locate him and let him know about it. Always in trouble, as he had been in the past, I couldn't imagine his schooldays had been the happiest days of his life. But I was regretful, all the same, that we'd be robbed of the opportunity to find out if he'd become as colourful a man as he had been a boy. Whether he'd ended up in jail or made a million. Surely it would be one or the other. I couldn't imagine Aaron having an ordinary, mundane life. If he *was* still alive, because it occurred to me that he was also the type to live hard and die young. Perhaps that was the reason no one knew what had become of him. Because he'd been killed in a road accident or some sort of violence that had got out of hand. The thought made me very sad, and I put it to the back of my mind, along, it has to be said, with most thoughts of the reunion.

I had enough to think about that spring sorting out the present and the future without worrying about the past. My job was keeping me fully occupied all week, and Saturdays and Sundays were spent making my house respectable for prospective buyers, and viewing properties that would be within my price range when David and I finally sold and split the proceeds.

To be honest, it was a depressing business. Nothing I looked at was quite right and I knew that half the trouble was that I'd been spoiled. I'd got used to space as well as convenience, and I found the rooms in the houses I looked at claustrophobically small, and the walls separating them from their neighbours worryingly thin. I didn't want to be cooped up in a little box with the neighbours' television for company; I didn't want to have to get rid of half my furniture and kitchen gadgets; I didn't want to move so far out of town that I'd face hours in traffic jams getting to and from work. But it didn't look as though I had much choice. David was becoming impatient, and I could hardly blame him.

In the end I settled on a cottage, the

middle one of a rank of three that had originally been built for farm workers in a village about nine miles out of town. The front door opened directly into a miniscule living room – my cream leather corner sofa and reclining chair with footstool would definitely have to go – and I'd have to rely on a septic tank because no mains sewage had ever been laid. But the walls were solid stone, about a foot thick, and there was a long strip of garden at the rear that graduated from lawn and flowerbeds through a vegetable plot to rows of well-established fruit bushes and a small orchard at the far end. Over the wall was a farmer's field with a herd of cows and a docile-looking bull. I'd never grown vegetables, but I rather liked the idea of giving it a go.

My offer was accepted and buyers materialized for my house. Things were moving now with astonishing speed. We completed on both deals and I moved into my new home two weeks before the date of the re-union. There were still packing cases un-touched in the tiny spare bedroom when I set out for Mowbury, and I was torn between frustration that they'd have to linger there for another week, and relief that I had the perfect excuse to turn my back on them and take the break that I thought I'd earned.

I locked the door just after five on the Friday afternoon, a little uncomfortable that there was no burglar alarm to set, though I wasn't sure what the neighbours would make of it if I had one fitted. The box would stand out like a sore thumb under the low, uniform eaves, and I could imagine they might well be scornful. 'You don't need that sort of thing out here. We all look out for one another.' I could hear them already. One set were middle-aged, the other positively elderly, and as far as I could make out they had lived here all their married lives, though their families had long since flown the nest.

I put my big squashy holdall in the boot of my car and set off along the lanes in the direction of the motorway feeling cheerful and enthusiastic if a little apprehensive at the thought of revisiting my past. But I had not the slightest premonition that the weekend ahead of me would turn into a nightmare. That it would not only open a Pandora's box of secrets, but also bring me face to face with dilemmas and divided loyalties, not to mention violent death and danger.

And that ultimately it would change my life for ever.

Two

The Beeches, as Laura had said, had undergone an impressive makeover some time during the last ten years – she would never have chosen it for the reunion otherwise. I remembered the place as shabby and run down, with trees and hedges overhanging the road and almost obscuring the peeling sign that had advertised 'B&B. Bar Snacks. Home Cooked Food'. I'd only ever set foot inside once – when my father had retired after forty years as a wages clerk for a local timber merchant, and they'd unwisely held his farewell party there. I remembered dark, narrow passages, an equally dim bar with ring-marked tables and rickety stools, and a draughty conservatory that looked as if it might lose its roof in a high wind.

That had all changed now, though. The reception area was bright and welcoming and the bar – much bigger than I remembered it – was old-world picturesque rather than depressingly dingy. The conservatory roof had been repaired, the old plastic furniture replaced with modern rattan, and it now looked out on to landscaped lawns and well-pruned shrubs instead of the tangled wilderness that had threatened to engulf it.

As for my room, I'd been allocated one in the newly converted stable block, and it was everything I could have wished for – tastefully furnished, with plenty of drawers and wardrobe space and a range of toiletries arranged along a shelf in the bathroom, which boasted a power shower. The window looked out on to the drive, which curved round the house to the main hotel entrance, and I rather liked that. I'd be able to see guests arriving and see if I could recognize them rather than suddenly being confronted with them in a crowded room.

In fact, of course, I had better things to do than stand at the window spying on cars that might be delivering ex-classmates. By the time I'd unpacked and had a shower it was almost six thirty and time to get ready to go to Laura's for a private get-together she'd organized just for Martin's Mermaids.

'We're never going to get enough time to catch up at the main reunion,' she'd said. 'With everyone else there, it's going to be chaos. I'll do supper on Friday evening and we can have a girlie night, just the four of us. It'll be like old times.'

'What about Mark?' I'd asked.

'Oh, Mark can go over to The Beeches for the evening,' Laura had said airily. 'Peter and

24

Stan are both staying there, and Mark and Ian can go and prop up the bar with them and have their own get-together.'

I have to say I was actually looking forward to our girlie night rather more than to the actual reunion. Catching up with the three girls who had been my closest friends was a great deal more appealing than making small talk with people I hadn't seen in almost twenty years and had never been that close to.

I chose a casual flippy skirt and camisole – chose? I'd only brought with me the things I'd planned to wear – then combed through my still-damp hair and put on a slick of lip gel and mascara. A quick glance in the mirror reassured me that I looked presentable. Older than they'd remember me, yes, of course. My hair cut now in a sharp bob instead of shoulder-length. And two whole dress sizes smaller than I'd used to be. I'd struggled for years to lose that weight, and then to keep it off. I'd never been fat, exactly, but I had been pretty solid. Swimming freestyle builds muscle – I'd worried about the size of my thighs and my shoulders. But now a good diet and sensible exercise had slimmed me down to an athletic shape I was secretly rather proud of. I grabbed a jacket, my bag and keys and headed out to my car, hoping I didn't bump into somebody I should recognize but might not. Having a room in the new stable block was a distinct advantage – it meant I didn't have to run the gauntlet of the reception area where people might be checking in, and the open plan bar where they could already be congregating for celebratory drinks, for all I knew. From what I remembered of the boys in our year, I could imagine congregating at the bar would very likely play a pivotal part in the weekend's programme.

The car park was only a few yards from my door, spreading from a narrow hard-standing into what had once been a copse, mainly cleared now, but with enough trees remaining to afford some shade on a hot day and the impression of graciousness rather than regimentation. To my relief, the only people I could see were an elderly lady and a younger man who, from the way he was supporting her on his arm and matching his pace to hers, was most likely her son or grandson. Clearly it was nobody connected with the reunion – unless the elderly lady was one of our teachers. The sudden thought shocked me a bit – to realize that some of those imperious dragons who had put the fear of God into me when I first went to the school could now be old and frail was a horrible reminder of the mortality of all of us. But the pair were some way off, walking in the same direction as I was, and they'd already passed the spot where my car was parked. If the woman was

Miss Day, let out from her residential home for the weekend, or Mrs Spearman or any of my other former members of staff, I was going to have to wait until tomorrow to find out.

If I'd thought I was going to escape without bumping into anyone, though, I was mistaken. As I unlocked my car a voice from behind me made me almost jump out of my skin.

'Hannah! How lovely to see you!'

I spun round. Tristan Forrester. Well, who else would it be? Typical of Tristan to creep up behind me like that, typical of my luck that of all the people I could have run into in the car park, it should be him.

'We really must stop meeting like this!' His tone was jocular but faintly suggestive, smooth as the silk shirt and suede shoes he was wearing.

'Like *what*?' I asked, a little tartly, and added: 'Hello, Tristan.'

'Airports – car parks...' He shrugged elegantly, smiled that smarmy smile. 'It was so fortunate we ran into each other that day, otherwise Laura might not have known where to find me.' Another sleek smile. 'I understand I have you to thank for pointing her in the right direction.'

More fool me...!

'I'm glad you were able to come,' I lied.

'I wouldn't have missed it for the world. I

27

flew in this afternoon. And now...' He laid a hand on my arm. *Actually laid a hand on my arm!* 'You are looking lovely, Hannah, I must say.'

I tried to back away – he was making my flesh creep – but really there was nowhere to go and I couldn't open my car door without physically thrusting him out of the way, which seemed unnecessarily rude.

'Thanks,' I said, jiggling my keys, willing him to remove his hand from my arm.

'Now, here's a suggestion I hope you'll find agreeable. I'm going into the bar to buy a bottle of the best wine they have in this rather God-forsaken place, and enjoy! So why don't you come too and share it with me?'

Oh-my-god! In your dreams...

'That's very kind of you, Tristan,' I said, 'but actually I am on my way to Laura's. We're having a girlie get-together – Laura, Jenny, Annabel and me.'

'Ah.' The smile faltered for a moment, then was back in place like a mask. 'Some other time then, perhaps.'

'Yes ... lovely...'

Coward. Why don't you tell him you'd rather leap stark naked into an alligator infested swamp...?

Someone else was heading across the car park rather purposefully and waving at us. My initial relief at the prospect of being

28

rescued from the appalling Tristan turned to dismay as I recognized Becky Westbrook. Nearly twenty years might have elapsed since I'd last seen her, and she'd put on a good couple of stone in weight, but there was no mistaking that rather pudgy face, pale freckled skin and carroty hair. As reunions went, this was really not turning out very well. The first two people I'd been reunited with were two whom I wouldn't care if I never saw again.

'It's Becky. Perhaps she'd like to help you drink your bottle of wine!' I said disingenuously – and rather wickedly.

That wiped the smile off Tristan's face – almost. It looked decidedly forced as he held out his hand to Becky.

'Good gracious! This is quite surreal...'

Becky practically ignored him. She was a little out of breath and patches of unbecoming scarlet stained her pale face and neck. The trot across the car park carrying all that extra weight had obviously taxed her.

'I saw you heading for the car park, Hannah. And I thought – I bet she's going to Laura's – that's lucky! If I can catch her, we can go together. It'll save taking two cars – yes?'

'You're going to Laura's?' I was miffed, to say the least of it.

'Yes, she is so good, isn't she, organizing all this? But then, that's Laura all over...'

'I'll leave you girls to it then.' Tristan treated me to yet another sickly smile and glided
off in the direction of the hotel.

'This is a surprise,' I said to Becky. 'I didn't
realize you...'

'But it makes sense to go together, doesn't
it?' she persisted.

'Well, yes ... I suppose so...'

'Your car or mine?'

Since we were standing right beside my
unlocked car it seemed a superfluous question. And in any case, I had even less desire
to be chauffeured by Becky, who might, for
all I knew, be the world's worst driver, than I
had to have her as a passenger.

'Might as well be mine,' I said with bad
grace. I had been looking forward to a
private catch-up with the girls who had been
my closest friends, and now Becky had
muscled in. Some things never changed.

'It was actually Mark who asked if I would
like to be included in the exclusive gathering,' Becky said rather smugly, as if she had
read my thoughts. She was settling into the
front passenger seat, yanking at the seat belt
to make it stretch round her ample frame.

'Mark? But Mark's not going to be there...'

'No, he's meeting up with the boys here.'
Becky seemed remarkably well-informed.
'But when he realized Laura had forgotten to
include me in the girls' get-together, he
insisted I should come along.'

'How did you come to see Mark?' The question was out before I could stop it.

'Oh, I often see Mark.' Becky sounded smug again. 'Not as much as I used to, of course, when I was his PA.'

'You were Mark's PA?'

'Oh, yes – for about a year. I was made redundant by the company I was working for, and he offered me a job. He is such a kind person. I mean – I was well qualified, of course – I did a really good secretarial course after we left school – but all the same, there are plenty of people who wouldn't lift a finger to help an old friend. They'd rather do you down. Not Mark. I'm not even sure that job really existed before he found out I was unemployed.'

'But you're not working for him now.' I was negotiating my way out of the car park, waiting for passing traffic before turning out on to the main road.

'No. As I say, for one thing I suspected he invented the post to help me out of a hole, and for another—' She broke off, swivelling to look after a car that had turned into The Beeches, passing us in the entrance to the drive. 'Was that Aaron?'

'I don't know, was it?' I had been concentrating on the traffic on the main road; now I looked over my shoulder, a little too eagerly, but I could see only the rear of a silver hatch turning into the car park.

'I'm sure that was him!' Becky glanced up and down the road. 'It's all clear. You can go now.'

I pulled out, resisting the temptation to tell her I could see perfectly well for myself. 'So you were saying,' I said instead, 'you aren't working for Mark any more.'

'No, I'm in local government. The recycling department, actually. Very green. They even had horse-drawn collection vehicles when I first went there, though they've replaced them now with lorries. Too many complaints that they were holding up the traffic. But at least they were *civilized* complaints. Not like the protests we had at Calvin Transport.'

I frowned. 'What on earth do you mean?'

'Oh...' Becky gave a little laugh. 'That was the other reason I decided it was time for a change. It got a bit hairy at times at Calvin Transport. The animal rights lobby making things difficult – you know.'

'No.' I was intrigued. 'I don't know what you're talking about, Becky.'

'Oh – I thought Laura would have told you ... Mark took on a contract delivering foodstuffs for Mowbury Poultry – you know, the battery farm on the Bath road? Well, the animal rights people have had their sights set on the place for some time, doing everything they can to get it shut down. They target everybody connected with the farm –

suppliers, contractors – any connection at all. It really wasn't very pleasant – we had all kinds of disgusting things dumped on the office doorstep, there were threatening phone calls, we even had to be careful opening the mail because we never knew what might be inside a package.'

'No! And is this still going on?' I asked, horrified.

'I wouldn't know. As I said, I don't work there any more. And that is one thing about being with Calvin Transport that I really don't miss.'

'I'm not surprised! That is just awful!' A thought struck me. 'If you're living locally, why are you staying at The Beeches?'

'I am seven miles away. And in any case, I thought it would be nice to be at the hub of things. Feel a part of it all.'

Typical, I thought. That was Becky. Desperate to be in on the action, desperate not to be left out. Always trying too hard, and thereby only managing to distance herself further, turning herself into a target for derision and pity rather than achieving her objective. And then I thought of her left motherless at fourteen and felt ashamed of myself, an echo of the same guilt I'd felt in those long-ago days when I'd resented her for butting in to our close-knit quartet.

I'd had a happy home, the best parents any girl could wish for, a brother and a sister, a dog, two cats, a hamster and a goldfish. I'd been blessed with three brilliant friends and a talent for swimming. Becky had none of these things. After her mother had died suddenly she'd been taken into care and lived in a succession of foster homes. I should have been more generous – been glad to allow her to share some of my abundance of good fortune. I should be more generous now. Clearly Mark and Laura had been good to her. That I was as impatient of her now as I had been then didn't make me a very nice person, and I was not proud of myself for wishing she was anywhere but here, in my car, on the way to Laura's.

'Here we are – this is the turning.' Becky pointed to a lane marked with a 'No Through Road' sign, and, biting my tongue hard to keep myself from saying I knew very well where Laura lived, I resolved to try to be nicer to poor, unfortunate Becky.

There were several cars drawn up on the gravel run-around in front of the Old Rectory – presumably some of the other girls had beaten us to it, as I couldn't imagine all of them belonged to Laura and Mark, affluent though they were.

As Becky and I got out of my car the front door of the house opened and Mark came out. In his dark indigo jeans – neatly pressed – white shirt and expensive-looking loafers he looked as handsome as ever, maybe even more so. His hair had receded a little at the temples, true, but the short-all-over cut made that unimportant, and the bit of weight he'd put on suited him. He looked fit, healthy and prosperous, as befitted a successful businessman.

'Hannah,' he greeted me. 'Great to see you! It's been far too long.'

'Good to see you too, Mark.'

'And Becky.' His glance slid over her, slid away again, displaying something that fell short of enthusiasm.

'Surprise – I made it you see!' She sounded a little breathless again, a little too eager, and I couldn't help but notice she had gone a bit pink.

So – Becky still had a thing for Mark, I thought. She'd been keen on him in the old days, I knew, even more anxious to insinuate herself into our group when he was with us than she had been when it was just we girls. It hadn't surprised me then – most of the girls had fallen in love with him at one time or another, myself included – remember how heart-broken I'd been when he'd finished with me after just three glorious weeks that long-ago summer? The difference was that I'd got over him years ago. Becky clearly never had.

Briefly I wondered if that had more to do with her leaving Calvin Transport than any of the other reasons she'd given me. I couldn't imagine she'd have been put off by thinking the job had been created especially for her or by the animal rights campaigners, or that she could have been wooed away by the Council Recycling Department if there hadn't been some kind of a problem between her and Mark. More likely she'd thought that him giving her a job meant she stood a chance with him, and she'd said or done something that had embarrassed them both. The one thing I was absolutely certain of, though, was that it hadn't been the other way around. Mark would never come on to Becky in a million years. The only puzzling thing was why he'd been the one to invite her along tonight, knowing, as he must have done, that none of the rest of us would really want her. But then, she'd probably placed him in an impossible position. He, man-like, had let slip without thinking that we four were getting together, and she'd asked if she could come too. Mark was too soft-hearted to have refused outright, and not quick-thinking enough to come up with an excuse.

Now he pushed the front door open again, holding it wide for us.

'Go on in. Annabel's already here.' He nodded in the direction of a dark green open-top sports car, parked at a rakish angle. 'Nice wheels she's got, too!'

'That one's Annabel's?'

'Oh, yes. I'm hoping against hope Laura doesn't see it. If she does, she won't be satisfied until she gets one just like it, and that, I should think, will set me back the best part of twenty-five grand.'

I shook my head ruefully, dismissing the five-year-old Renault that was the best my salary could run to. 'How the other half live!'

'Go on, you wouldn't change what you do for the world. Teaching those horrible kids is your life.'

'They're not horrible! At least, not all of them.'

Laura must have heard our voices. She suddenly erupted into the hall, a glass of wine in one hand and a cigarette in the other.

'Hannah! Oh, Hannah!' She rushed towards me and tried to hug me – impossible with both hands occupied. 'Oh, take this!' She thrust the wine glass at Mark, and managed a one-handed embrace.

'Put your cigarette out, that's the answer. And what are you doing, anyway, smoking in the house?' Mark sounded good-humoured enough, but at the same time exasperated.

'I know ... I know ... but it's a special occasion, and I intend to enjoy myself!' Vivacious as ever, Laura tossed the cigarette on to the flower bed outside the door and retrieved her glass of wine from Mark. 'Come on in, girls. I don't know why you're still here, Mark. Ian and Stan will be wondering where the hell you are. And we girls want some quality time in a man-free zone, isn't that right, Hannah?'

'Right.' I threw a wry, apologetic look at Mark, and went inside. Becky followed.

'We're in the kitchen,' Laura called after us. 'Why does everyone always congregate in the kitchen?'

'Because that's usually where the booze and the food is.' Annabel was leaning against Laura's granite work island, chewing on a carrot baton. She looked great – much slimmer than I remembered her, tanned, and...

'Annabel, you've gone blonde!'

'Oh, just highlights, darling.'

'Highlights, my foot! You were–' it seemed a bit much to say 'mousey' to anyone, even as old a friend as Annabel – 'brown. Definitely brown.'

'Was I? It's such a long time ago. It feels like I've been this colour for ever.'

'Annabel,' Laura said, 'has a very glamorous life. She's put the rest of us to shame.'

'What do you do then?' I asked, thinking blonde highlights, St Tropez tan, very expensive sports car...

'Oh, I'm just a solicitor.'

A solicitor! Last time I'd heard, Annabel had been a general dogsbody in ... yes, a solicitor's office.

'How did that happen?' I asked.

'They paid for me to go to college. I did my articles with Browne, Browne and Timpson.'

It was the local firm she'd joined straight from school.

'And now she's a junior partner with a *very* upmarket firm in London,' Laura finished for her. 'Specializing in family law. You wouldn't believe the people she's got on her client list! Really famous – uh? Oh, look – I'm being a terrible hostess. What are you going to have to drink, Hannah? I've just opened a bottle of Chablis, and there is fruit punch if you must, but I've got a bottle of best bubbly on ice for later – we could open that, but I suppose we ought to wait until Jenny gets here...'

'Just a soft drink for me,' I said regretfully. 'I'm driving.'

'I'm not,' Becky put in triumphantly. 'I'd love a glass of Chablis.'

'Oh, have just one and then go on to the punch,' Laura pressed me. 'One can't do any harm, surely. And if you get stopped by the police, Annabel can always get you off.'

'I can't risk being breathalysed. And in any case, I thought you said Annabel specialized in family law.' I was still stunned by how well Annabel had done. Of all of us she was the one who'd done least work at school. 'Oh, all right, go on then – just the one. But then I'm definitely on the fruit punch.'

'Well...' Laura was dithering. 'You've absolutely got to have some champagne. This is a special occasion ... But I guess we can make it a Buck's Fizz with more orange juice than bubbly.'

She poured me a too-large glass of Chablis; I figured most of it would have to go down the sink when no one was looking. Not a very fitting fate for expensive wine, but I had no intention of falling foul of a roadside breathalyser test.

'Where *is* Jenny?' Laura refilled her own glass and slurped at it as if it were lemonade. 'Why is she always late? No – don't answer that. Playing mother hen to her ever-growing brood, I suppose. Do you know she has four now – and another on the way? But wouldn't you think that just this once that husband of hers could put them to bed? Jenny is just so ... frazzled.'

'That sounds like a car now,' Annabel offered. 'Could that be her?'

'I jolly well hope so! How can we have a reunion of Martin's Mermaids without Jenny?' Laura dumped her glass of wine on the counter and headed out along the hall.

'Where are you staying then, Annabel?' I asked. 'You're not at The Beeches, are you?'

'No. I'm at The Farm.'

'Ah.' The Farm. Not as in an agricultural undertaking or small-holding. The Farm as in Country Club and Health Spa, retreat for the well-heeled and B-list London celebrities – well, maybe A-list as well, for all I knew. Very expensive, very exclusive, set in acres and acres of grounds about six miles out of Mowbury. I had a feeling I'd read that a member of a well-known boy band and a glam TV presenter had celebrated their nuptials there, to name but two.

'I'm a member there,' Annabel said carelessly. 'I often come down for the weekend.'

'That is fantastic, Annabel! You really have made it, haven't you?'

Becky said nothing but I could practically read her mind. Her rather suety features had gone very shut in, and her eyes narrowed so that they almost disappeared into her puddingy cheeks. She was jealous. Well – so was I ... not *jealous* exactly, perhaps, but certainly envious. But Becky... *'It's not fair,'* I could almost hear her thinking it. *'I arrange for people's empty bottles and old newspapers to be collected for recycling, and she hobnobs with celebrities. It is just not fair...'*

Voices in the hall.

'She's here at last,' Laura called. 'Jenny's here!'

I turned expectantly towards the door. I'd always been extremely fond of Jenny, she was always the quiet one. The perfect antidote to Laura's vivacity and Annabel's wicked streak. Jenny, who listened when you talked to her, and then came out with something wise – or at least, sensible. Pretty Jenny, who was blind without her glasses and had frequently bashed straight into the end of the

41

pool because she hadn't seen it coming. Jenny, who worked hard and methodically without ever managing to get a single 'A' grade in anything, except perhaps once, in cookery, but rarely failed either.

She'd been small and slight, though surprisingly strong, and she was still small and slight. Apart from the enormous baby-sized bump that she carried before her. She wasn't wearing glasses though – somewhere along the line she must have swapped them for contact lenses. And her shoulder-length hair was cut to an easy-care bob.

'Jenny! Oh, Jenny! It's so good to see you!'

'Sorry I'm late, Laura. Friday evening is Jack's kick-boxing class. And then just as I was leaving Noah was sick...'

'Never mind, you're here now. We're all here! Martin's Mermaids!'

I caught sight of Becky, lurking awkwardly. 'And Becky too.'

'Oh, yes – and Becky.' Laura was at the huge, American-style fridge. 'I think it's time to open that champagne. Why don't we take it out and have it by the swimming pool?'

'Oh, the luxury of it!' Jenny said wistfully.

'Nothing but the best – we deserve it!' Laura bubbled. 'Girls, we are going to have one hell of a reunion!'

The cork popped, the champagne fizzed. And none of us guessed for a single moment how apt Laura's words would prove to be.

42

Three

Everything was set for a great evening. Laura had prepared the sort of cold buffet that a professional caterer would have been proud of – a whole side of salmon garnished with cucumber and lemon, a selection of quiches that had Waitrose written all over them and several interesting salads, not to mention a tiramisu and a huge bowl of strawberries and cream. There was far more than just the five of us could possibly demolish and enough wine to sink a battleship, though neither Annabel nor I were drinking since we both had to drive, and Jenny, in her advanced state of pregnancy, was being equally abstemious. But we had so much to catch up on, so much to talk about, that the time flew by on wings.

'When is the baby due?' I asked as she shifted around in her chair trying to make herself comfortable.

'Not for another three weeks, would you believe. I seem to get bigger sooner with each one.'

But she looked good on it, I though. Rosy

and contented, and I told her so.

'You should try it, Hannah,' she rejoined, then bit her lip. 'Sorry, I shouldn't have said that. You've split up with your husband, haven't you?'

'It's OK. It was two years ago. I'm over it now.' But I felt a pang, all the same, for the dreams David and I had once shared, and the longing that still gnawed at me for a child of my own.

'I, for one, have no intention of going down the motherhood route,' Annabel said emphatically. 'Broken nights, stinking nappies, puke everywhere – not my scene. My partner does on occasion turn a bit broody, but I manage to talk her out of it.'

Four sets of jaws dropped.

'*Her?*' Jenny echoed.

'Deanne. We've been together for three years now.'

Annabel was gay. I was staggered. I should not have been, I suppose, plenty of people are, and they thankfully don't have to hide in the closet any more. But it was a shock, all the same, to learn something so fundamental about someone you thought you knew so well. And yet, when I came to think about it, Annabel had never been one for the boys. She'd gone out with a few, but it had never lasted, and she'd never mooned around after anyone as the rest of us had.

'Well, good luck to you I say!' Laura raised

her glass in a toast and took a healthy swig. She was, I thought, drinking rather a lot. 'Who needs a man on a permanent basis? Men are from Mars, Women are from Venus!'

'Don't say it like that,' Jenny objected. 'You're happily married, Laura – aren't you?'

Laura tossed back the rest of her drink. 'I suppose so.'

'You are! You adore Mark, and he adores you.'

'And we've been together since we were eighteen years old. Nearly twenty years, for God's sake! I know all his faults and he knows mine, and we've both realized neither of us is ever going to change. And let's face it, sometimes it does get just the teeniest bit boring.'

'You should have children. Then you wouldn't have time to be bored,' Jenny said.

'It hasn't happened though, has it?' Laura threw it away, but there was an underlying tone of something that might have been despair, and for a moment it cast a cloud over our jollity.

On the surface, Laura seemed to have everything. In fact, there was a great aching hole in her life, a sadness eating away at her. Perhaps that was the reason she kept so busy, threw herself into projects like organizing this reunion. To try to fill it.

'Have you tried IVF?' Annabel asked into the silence.

'Three times. No joy. Look, we don't want to talk about it now, do we?' She waved the wine bottle. 'Who wants a refill? I know I do!'

Somehow we got the conversation back on track, but I think we were all a little wary now, realizing that catching up with the way our lives had turned out could be a minefield none of us had suspected.

I'd noticed too that, inevitably, Becky was being a bit left out.

'Becky was telling me she used to work for Mark,' I said, hoping that that, too, was not dangerous ground. 'And she said you had trouble with the animal rights people, too. That is just awful, Laura.'

That steered the conversation into a whole new area and we all relaxed. The problems these fanatics had visited on Mark and Laura were pretty nasty, as Becky had told me. All kinds of harassment that the police seemed unable – or unwilling – to prevent, but at least none of it was personal.

Pretty scary stuff, though!

'They tried to kidnap me once,' Laura said. 'At least, I suppose that's what they were trying to do. I was driving along the lane, and there was a girl in the middle of the road, waving at me to stop. I thought there'd been an accident or something, so of course I did. And then these men appeared from no-where. They must have been hiding in the hedge, I suppose. It was awful! They were all wearing balaclavas or hoodies and they surrounded the car. Luckily I had the presence of mind to hit the central locking button and I dialled 999 on my mobile, and they all ran away.'

'My God, Laura!' Annabel exclaimed. 'They could have killed you!'

'They could – though I think they probably just wanted to frighten me. And they certainly succeeded. They got what they wanted, anyway, as far as we were concerned. We'd had enough. Mark gave up the contract after that. He said targeting his office was one thing, but he wasn't going to have me put at risk.'

'So you're all right now?' I asked. 'They're leaving you alone?'

'More or less. There was still the odd incident – splinter groups, Mark thought, who either didn't know he'd stopped running deliveries to the poultry farm, or were still dealing out reprisals, but they seem to have gone quiet. We haven't heard anything of them for a long while now.'

'Well, thank heavens for that!' Annabel said. 'I know it goes against the grain to give in to that sort of intimidation, but people like that are very dangerous. They're completely obsessed.'

'But they have a point. Those battery farms are terrible places. No living creature should

47

be kept in conditions like that.' Jenny was very pink.

'We all agree with you,' Annabel said. 'Factory farming shouldn't be allowed. Or the export of veal calves, or animal testing for cosmetic purposes, or pheasant shoots, if it comes to that. But that doesn't mean it's right for these people to take the law into their own hands and terrorize law-abiding citizens who are just doing a job to earn a crust. Most of the extremists don't give two hoots about the cause, anyway. They're just looking for an excuse for violence and anarchy.'

'If I didn't have my hands full I'd start a group of my own,' Jenny said. 'I wouldn't send letter bombs or try to kidnap anyone, but I would stage a peaceful protest outside the gates of that horrible place.'

'And wear a bobble hat and dungarees and carry placards, I suppose.' Annabel grinned. 'And get arrested and carried off to a police van. Oh, Jenny, you never change, do you? Thank God!'

'We've none of us changed really,' Jenny said thoughtfully. 'We've grown up and taken the experiences life has thrown at us on board, and adapted, and we might be a bit older and wiser and less full of shit. Or maybe a bit more! But inside ... inside we're still the same people we always were. And always will be. Your basic personality – that's yours for life.'

'I'll drink to that,' Laura said, filling her glass yet again.

When we'd exhausted every detail of our lives that were fit for public consumption, the topic changed to the people who were attending the reunion.

'I think we've done really well,' Laura said. 'There were one or two we couldn't seem to find, and poor old Robert Hepburn's not with us any more...'

'*What?*'

'Robert Hepburn – not with us? Why? How?'

'Road accident. Ran his car into a tree not so long after we left school.'

'Oh, no! How awful! Poor Robert!' I exclaimed.

'But on the whole, we've managed to contact virtually everybody – and most of them are coming.'

'Great! You've done a sterling job, Laura.'

'I'm pleased, though I say it myself.'

'What about Aaron Flynn?' Becky asked. It was the first time she'd spoken for ages. 'I thought I saw him driving into The Beeches just as we were leaving.'

'Hannah, your glass is empty. I've got another jug of fruit punch in the overflow fridge in the utility room.' Laura, ever the perfect hostess, disappeared to fetch it, and

Jenny answered for her.

'Aaron was one of the ones Laura thought she'd failed with. We left messages with everybody we could think of, and someone came up with an address in Bristol. Laura wrote, but I haven't heard that she ever got a reply.'

'Really? Are you sure?' Becky interposed. But as usual, nobody took much notice of her.

'He'd moved on, I suppose,' Jenny went on. 'Or simply didn't want to get involved. I'm not sure Aaron and reunions mix.'

'I thought the same,' I said. 'He really was not the retrospective type, was he? I didn't see the man myself, but Becky thought it looked like him.'

'I'm sure it was.' Becky nodded emphatically. 'He looked older, of course, but then so do we all. It was Aaron, I'm sure it was.'

'Oh, I do hope so!' Jenny enthused. 'I'd love to see Aaron again. What a character, huh?'

'What a hunk!' I said softly.

The others looked at me in surprise.

'You *fancied* him, Hannah?'

'Too true! It was that edge of danger that got me.'

'You little devil! And you never let on!'

'He's probably old and staid now.'

'Aaron? Never!'

'Well, if it *was* him, you'll find out tomorrow,' Annabel said.

'What about the staff?' I asked, anxious to change the subject. 'Are any of them coming?'

'More than you'd think! They're positively chomping at the bit!' Laura, back with a fresh jug of fruit punch, began reciting a list, which resulted in more reminiscing, some with horror: 'Oh, not Miss White! She was terrible!'; some with hilarity: 'Poor Mr Blake! He could never control a class! How we used to play him up! Do you remember...?'

Oh, yes, we all remembered. Mr Blake taught music; we'd all pretended to be tone deaf. Passed notes to one another. Giggled. Pulled silly faces. Once, someone had let down the trestle table that had all the music stacked on it in the middle of one of Mr Blake's renditions of a piano concerto. The table had gone down with a tremendous crash and all his carefully sorted four-part choir scores had flown all over the floor. We, of course, pretending to help by collecting them up again, had managed to muddle them up even more. It had seemed like harmless fun at the time, a good way of passing an hour. Now, I realized we had been cruel and heartless. Mr Blake had been a talented musician and a kind and gentle man driven to distraction. I couldn't believe he'd actually want to come back and meet his tormentors again, but apparently he did.

'And Martin Golding is coming, isn't he?' I said. 'He's still teaching at the school, you said, Laura.'

Laura nodded. 'Yep. Still there. One of the few that is.'

'I'm really looking forward to seeing Martin.'

Annabel snorted. Very loudly. Very contemptuously. We all turned to look at her.

'Lech,' she said viciously.

'*What?*' I was dumbfounded. 'Mr Golding?'

'Who else?'

'Annabel – no! Not in a million years!'

She arched an eyebrow. 'Why else do you think he put in so much of his own time training us? Two evenings a week – early mornings – treating us to bacon sarnies at the Greasy Spoon...'

'We were good, that's why,' I objected. 'We won medals for him. He was proud of us.'

'He liked seeing us in our swimsuits.'

'Annabel, you are so wrong.'

'Well, he certainly tried it on with me.'

There was a shocked silence.

'Annabel, you imagined it.' That was Laura, sober suddenly.

Annabel shrugged. 'Suit yourselves. Believe what you like. But I am telling you Martin Golding wasn't quite the perfect hero you all seem to think he was.'

'Stop it, Annabel.' Jenny got up laboriously

from her chair, resting her hands protectively over her bump. 'You know you like nothing better than to set the cat amongst the pigeons. But we're not biting. We're going to have a great reunion and nothing is going to spoil it. OK?'

Annabel raised her hands in surrender. 'OK – OK. I won't mention it again. Nothing happened. I made it all up.'

Laura was waving the wine bottle dementedly. 'Who's for another drink?'

The party resumed and no more was said about Martin. None of us, I thought, wanted our hero tarnished. But I was remembering, all the same, the time not long before we left school when Annabel had definitely been 'off' him, how they'd sat in his car for ages, talking, how she'd pointedly ignored him for a while – days? weeks? I couldn't be sure. We'd assumed he'd given her a ticking-off for not putting a hundred per cent effort into her training; now I wondered if there had been something else behind it. Annabel might have liked stirring up trouble – and clearly still did – but she could also be very secretive. As witness how she'd hidden from us the fact that she was gay.

Or perhaps she hadn't known then. Perhaps it was something she'd only found out later. Maybe even as a result of this encounter with Mr Golding ... if it had ever happened at all.

Another half hour slipped by. Jenny was beginning to wilt.

'Sorry to be a party pooper, Laura, but I am going to have to go home,' she said. 'If I don't get some sleep I'll be good for nothing tomorrow.'

'Are you all right to drive?' Laura asked.

'Yes, absolutely. I'll just pop to the loo before I go, though. Frequent visits are all part of the condition.'

'You know where it is? Through the kitchen and the utility room, turn right … Unless you want to go upstairs?'

'No, the cloakroom will be fine.'

When it had got dark we'd adjourned to what Laura referred to as 'the drawing room', though I'd thought it was still quite warm enough to be outside, and we'd smiled and reminisced over some photographs Laura had displayed there of the four of us in our heyday as 'Martin's Mermaids', one with our medals, another with a cup we'd won at a big gala. Now, Jenny headed off across the hall in the direction of the kitchen.

'Actually I think we ought to be making a move too,' I said. 'It's been lovely though, Laura.'

And Jenny screamed. A terrified, ear-splitting scream that made us all go cold.

There was a fraction of a moment's shocked silence, then we all dived for the door. I was closest, so I got there first, with Annabel close behind me. Laura's reactions had been slowed by all the alcohol she'd consumed and Becky ... well, Becky was hanging back, I think, not wanting to be the first to find out what the hell was the matter.

We practically bumped into Jenny in the hall. Thankfully she was in one piece.

'There's a man in the kitchen!' she gasped hysterically.

A man. In the kitchen.

I flew across the hall. And sure enough, there was. Tall. Skinny. Long hair tied back in an untidy ponytail. Earrings. Nose stud. Grubby jeans. Doc Martens. I'm not sure just how much I registered of that in that first instant, but the impression was un- mistakeably unreassuring.

Oh my god, it's the animal rights activists! I thought. They've broken in!

'What do you think you are doing?' I yelled, half-expecting the man to come at me with a knife or even a gun. But he didn't. He actually looked as shocked as I felt. Just standing there, staring at me glassily.

And from behind me Laura's voice, not frightened, but a little slurred – and very angry.

'Darren! What are you doing in here?'

'Nothing. Just looking for some cheese...' He sounded, I thought, a bit spaced.

To my amazement, Laura marched to the fridge, got out a lump of cheddar and thrust it at him.

'Here you are. Now – go. I told you I had visitors tonight. Go on ... scarper!'

'Sorry. Didn't mean to...'

'Just go!'

And he went. Out of the back door, quiet as a lamb.

'Oh!' Laura fumed. 'I am so sorry about that, girls. Jenny, are you all right?'

'Yes, fine. He just gave me such a fright...' Jenny had appeared in the kitchen doorway. She looked a bit pale and shaken but otherwise OK.

'I am so sorry! I told him...' Laura took a deep breath. 'That's Darren, Mark's nephew. He's had a few problems and we've let him have the use of our motor home. He doesn't normally bother us ... I specifically told him the house was out of bounds tonight, but he sometimes gets this craving for cheese...'

'I thought he was one of the animal rights lot,' I said.

'Well, he could be, couldn't he? But he's not. He's just Darren. And we're doing our best for him.'

It didn't seem the right moment to ask Laura exactly what was wrong with Darren, what he was doing living in their motor home, or exactly how they were trying to help him, since Laura didn't seem to actually want to explain. But I had a pretty good idea. Mark's nephew looked like a lad who had dropped out of society, and was probably on drugs.

Now we were all on our feet it seemed pointless to sit down again given that it was getting late. Jenny, Becky and I all headed for the door, though Annabel seemed in no hurry to leave. She was still in the hall cradling a glass of fruit punch as we said our goodnights and drove away.

'So what's with this nephew of Mark's?' I asked Becky, as I pointed my car down the lane in the direction of the main road. 'Has he been staying with them long?'

'I didn't know that he was. I don't think he can have been there when I was working for Mark.' Becky sounded faintly put out. I guessed she hated not being the fount of all knowledge where Mark was concerned.

'He looked like trouble to me.' I shifted gear. 'Which of Mark's brothers is his father?'

'Paul, the older one, I think. He's a bank manager in Bristol.' Becky was happier now she had information she could impart. 'He's not exactly over the moon with the way his son has turned out, I imagine.'

'No, I imagine not.'

I could see it all. A young man kicking against a respectable, maybe stifling, upbringing, parents despairing of getting him back on course, especially in a city environment, perhaps even a big falling-out over the way he was living his life, Mark and Laura riding to the rescue and taking him under their wing. Very admirable, but not something I'd care to take on. At best it must be stressful. At worst, if he *was* into drugs – and I felt fairly sure he was – heaven alone knew what they'd let themselves in for. From my own experience with former pupils who'd gone down that road I knew that addicts could be unpredictable and would stop at nothing to get the money to buy their next fix. Burglary, mugging, prostitution, stealing from their own families, perhaps dealing themselves. I certainly wouldn't want a drug addict living in my backyard with access to my home, even if it was my nephew.

But then, I wasn't Laura. I didn't have her single-minded determination and self-belief. And in any case, I could be wrong. Perhaps it wasn't drugs that had made Darren appear so spaced. Perhaps he was suffering from some mental disorder, schizophrenia maybe. Perhaps Mark and Laura had offered him the use of their motor home so that they could keep an eye on him and make sure he took his medication whilst at the same time allowing him a certain amount of independence. He was, after all, Mark's flesh and blood, and remembering how upset Laura was at their inability to have children of their own it was possible that caring for him was fulfilling some deep-seated need in her. But all the same, I didn't like it. Docile as he had seemed this evening, I still couldn't escape the feeling that the boy was a disaster waiting to happen.

'I wonder if the men are still drinking in the bar,' Becky mused as we turned into the drive of The Beeches.

'Well, Mark wasn't home when we left, so it's a possibility,' I said.

'I think I'll go and see. Drop me by the door, will you?'

I gave a mental shake of my head. Had Becky no more sense than to gatecrash what was basically a stag night? But if she couldn't work it out for herself, it wasn't up to me to do it for her. I pulled up at the hotel entrance and she got out.

'Thanks, Hannah. See you tomorrow.' But already she'd put our evening behind her, I could tell, and was hightailing it towards her next session – with Mark, if he was still there. I could well imagine his reaction when she barged in like an eager puppy – and I didn't think it would be pleasure at seeing her.

I drove on into the car park. It was fuller than it had been earlier – the spot I'd been parked in was now occupied and I had to go much further into the trees before I found a space. I turned off the engine, hitched my bag out of the back seat and on to my shoulder, and locked the car.

With the headlamps off, I realized it was very dark. The lights at the hotel end of the car park were almost hidden by the trees, and if there was a moon, I couldn't see it. I should have brought a torch. Oh well, too late now. The path back to the hotel was pretty well defined and I could scarcely fail to follow it safely – unless there were tree stumps between it and me, or potholes in the tarmac that I couldn't see.

I'd only covered a few yards when I had the strangest feeling I was not alone. I stopped abruptly, head cocked, senses alert, and peered about. Nothing. No one. I started off again; stopped again. There *was* something, I was sure of it, something that had sounded like the rustling of a bush, or a footfall in deep leaf mould. Yet now, once again, apart from a car out on the main road, there was absolute silence.

For goodness sake don't be so stupid! I told myself. *You've just been spooked by a strange boy in Laura's kitchen. Your nerves are a bit frayed, that's all.* But I couldn't shake the deep feeling of unease. It whispered over my skin like a sharp chilling breeze and knotted in my stomach; it was more the sensation of being watched now than anything else. If there was someone in the shadow of the trees, wearing dark clothing, I had no hope of seeing them. They could creep up on me without my knowing, just as Tristan had crept up on me earlier, and it had still been daylight then.

Tristan ... the thought of him lurking made my flesh creep even more, even though I was sure he was perfectly harmless.

'Is anyone there?' I called out. My voice sounded panicky.

Silence. I felt a little foolish. An owl hooted somewhere out there in the darkness, nearly making me jump out of my skin. But otherwise nothing. I set off at a fast pace along the track between the trees, careless now of any unevenness on the path, tense and frightened, and still not really knowing why. Only when I reached the open area behind the hotel did I slow down, looking round again and seeing nothing. I was enormously relieved, all the same, to reach the converted stable block. It was well-lit there, and as I fumbled my key out of my purse a couple came out of the hotel, chatting and walking towards the car park. I opened my door, switched on the lights and went inside. But it was only when I'd locked the door behind me that I truly relaxed, scolding myself for behaving like a frightened rabbit.

Why the hell had I been so scared? It just wasn't me. I wasn't the nervous type. Yet out there in the dark between the trees I'd been absolutely certain I wasn't alone. That someone was watching me, following me.

Some sixth sense had kicked in, warning me...

'Rubbish!' I said aloud. I must just be overtired and over-excited. It wasn't even as if I'd had too much to drink. A small glass of wine and a Buck's Fizz hardly constituted over-indulgence in that department. There was nothing to stop me now, though. Feeling madly extravagant, I raided the minibar for a miniature of gin, topped it up with tonic, and demolished it. And then I really did feel better.

As I got ready for bed I thought of all the things I'd learned already about my former friends and classmates, not to mention Martin Golding. If nothing else, this was going to be an interesting weekend.

And, for the first time, I wondered if it was really such a good idea after all.

Four

Perhaps it was the effect of the gin on top of the wine and the Buck's Fizz, perhaps I had been more tired than I realized, but I fell asleep the moment my head touched the pillow and slept the sleep of the just. It was well past eight when I came to and drowsily checked my watch; by the time I'd bathed and dressed it was almost nine. What luxury! I could scarcely believe it, and I had nothing to do all day but please myself. Apart, of course, from catching up with people I hadn't seen for almost twenty years.

My fright of the previous night was completely forgotten now. In the light of day it seemed ludicrous that I could have been so silly as to believe someone was watching or following me. I set out for the dining room which was, of course, situated in the main building, wondering if any of my former classmates would be there eating breakfast and whether I'd recognize them. Quite a few were staying here, according to Laura – Stan and Peter amongst them. I very much hoped I'd manage to avoid Becky – I really felt I'd had enough of her company already, and I knew she'd latch on to me given half a chance – but thinking it still made me feel vaguely guilty. I had no such qualms feeling the same way about Tristan Forrester, though. He gave me the creeps and he was not my responsibility. The boys could look after him – if he needed looking after.

To my relief neither of them was in evidence when I went into the dining room, but Stan and Peter were. For all the years that had passed since I'd last seen them, I knew them at once – not so much from the way they looked as from the way they were sitting: sprawling and relaxed over the remains of their full English breakfasts, just as they'd used to sit in the canteen at school and by Stan's unmistakeable hearty laugh which I heard the moment I went into the dining room. I made a bee-line for them and they got up to greet me. Peter holding out his hand a little stiffly, Stan enveloping me in a bear hug. After the initial shock of seeing the effect of the passage of nearly twenty years on their faces, it seemed to me they hadn't changed at all – Peter was athletic, good-looking and reserved, every inch the vet he had become; Stan, who had been one of the mainstays of the rugby team, a big bear of a man with a personality to match. They dragged an extra chair up to their table for me and Peter fetched me a glass of orange juice from the buffet table while Stan waved for a waitress to come and take my order.

'Got to get it in, Hannah – they stop serving in quarter of an hour.'

'I don't know that I want anything,' I protested weakly.

'Course you do! Bacon, egg, sausage, beans, mushrooms ... you'll need a full stomach to cope with all the drinking we intend to do later.'

'That *you* intend to do!' I laughed. 'Leave me out of it!'

'Oh, you'll have your fair share, Hannah,' Stan assured me. 'Isn't that why we've booked into the venue where the reunion is being held? So we can get legless and not have to worry about it?'

'I'll just have scrambled egg and toast,' I said, looking at the menu.

'And tomatoes and bacon on the side,' Stan instructed the waitress who was hovering, pad in hand. 'If she can't finish it, we will.'

'Stan, you are incorrigible!' But it felt great, all the same. Just like old times. And when my breakfast arrived, a mound of fluffy egg flanked by grilled tomatoes and crispy bacon rashers, I found I was hungrier than I'd realized, and cleaned my plate – much to Stan's disappointment.

'Has anyone else from our year been in for breakfast?' I asked, scraping butter on to the last piece of toast.

'A few...' Peter named a couple of former classmates. 'I think they've gone off to have a look round the town, see how it's changed.'

'And that bore Tristan Forrester,' Stan added. 'He must be an early bird – he'd more or less finished by the time we got here. God knows where he's taken himself off to, but I hope he stays there.'

'What about Aaron?' I hated myself for asking, but somehow couldn't stop myself.

'Haven't seen him this morning. He was in the bar last night though,' Stan said, and my heart lifted.

'Really? He's here?'

'Yeah – bit of a surprise, that.'

'So – what's he doing now?'

'Search me.' Stan emptied my coffee pot into his cup and signalled to the waitress for a refill. 'Aaron's a bit of a mystery man, but then he always was, wasn't he?'

'Stan, if we're having more coffee, perhaps we should have it out in the lounge,' Peter said. 'I think they're waiting to clear the tables in here.'

'More coffee – in the lounge,' Stan ordered the long-suffering waitress, and we trooped through to a pleasant room where deep armchairs and small sofas were grouped around low tables.

'What does he look like now?' I asked, returning as gently as I could to the subject of Aaron.

'Look like?' Stan sounded baffled. 'Well …
I dunno.'

'Just the same as ever,' Peter offered.

'Yes, Becky said she thought she recognized him in a car last night.'

'Becky!' Stan interrupted. 'Don't mention that girl. She barged into the bar last night and had everyone buying her drinks. We couldn't get rid of her. What a plonker!'

'Oh – you've got to make allowances.' I was miffed that the conversation had moved on from Aaron, but felt obliged, for some reason, to defend Becky.

'Why the hell should I?' Stan demanded bluntly.

'She had a pretty hard life…'

'Because she was always a plonker.'

'But her mother dying like that and everything…'

'That's more than twenty years ago now,' Stan declared unsympathetically. 'Surely we're not still expected to feel sorry for her twenty years on?' He slurped his coffee. 'If you ask me, the poor woman threw herself down that staircase to escape her ghastly daughter.'

'Stan, that is a terrible thing to say!' I scolded him.

'Well, at the very least, she was drunk.' Stan looked a little sheepish momentarily, then quickly recovered. 'Small wonder, if you ask me. I'd turn to the bottle if I had a daughter like that. And speaking of daughters...'

He eased his wallet from a back pocket and extracted a couple of photographs of three bonny little girls, all miniature female versions of Stan. 'My brood,' he said proudly. 'Got my comeuppance, didn't I, ending up with a houseful of women? Even the dog's a bitch.'

'Oh, Stan – they're gorgeous.' I was admiring Stan's family, saying the right things, but still thinking about poor Becky and how dreadful it must have been for her to arrive home from school to find her mother at the foot of the stairs with a broken neck. Stan was probably right, of course, she had fallen because she was drunk – Becky's mother's alcoholism had been common knowledge in Mowbury, though we hadn't called it that in those days. 'She hits the bottle,' my mother used to say. I remember her using that expression to explain the situation when I'd come home from school one day full of how Becky's mother had burst into our classroom to upbraid the teacher for failing to prevent Becky being bullied by some older girls, screamed at her, tried to pull her hair – 'See how *you* like it, Lady Muck!' – and then fallen over her own feet and ended up in a heap in front of twenty-eight astonished pupils.

Becky's mother had had a drink problem

all right, and she'd probably been well and truly inebriated when she fell down those stairs and broke her neck, but that didn't make it any the less terrible for poor Becky, finding her there, and it didn't make it her fault either. Rather, it explained a lot.

We stayed in the lounge chatting for a very long time. A few former classmates drifted through and we exchanged greetings and briefly caught up. Tristan put in an appearance once, to our dismay, but he didn't stay long. He was on his way to check out the little local volunteer-run museum that had opened in Mowbury. But there was no sign of either Aaron or Becky. Becky was probably nursing a hangover, I thought, relieved not to have to put up with her annoying ways and be nice to her. But I was yearning to catch a glimpse of Aaron.

'You don't think he's changed his mind and decided to cut off home, do you?' I suggested.

Stan looked bemused. 'Why would he do that?'

'Well, if you were asking him a lot of questions he didn't want to answer he might have taken fright.'

'His parole's up, more like!' Stan laughed his hearty laugh. 'I always said he'd end up in jail.'

'Stan – stop it! Why would Aaron end up in jail?'

'I reckon he's either a jailbird or the modern equivalent of 007.' Stan fixed me with an amused look. 'You're very interested in Aaron, Hannah. Don't Peter and I do it for you?'

'No, you certainly don't!' I laughed. 'Sorry, Stan, we just know one another too well.'

'I'm deeply hurt.' He didn't look it but I thought it was time I stopped mentioning Aaron. I was giving things away that I hadn't even realized myself until now.

'Bar's open,' Stan said. 'I'm having a pint. How about you, Peter?'

And that, I thought, was likely to be the trademark of the weekend!

The visit to the old school had been scheduled for two thirty p.m. Stan and Peter offered me a lift with them, which meant I was able to avoid being lumbered with Becky, who arrived in the bar obviously hoping we could team up. And though I felt sure there would be room in his car, Stan didn't suggest she could ride with us.

'Not bloody likely!' he said bluntly.

Laura and Annabel were already there waiting for us as we disembarked in what used to be the playground but was now a car park, Laura ticking off names on a list attached to a clipboard. After enthusiastic greetings all round, Laura suggested we went on in to the hall, which was to be the starting point of our tour.

'Not the old hall – it's a new one in the new block. Through the main doors, turn left, along the corridor and you can't miss it,' she instructed. 'I have to stay here to direct people, but Mark and Ian are in there already, and I'll be in very soon.'

We did as she suggested, marvelling at the way the school had been enlarged and modernized since our day, and stopping en route to look at the panoramic framed photographs that lined the corridor, one for each year of the school's history. It was great fun, spotting ourselves as we'd been between the ages of eleven and eighteen, and caused some merriment on the lines of: 'Oh my goodness, look at me!' and 'Get that haircut! How could you see out from beneath that?'

Quite a few ex-pupils and members of staff were already gathered in the impressive new hall – all smoked glass and pine – Mark and Ian amongst them. Mark looked tired; a result, perhaps, of a long and heavy drinking session last night. But he greeted Stan and Peter affably enough, and as they started reminiscing about the long ago exploits of the rugby and cricket teams, Annabel and I wandered off together, stopping to exchange a few words with other girls and with Mr Blake, our old music teacher, who now looked like a round, rosy-faced and slightly wrinkled pixie, and who seemed incredibly excited to see us all despite the terrible dance we'd led him all those years ago.

'Mark doesn't seem quite himself,' I said to Annabel in a quiet moment.

Annabel pulled a face. 'Hardly surprising! I shouldn't think he could sleep soundly in his bed with that ghastly nephew of his on the scene. I know I wouldn't. Do you know he came back *again* last night after you left – looking for whisky, would you believe? They shouldn't have him there. It's asking for trouble.'

'What is his problem – drugs?' I asked.

'I think that's the root of it, yes ... Oh, Miss Day. How lovely to see you!'

Miss Day, looking surprisingly spry – and almost human without her flowing black gown.

'Jenny's late again,' I said when we extricated ourselves.

'Oh, she's not coming this afternoon. Her eldest daughter is at the school now, and Jenny's on the PTA, so a guided tour would be a bit of a bore for her. She'll be at the reunion proper tonight, though.'

I couldn't spot anyone who looked remotely like Aaron either, but this time I refrained from saying so. I was in danger of making a fool of myself over that man! But even as the thought crossed my mind I saw someone I certainly did recognize making a bee-line for us.

72

Martin Golding really hadn't changed at all. Still handsome, still athletic-looking, a full head of hair, though shot through with grey at the temples, casual cotton trousers and open-necked shirt worn with sandals and no socks.

'Well, if it's not one half of my swim team!' he greeted us. 'The most successful quartet I ever trained. How about it, girls – are you ready to go in at the deep end?'

'I don't *think* so!' Annabel tipped her head back, looking at him speculatively from behind her permanently tinted lashes.

I was suddenly very afraid she might make some comment similar to what she'd said last night, some reference to the effect that she thought he'd been more interested in our bodies than our swimming prowess. She was, after all, a grown woman now, not a naïve teenager overawed by the attentions of a teacher and swimming coach. The demarcation lines had gone now; we were all on a level playing field.

'We wouldn't win any medals if we did, I'm afraid,' I said hastily. 'I haven't done more than a few lengths in years, Annabel wouldn't want to get her hair wet, and Jenny is seven-and-a-half months pregnant and huge – she'd be mistaken for a bell buoy or a visiting whale.'

'And Laura?'

'Ask her yourself,' Annabel said.

'Ask me what?' Laura had come up behind us, still clutching her clipboard.

'If you'd be up for swimming a relay this afternoon.' Annabel's eyes were dancing with mischief.

And it was Laura who jumped in with both feet and created the awkward situation I'd thought Annabel might.

'You are joking! I rather think your fun days are over, Mr Golding. For good. Or do you have another little team you're coaching like you coached us?'

I caught my breath, horrified and embarrassed, but before I could think of anything to say that would defuse the situation, Laura went on in a lighter, more conversational tone.

'They must be a great temptation, this new generation. They mature earlier these days, don't they?'

'Are we going to start the tour soon?' Annabel asked coolly.

Laura's gaze lingered for a long moment on Martin Golding's face. Then she nodded. 'Yes, I think we're all here. Bar Aaron. Mr Golding is going to conduct it since he still teaches here, aren't you, Martin? He'll make a really good job of it, I hope. After all, I know a lot of people with children at the school, and it wouldn't do for me to send back a bad report, would it?'

Was it just my imagination or did Martin

Golding stiffen? Laura's veiled threat was so clear to me I could scarcely believe he hadn't understood what she was saying too. But then, of course, that would depend on him being guilty of the accusations Annabel had levelled at him and I still wasn't a hundred per cent sure they were true.

'If Mr Golding is as good a guide as he was a teacher, I'm sure the tour will be a great success,' I said as confidently as I could manage.

'OK then, let's get this show on the road.' Laura grabbed the assembly bell pull and yanked on it. She seemed to have put the barbed comments behind her. 'Right, everybody, are you ready?' she called once a respectful hush had descended.

There was a chorus of agreement.

'That was a nasty moment,' Annabel said softly.

'You can say that again,' I agreed.

'Let's hope she'll soon forget about what I said.'

'I'm not so sure she will,' I whispered anxiously. 'You know what Laura's like when she gets the bit between her teeth...'

We set off with the others, following Martin Golding, but I was wishing most heartily that Annabel had kept to herself the information about him that she had chosen, after all these years, to share with us, and a little worried as to what was likely to happen at the reunion proper tonight, when free-flow-ing drink loosened tongues and made people less inhibited than they might normally be. If there were any skeletons, I hoped very much that they would remain safely in their cupboards where they belonged.

When we parted company after the school tour, Laura asked me if I could be on hand in good time this evening to help her welcome the guests and get things going smoothly.

'I've got name tags to hand out, and a wel-come drink, and if someone keeps me talking everything will grind to a halt. As you're staying at The Beeches it would seem to make sense...'

'Fine.' Since most of us had already met up this afternoon, I couldn't quite see the neces-sity for name tags, but if that was what Laura wanted, who was I to argue?

Back in my hotel room I put my feet up and relaxed for half an hour, then showered, changed and made my way over to the main building.

Laura hadn't arrived yet, and when a rather officious receptionist approached, asking me where we would like the glasses and drinks to be set out, I began to regret having agreed to share responsibility.

'It's not really my decision, but I should think here in the foyer. Laura may want to change things, though ... I'm sure she'll be here soon.'

Then, to my annoyance, Becky came lumbering in, dressed in floaty puce georgette.

'I heard Laura ask you to help her. I thought perhaps you could use an extra pair of hands.'

'There's nothing to do, Becky, really, thanks all the same.' She looked crestfallen, and I felt guilty all over again. 'Well, just make sure they've set out plenty of chairs in the function room. We don't want the elderly guests to have to stand.'

Becky did not look best pleased. 'Surely that's the hotel's job?'

'Well, yes, it is really, but...' Meeting and greeting was more what Becky had had in mind, I guessed, and given her general unpopularity, that really was not the best idea in the world.

To my immense relief Laura arrived then, a little flushed, laden down with box-files and what looked like two or three rolled-up panoramic photographs, copies of the ones that adorned the corridor at the old school.

'I thought we could put these up. Make a sort of display of memorabilia. I think some of the others will be bringing stuff too.'

'Becky's offered to help,' I said, anxious to get her away from the reception area, but not too sure that entrusting her with setting up a display was wise either.

'Oh, well done, Becky!' Laura transferred the load to a rather startled Becky. 'There should be a table for bits and pieces, there's certainly a white board, and you'll find Blutack in the top box.'

Becky had no option, really, but to do as Laura asked.

'She'll do a good job,' Laura said, sensing my reservations. 'She's quite artistic actually.'

'Laura – you look fantastic!' I said. She was wearing a concoction in ecru lace – lots of leg, lots of cleavage. I'd settled for silk palazzo pants and camisole; now, by comparison, I felt underdressed.

'Thanks. I thought I should make the effort. And you look good too.' But her mind was obviously on the evening ahead. 'Hannah, this is going to go well, isn't it? If it flops, I'll just die!'

'It's going to be great,' I assured her, and then risked qualifying: 'No more digs at Mr Golding, though. It was all a very long time ago ... if it happened at all.'

'Oh, it happened.' There was a certainty in her tone that made me wonder briefly if there was yet more I still didn't know. 'And he's still teaching, Hannah. Vulnerable young girls ... You're right, though, I'll put it out of my mind for tonight, at any rate. Then I'll think what I'm going to do about it.'

My heart sank. There *was* more to this than

met the eye. There was something Laura had been hiding too, and Annabel's revelations must have brought it all to the surface and made her realize she hadn't been the only one. But before we could say any more about it, Stan and Peter emerged from the bar, already well-oiled from the look of them.

'Laura! Hannah! Well, just look at the pair of you. To think you were the inky kids we used to know.'

'We were not inky!' I objected.

'Where's that husband of yours?' Peter asked Laura.

'Oh, he'll be here later.' There was something faintly dismissive in Laura's tone. 'I needed to be here early to get things set up, so we decided to come in separate cars.'

'Nice one.' Stan was eyeing Laura appreciatively. 'Though if you were my wife, I'm not sure I'd let you out of my sight looking like that, especially with a load of old admirers sniffing around.' He put an arm around her waist, leering at her, but it was a Stanleer, not a Tristan-leer, and somehow not in the least offensive.

Laura spun away and tapped his hand sharply. 'Behave yourself, Sean Bennett!'

Stan laughed, his chortling laugh. 'I think I've got our Laura mad. That's the first time anyone's called me that in years!'

We were more or less ready by the time any

of the others started arriving, some by car, others drifting down from their hotel rooms. Most of the chaps made a bee-line for the bar, whilst the girls stood in groups sipping sparkling wine or fruit juice. The members of staff who'd made it all looked every bit as excited as Mr Blake had done, chatting proudly to their former pupils as if they, single-handedly, were responsible for the people they had become. Martin Golding was steering clear of Laura and Annabel, I noticed, though when Jenny arrived – late as usual – he had quite a long chat with her, and I made an effort to talk to him as if nothing was wrong. As I say, he'd never been anything but nice and perfectly properly behaved as far as I was concerned and I didn't want any unpleasantness tonight.

He was edgy, though, I could tell. There was an awkwardness in his manner that might have been due to the fact that so many years had passed since we'd last talked, but equally might have been embarrassment, or even guilt.

I was halfway through telling him about the school where I now taught when, over his shoulder, I caught sight of Aaron. I knew him immediately, just as Becky had known him. There was no mistaking it really – he stood out from the crowd. Whereas most of the other chaps wore jackets and ties, Aaron was dressed almost casually – dark, open neck shirt, dark trousers. He looked just as, let's face it, he'd always looked – mean, moody. Except that I knew he wasn't mean, just scarily fascinating in a dangerous way.

He was talking to Laura and I have to say there was something about her body language that made me think I wasn't the only one who found him fascinating. She'd already had several drinks that I'd seen, and she'd always been a terrible flirt, but all the same ... The tilt of her head, the way she was looking up at him under her lashes ... alarm bells rang in my head. When I'd finished my conversation with Martin Golding, they were still together, and I made my way across to join them.

'Hello, you! I thought you weren't coming.'

Laura, I thought, did not look best pleased at being interrupted, but Aaron grinned – that wicked grin I remembered so well. 'Hannah! Good to see you.'

'I told you I'd found him,' Laura said.

'No you didn't. The last I heard was that you hadn't got a reply. Where have you been hiding, Aaron?'

'Scarcely hiding. I've been in Bristol for the last ten years.'

'Doing what?' I asked.

'Oh, a bit of this and a bit of that...' Aaron smirked wickedly. He was enjoying this, I could tell.

'You don't have to say anything–' Laura

dimpled, teasing him with her eyes – 'but a bit of this and a bit of that isn't a job.'

'It is as far as I'm concerned,' Aaron said airily, then turned to me. 'Wheeler-dealer, I expect you'd call it. Buying and selling. You want something, I get it for you.'

'You mean like Del Boy in *Only Fools and Horses*?' I said, teasing him.

'Yes, except that I don't have a Robin Reliant.'

I thought of the car that had passed us in the hotel entrance last night. No, Aaron was a good bit more successful than Del Boy – or else he was spinning us a yarn and he wasn't a wheeler-dealer at all. You never could tell with Aaron.

'Laura – the photographer is here!' That was Jenny, materializing out of the crush.

'OK, come on then. Let's get everybody lined up.' Laura was back in organizer mode, arranging for a row of chairs for the former members of staff with the rest of us lined up behind, drinks in hands. Aaron was on one side of me, Stan on the other, and just as the flash went off he pinched my bottom so that I was captured for posterity turning towards him with my mouth open in an expression of surprise and outrage.

The reunion was well and truly underway, and so far it seemed to be being a roaring success.

Five

It was about eleven o'clock, I suppose, when things began to go horribly wrong. Until then the evening had been an unqualified success. Now, the first early birds – mainly elderly former teachers – had said their reluctant goodnights and left, and most of the other guests appeared to have settled in for the duration. Even Jenny was still partying, although she regularly announced that she 'really must go home!'

Thankfully, I don't think many of the others were aware of the altercation, but it so happened that I'd paid a visit to the cloakroom, just along the passage from the main entrance, and I was just about to emerge when I heard raised voices in the corridor outside.

'Mark, please – stop it! It was nothing!'

'It didn't look like nothing to me.'

It was Laura and Mark, and they were having one hell of a row. I froze, gripping the handle of the door, unwilling to intrude at this precise moment.

'I've had enough!' Mark shouted. 'Come

on. Get your bag. We're going home.'

'Don't be so stupid! I can't go home.' Laura was shouting too.

'You mean you don't bloody well want to!'

'I can't! I can't just leave! What would people think?'

'I don't give a damn what they think. We're going – now!'

'I am not going home! You can't make me!'

'What's going on?' Another voice – Aaron's – a little puzzled, a little alarmed. 'Is everything all right?'

'No, it's bloody well not. And you ... you can stay away from my wife!'

'Mark! For God's sake...' Laura's voice rose sharply, almost hysterically, and without stopping to think I wrenched the cloakroom door fully open and ran out into the corridor.

Mark had Aaron up against the wall, jabbing his finger threateningly into Aaron's face. Aaron, shorter than Mark by several inches and much slighter in build, had his hands raised in surrender. 'OK. OK. Calm down, mate.'

'Just leave her alone, right?' Mark jabbed furiously millimetres from Aaron's eyes. 'She is my fucking wife.'

'Yeah – like I say – OK. Now, cool it...'

'Randy bastard!' I had never seen Mark so angry. It was frightening to say the least of it. For another long moment he eyeballed

84

Aaron, his lip curled back in a snarl, then he turned abruptly away, directing his fury at Laura. 'Come on. We're going.'

'I am not going anywhere with you. You animal!' Laura was almost in tears now. Mark grabbed her arm as if to frogmarch her out, but she stood her ground, staring at him defiantly, and he let go of her.

'Are you coming home with me or not?'

'For the last time, no!'

'OK, suit yourself. You usually do.' As if he'd suddenly lost the will to continue the fight, Mark swung round and strode out. As the door slammed behind him, a couple of guests, clearly unaware of what was going on, emerged from the direction of the function room, chatting and laughing, and Laura crumpled suddenly, rushing for the cloakroom. Without a word to Aaron, I followed her.

I found her slumped against the vanity unit, sobbing uncontrollably.

'Laura!' I said urgently. 'What on earth is going on?'

For a minute she couldn't speak. Then: 'Oh – it's just Mark being Mark,' she managed between sobs. 'Oh, he's so jealous, Hannah, you just wouldn't believe ... Why does he have to be so horrible? Why does he ruin everything?'

'Oh Laura, come here.' I put my arms around her and she cried some more.

'But what started all this off?' I asked when her sobs subsided a little – though I thought I knew the answer. Laura confirmed it.

'Oh, he thought I was up to something with Aaron.' She looked up at me, a parody of the vivacious, attractive girl she had been earlier in the evening. Her eyes were swollen and swimming, her cheeks streaked with mascara and her nose running. I pulled a handful of tissues out of a silver box on the vanity unit and handed them to her. She blew her nose and wiped away the tracks of her tears.

'It was just awful, Hannah. We were just talking, that's all, and Mark came out and went berserk.'

'Came out?' I echoed, puzzled.

'We were out on the terrace. You know – the French windows were open to let in some air and we just went outside for a chat.'

Oh, yes, I thought, pull the other one. I'd seen the way she was flirting with Aaron, and I suspected she'd had more than a chat in mind when she'd gone outside with him. But it wasn't for me to judge – though I must admit to a bolt of jealousy. I wouldn't have minded going outside for 'a chat' with Aaron myself.

'I thought Mark was going to hit him, I really did,' Laura went on. 'But he just grabbed hold of me and yelled at Aaron. He said he knew what was going on, and to leave me

86

alone. Then he dragged me back inside and said we were going home. I went so far with him because I didn't want to make a scene in front of everybody, but there was no way I was going to let him make me go home – just like that – for no reason. This is *my* party! I've worked so hard ... Oh, Hannah...' Then she burst into tears again.

'Come on, Laura,' I urged her. 'You've got to pull yourself together. Somebody might come in. You don't want them to see you like this.'

She gave a huge snuffle and dried her eyes again. 'You're right. I won't let him spoil everything. I won't! Oh, why does he do it? I can't bear it, Hannah. He's just impossible.'

'You mean ... this isn't the first time?' I asked.

'Oh, no. He's always getting it into his head that I'm having affairs. I only have to look at somebody and he thinks ... But it's this temper of his that really gets to me. When he loses it, he's like ... you see his face change and his voice, and he's not Mark any more. He's like a wild beast. It is so scary. Well, you saw what he was like.'

'Yes, he was rather...' I broke off, at a loss for words. 'He wasn't at all like the Mark I know,' I finished lamely.

'Exactly. Not like the Mark *anyone* knows, except me. They all think he's even-temper-ed and reasonable and solid and reliable, but when he loses it ... He did let fly once, at one of those animal rights protesters. Mark caught him dumping a load of dead chickens in our swimming pool and he gave him such a beating! Honestly, I thought he was going to kill him.'

'So, what happened?'

'Oh, the boy managed to get away – I think they had a van parked out on the road. We never heard any more about it – well, they were hardly likely to go to the police, were they? Not with all the harassment they were perpetrating. And to be honest, I didn't really blame Mark for losing it with him. We'd put up with so much. But the point is ... I've seen just what he is capable of, and it's worried me ever since. If he'd gone for Aaron the way he went for that boy—' She stopped suddenly, jamming the screwed-up tissue against her mouth.

'Laura...' I was anxious suddenly. 'He ... he doesn't hurt you, does he?'

Laura shook her head emphatically. 'Oh, no – no! I'd never stay with him if he did. He raised his hand to me once, and that was enough. I told him – if ever he laid a finger on me, I'd be out that door so fast my feet wouldn't touch the ground.'

'That's all right then.' I was relieved, but still concerned. I'd been so certain Laura and Mark were rock solid. Had a really good marriage apart from the odd blip. Now it was emerging that behind closed doors, things were not what they seemed.

Footsteps in the corridor outside. 'Someone's coming!' I bundled Laura into one of the cubicles. 'Stay there until they've gone. I'll wait for you.'

She disappeared, slamming the cubicle door closed just in time and I busied myself at the vanity unit, fiddling with my hair at the mirror.

To my relief, it was Jenny who came in.

'Hannah!' she greeted me. 'We were wondering what had become of you. And nobody knows where Laura is either. She's been missing for ages, and Tristan is looking for her.'

'Spot of bother.' I nodded meaningfully towards the cubicle. 'It's OK, Laura,' I said in a louder voice. 'It's only Jenny.'

The door opened and Laura emerged. She'd obviously made an effort to make herself look a bit more presentable, but there was still no mistaking that she had been crying.

'Laura – whatever is wrong?' Jenny asked anxiously.

'It's a long story,' I warned.

'Then I must go to the loo first. I'm absolutely bursting.' Jenny disappeared into a cubicle.

'I've got to get back to the reunion,' Laura said distractedly.

'You're in no fit state,' I told her.

'I'm all right now. And I heard Jenny say people are wondering where I am.'

'They'll just have to wonder,' I said. 'You've got to tidy yourself up a bit first. You haven't got any make-up with you, I suppose?'

'No, it's all in my bag, and I left that in the hall.'

I rummaged in my own bag for concealer, mascara and lipstick and dumped them on the vanity unit. 'Here you are – use these.'

'Oh my God, look at the state of me!' Laura was regarding her image in the mirror with horror.

'Nothing that can't be fixed,' I said, determinedly cheerful. 'Just don't start crying again, that's all.'

'I won't. I'm just angry now.'

By the time Jenny emerged, anxious and curious, Laura had cleaned up her face and was smoothing some of my concealer on to her eyes to hide the redness.

'Laura had a bit of a spat with Mark,' I explained. 'He's gone off home in a huff. Why don't you stay here with her while she fixes her make-up and I'll go back in and cover for her.'

'Yes, sure. I'll look after her.'

She would, I knew. The old bonds were still there, twenty years on, and sensible, mother-ly Jenny was probably the best one to calm

90

Laura down. Leaving them in the cloak-room, I went back to the function room.

The minute I walked in through the door, Tristan pounced on me, though 'pouncing' is not really a very good word to describe Tristan's slithery approach.

'Have you seen Laura? I can't find her any-where, and someone said they saw her leav-ing.'

'Oh, no, she's just taking a breather,' I im-provised.

'That's all right then.' He smiled his sickly smile. 'We've got a little something for her as a token of our appreciation for all her efforts organizing this weekend, so I was very con-cerned when I heard she'd left. I wouldn't like her to have gone home without being thanked properly for all her hard work.'

'Oh, right. Well, that's a very nice thought.' I felt a stab of guilt that such a thing had not even occurred to me. It was typical of Tristan, though. He didn't miss a trick. Then I felt guilty all over again for thinking of him so uncharitably.

'She'll be back in a minute,' I said. 'It's Mark who has gone home. That's how the confusion arose, I expect. He had a headache I think,' I lied.

'Oh, dear, what a shame. So Laura is now unescorted?'

Probably not for long, I thought ruefully,

looking around for Aaron. But he was nowhere to be seen. I spotted Annabel, though, who had been cornered by Becky, excused myself from Tristan and went over to her.

'Can I have a word, Annabel?' We moved away from Becky. 'Tristan is looking for Laura to do some sort of presentation. She's a bit upset. Mark has gone home and...'

I broke off. Becky was hovering again, pushing in.

'Mark's gone home? Whatever for?' She sounded dismayed. Disappointed that she would see no more of her idol tonight, I supposed. I didn't want her to know about the row if I could help it; she would delight in all the gory details.

'He wasn't feeling well,' I said.

'Laura's here now,' Annabel said.

I looked round; Laura and Jenny were coming through the swing doors. Jenny looked worried; Laura, her make-up successfully repaired, was smiling brightly. Too brightly. But I supposed that most of the guests would take that at face value – just Laura being Laura.

Tristan must have seen her come into the room too; he made for the bar, said something to the bartender and clapped his hands to get everyone's attention.

'I'd just like to say a few words,' he said when a hush fell. 'I'm sure I speak for everyone here when I say this reunion has been a wonderful experience and a roaring success. But without the tireless efforts of just one person, it would not have happened. Laura. Will you join me?'

For a second, Laura's smile wavered and my heart missed a beat. Then it was back in place and she moved towards Tristan like an actress going on stage for a starring role.

'Laura.' He smirked at her, laid a hand around her shoulders. 'Thank you for having the idea, and for all your hard work. And on behalf of all of us–' he nodded to the barman, who, on cue, produced a huge cellophane wrapped bouquet of flowers from beneath the counter, took them, and held them out to Laura – 'we would like you to accept this small token of our appreciation.'

'Oh, thank you so much!' If there were tears in Laura's eyes now, the casual observer would think they were there because she was touched. 'There was no need, honestly. But they are beautiful. And I would like to say thank you, too, to all of you, for coming from the four corners of the earth...'

'We'll go anywhere for a booze-up!' Stan called out, heckling. There was a ripple of laughter.

'I'll ignore that remark,' Laura said. 'Thank you all once again. And I do hope you have enjoyed it as much as I have.'

I glanced around the room. From the smiles on most of the faces, I felt sure that they had. Only one person looked less than happy. Martin Golding, standing alone in a corner, arms folded, did not look happy at all. He looked like a man with the weight of the world on his shoulders, and I could guess why.

For Martin, the reunion had meant the past had caught up with him. And worse, if Laura decided to spill the beans, it could well stretch long tentacles to destroy his future. Whatever had happened might have been almost twenty years ago, but that wouldn't save him. His career, his marriage, maybe even his liberty, would come under threat. No, what had been a pleasant week-end for most of us could very well have been a nightmare for Martin Golding.

I felt very sad suddenly. Shattered illusions, tarnished memories, dashed hopes. Perhaps reunions were not such a good idea after all.

'How are you going to get home, Laura?' Annabel asked.

It was past midnight, most of the guests had left, some arranging to meet up again at lunchtime tomorrow, others vowing to have another reunion soon – next year certainly – they didn't want another twenty years to elapse before they saw one another again. Ian, who was heading off on holiday on an early flight in the morning, had said his goodbyes, Stan and Peter had adjourned to the hotel bar for a nightcap since the one that had been set up in the function room had closed at twelve, and Jenny had finally given in and gone home. Now it was just me, Laura, Annabel and, needless to say, Becky, packing away the photographs and other memorabilia that Laura had brought, whilst long-suffering hotel staff cleared the detritus of the party around us.

'No problem. I've got my own car, remember?' Laura was more or less back to normal – or at least, putting a brave face on it.

Annabel fixed her with a straight look. 'Should you be driving? You've had quite a bit to drink.'

'Well, I'm certainly not going to walk!' Laura laughed, a bit brittle, but a good approximation of the old Laura, but she definitely sounded slightly tipsy.

'I've got a taxi coming in a few minutes. We could share that,' Annabel offered.

'Thanks, but I'll be fine, honestly. It's only a couple of miles for me, but it's right out of your way. And I haven't had *that* much to drink.'

Annabel raised an eyebrow but didn't argue. 'I guess you know best. But the offer's there.'

'I don't want to leave my car here. I'll only have to find a way to get back for it tomorrow.'

And Mark might not be in the mood to drive

me, was the unspoken addendum.

We each picked up some of the memorabilia, Laura rescued her bouquet, and we trooped out to load it all in her car, which was parked close to the main doors.

'Are you sure about this, Laura?' I asked. I thought she'd looked a little unsteady.

'Sure. Stop fussing.' She started the engine, said her last goodnights, and drove away.

'She's only got on her sidelights,' Annabel said anxiously.

'She'll soon find that out when she gets into the unlit lanes.' I was trying to be prosaic.

'If she doesn't get stopped by the police first,' Annabel said grimly.

'There's nothing we can do about it.'

'Suppose not. And where the hell is my taxi? I had it booked for half twelve.'

I checked my watch. 'It's only twenty-five past now. He'll be here, I'm sure. I'll wait with you until he comes.'

'I think I'm going to say goodnight, girls,' Becky said. 'I'll see you in the morning, Hannah.'

'Yes, OK,' I said resignedly, but as Becky disappeared back into the hotel I groaned. 'I know it doesn't make me a nice person, but that girl drives me mad.'

'And so say all of us! Now she's gone ... should we go over to Laura's tomorrow, do you think? Just the two of us? Make sure she's all right?'

'Good idea. Say about half eleven? Meet you there.'

'Yes.' Annabel paced impatiently. 'Where *is* my taxi?' She fumbled in her bag for her mobile. 'I'm going to give him a ring. Chase him up.'

'Don't be so impatient! Listen – that sounds like a car coming now.'

'Yes, it does. Oh, good.' Annabel slipped her mobile back into her bag, but the lights that turned through the gates were sidelights only – no headlamps.

'It's Laura!' I said. 'She's back!'

The car pulled up beside us, the electric window slid down. 'Oh, good, you're still here.'

'What's wrong, Laura?' I asked.

'I've realized – I don't really feel too good. Can I take you up on your offer, Annabel? I don't think I ought to be driving.'

At that precise moment the taxi swung into the drive. 'Hurry up, then,' Annabel said.

Laura pulled into the parking area outside the converted stable block and I held my breath as she manoeuvred into a space. Whilst Annabel got into the cab, and presumably, instructed the driver about the detour, I went over to Laura's car to help her with her things.

'Oh, leave it all here. It's not going to come

to any harm,' Laura said.

'You must take your flowers. They'll die if they don't go into water.'

I carried them for her; she locked her car, wobbled over to the taxi and piled into the back beside Annabel.

Well, thank goodness for that, I thought, as the taxi pulled away. At least she'd had the sense to realize she wasn't fit to drive. I only hoped that when she got home Mark wasn't unkind to her. I really didn't think she was in a fit state to cope with another row. But most likely he was already in bed and fast asleep. Men could do that – turn their backs on hassle and switch off. It had been one of the things that had infuriated me when David and I had rowed – I'd be lying awake, going over and over it and getting more and more worked up, and he'd be lying there snoring. Ah well, *c'est la vie...*

With a little sigh I turned and headed back in the direction of my room, and my bed.

What the hell was that racket? In the middle of the night, for goodness sake! Blearily I fought my way through the layers of sleep and realized one thing for sure – it wasn't the middle of the night, it was broad daylight. Sunshine was streaming in between a gap in the curtains. And as I came to, I identified the noise that had woken me. Someone was hammering on the door of my room.

'OK – OK. I'm coming!'

I pushed aside the covers, stumbled out of bed, staggered across the floor, fumbled with the unfamiliar lock, opened the door a crack, and blinked in surprise.

'Stan!'

'Hannah. Were you still asleep?'

'Yes. What's the time? Have I missed breakfast?'

'Yes – no. Can I come in?'

'For goodness sake, Stan!' I was very aware I was wearing nothing but my very brief tee-shirt nightdress.

'Hannah, it's important.'

Something in his tone chilled me. 'Wait a minute...' I staggered back across the room, grabbed the fluffy white hotel robe from the bathroom, and pulled it on. Then I went back and opened the door. 'What the hell is going on?'

Stan came into my room and just stood there, looking awkward, saying nothing. Suddenly I was filled with sick dread, the stuff of nightmares.

'What's the matter, Stan?'

'I think you'd better sit down.'

'Why? What's wrong? Tell me!'

Stan sighed. He seemed to have aged ten years since last night.

'It's Laura.'

'Laura? What's wrong with Laura?' A picture of Laura getting into the taxi flashed before my eyes. 'She's fine, Stan. She didn't drive. She went home with Annabel.'

'She's not all right, Hannah.'

'What the hell are you talking about?'

'Oh, Hannah,' Stan said in an anguished voice. His eyes met mine and my stomach contracted. 'Oh, Hannah. Laura is dead.'

Six

The world spun. My legs would not support me. I felt the rim of the bed against the back of my knees and sank down on to it.

'Laura?' I said blankly.

'She's dead, Hannah.'

'No. No! Why are you saying this? How do you know?'

'Mark phoned.'

'Oh my God. I don't believe it! Laura – dead? But how? What happened to her? Was she taken ill? She was fine when she left here. A little bit drunk, but...' I was gabbling, I knew, but somehow I couldn't stop myself.

Stan was at the little sideboard, switching on the kettle, putting complimentary tea bags into cups, breaking open paper phials of sugar.

'She drowned,' he said flatly.

'Drowned?'

'Mark found her this morning – in their swimming pool.'

'She'd been *swimming*? Last night? Or early this morning?' I was struggling to grasp what he was saying.

'No, as far as I can gather, she was fully clothed. Wearing the outfit she had on last night.'

'You mean she fell in? But what was she doing out by the pool in the early hours?' I was trying to answer my own questions, imagining Laura a little bit tiddly, not wanting to go to bed, taking yet another drink out on to the patio. But it didn't add up. Difficult to believe that Laura was dead, let alone that she had drowned. Laura – backstroke. One of Martin's Mermaids. A brilliantly strong swimmer. She couldn't have *drowned*. Even if she was fully clothed. Even if she was drunk. The cold water would have sobered her, surely, and her natural response would take over. She couldn't have *drowned*.

'Are you sure?' I whispered. 'This isn't some kind of sick joke, is it?'

His face told me it was not. The kettle had boiled. Stan poured water into the cups, squashed the tea bags and tore the plastic coverings off two miniature cartons of milk.

'Drink this.' He pushed a cup into my trembling hands. 'You're in shock. We all are.'

I sipped my tea, scaldingly hot and very sweet, but it didn't help much.

'It's just crazy. She can't be dead. Not Laura.'

Stan sat down on the bed beside me. I was suddenly very glad that he was the one who had told me, him who was here with me now. He might play the fool, act sometimes like an overgrown schoolboy, but in a crisis there was also something comfortingly solid about him. If I fell apart, Stan would pick up the pieces.

'Peter and I are going over there now,' Stan said. 'We wondered if you might like to come with us.'

'Oh – I don't know...' A sort of cold panic started in my stomach, a shying away from going to the house where it had happened. Laura's house. They'd have taken her away by now, I supposed, but I didn't want to see her things lying around, didn't want to see the pool, didn't want to have to face Mark. I wouldn't know what to say to him. Bad enough to know what to say to any recently bereaved person, but under the circumstances...

'They had a terrible row last night,' I said. 'Mark really lost it with her. He is going to be in such a state, especially knowing the last things they said to one another were said in anger.'

'He is going to need his friends,' Stan said

102

stoically. 'That's us, Hannah. Peter and I are definitely going. What you do is up to you, but I think a woman's touch might not go amiss.'

'OK.' I made up my mind and being decisive helped. A sort of unnatural calm descended on me. 'Does Annabel know?'

'Peter was going to phone her.'

'And Jenny? We have to be careful about telling Jenny. She shouldn't have a shock like this in her condition, but she has to be told. She'd never forgive us if we knew and she didn't. We were all so close. Well, you know we were–' for some reason, I couldn't bring myself to say 'Martin's Mermaids'. What with finding out that something inappropriate had been going on between him and Annabel and possibly Laura too, added to the fact that Laura had drowned, it seemed gruesome somehow – 'the Inseparables,' I finished, reverting instead to the earlier nickname for the four of us.

'We thought it would be best to leave telling Jenny to you and Annabel,' Stan said.

'Yes, I think so, definitely. We can do it together. Or maybe...' I broke off, my mind racing ahead. 'Maybe it would be better if we told her husband – got him to do it. It would be a hell of a shock if the two of us turned up at her door with news like this. I don't want her going into premature labour or something. You say Peter is ringing Annabel now?'

Stan nodded, and right on cue there was a tap on the door. It was Peter.

'Oh, Peter, this is just terrible!' I greeted him.

'I know.' He, too, looked pale and shaken, but when I went to squeeze his hand he recoiled, ramrod stiff, all his shock and grief locked inside him. 'I've spoken to Annabel and she is going to meet us in the lay-by on the main road just before the turning to Mark's house. We don't want umpteen cars rolling up the drive as if it were a circus. In fact, I'm not sure we should go at all. Ian will be there, for sure.'

'Ian will be on the plane by now,' Stan said. 'Don't you remember him saying he was off to Minorca or Majorca or somewhere on an early flight? No, I'm going definitely. You two can please yourselves.'

'I'll come with you,' I said. 'Just give me five minutes to get dressed.'

Stan nodded and he and Peter left. For a moment I stood, my hands pressed to my mouth as the shock ran through me again in waves. This couldn't be happening. It couldn't! But it was.

I sorted myself out some clothes – the trousers and top I'd worn to drive down – and slipped them on. The last time I'd worn these things, Laura had been alive, I thought, and stopped myself short.

Don't go down that road. If you do you'll fall

104

apart. Just think about doing what you have to do...

There would be time for tears later. For the moment it was all action.

Annabel's flashy sports car was already parked in the lay-by when we got there. Thankfully, I'd managed to avoid seeing anyone from our class before leaving The Beeches – I'd simply thrown on my clothes, grabbed a packet of biscuits from the courtesy tray and hurried out to where Stan and Peter were waiting. I didn't feel like eating, but I thought I might need something later, and as I left my room I cringed to see Laura's car still parked where she had left it last night.

Annabel was in just as great a state of shock as we were. She was standing beside her car smoking a cigarette. I'd never seen Annabel smoke before.

'I know – I know,' she said distractedly. 'I gave up five years ago, and haven't had so much as a puff since. But, my God, this morning I needed it!'

I knew how she felt. I'd never smoked in my life, but right then I wished I did.

We discussed tactics and decided that after all we would take two cars, as it gave us greater flexibility. If Annabel and I weren't wanted, we could leave again. I insinuated myself into the passenger seat of her car and we set off following Stan's people carrier down the lane.

'I don't believe this is happening,' I said. 'Not Laura.'

'I know.'

'How did she seem when you dropped her off last night?' I asked. Annabel had, after all, been the last one to see Laura alive.

'No different. She was a bit tiddly, but she certainly wasn't incapable. I asked the taxi driver to wait until she was safely inside the house but she went around the back way. We left when she disappeared from view.'

'I just don't understand it,' I said. 'How the hell did she come to fall into the swimming pool? How the hell did she *drown*?'

We were at the house before Annabel could answer – not that there was really any answer she could give.

I'm not sure what I expected to find – my experience of sudden death was, thankfully, very limited, but everything looked bizarrely normal, apart from a police car pulled up on the turnaround. The four of us had a discussion about our best course of action and decided Annabel and I should wait outside while the boys tested out the ground. As they approached the front door, however, it opened and two uniformed officers came out. Both wore flak jackets over their short sleeved white shirts – a sign of the times, I supposed, as was working in pairs even for something as routine as this.

They nodded to Stan and Peter, but in all honesty seemed more interested in Annabel's car, which they had a jolly good look at before getting into their response vehicle. Stan and Peter went into the house and a moment later Peter came out again and crossed to where Annabel and I were waiting.

'Mark says to come in.'

My stomach lurched. 'Is Laura...?'

Peter seemed to read my unspoken, rather foolish, reluctance. 'Don't worry, she's not here any more,' he said soothingly.

'The police...?'

'They'll have been taking details from Mark,' Annabel said. 'Come on, sweetie, let's go and offer our moral support.' She linked her arm through mine and we followed Peter back to the house.

Stan and Mark were in the kitchen.

'Annabel. Hannah. Thanks for coming.' To my surprise, Mark sounded almost normal, if a bit robotic. He was in shock, I guessed. The terrible enormity of what had happened hadn't hit him yet.

'Oh, Mark, I am so sorry.' The words seemed hopelessly inadequate. But what else was there to say?

'Thanks. Can I get you a cup of tea? Or coffee?' As he spoke he was automatically collecting used mugs from the table, dumping them in the sink. He'd obviously made tea for the policemen we'd just seen leaving. It seemed wrong that he should be waiting on others.

'I'll see to it. You sit down.' I refilled the kettle, put it on to boil and found clean mugs in the china rack. But Mark didn't sit down. He paced aimlessly behind me.

'Sit down, mate!' Stan pulled out a chair and more or less forced Mark into it.

'I'm sorry.' Mark shook his head woozily, like a boxer who has just taken a heavy punch to the jaw. 'I'm not being ... I just can't seem to get myself together.'

'Hardly surprising,' Stan said. 'You've had one hell of a shock.'

'It was a shock, yes.' Back to robotic, semi-normality. 'I mean – I knew she hadn't come home. Or at least, she hadn't come to bed. I woke up in the middle of the night – about three a.m. – and her side of the bed was empty. But I thought she'd gone in the spare room. If she was late. Didn't want to disturb me...' He broke off, not saying what I think was in all our minds – that he'd thought that Laura hadn't wanted to share a bed with him because of the row. Or maybe hadn't even come home at all. His first words had given that away, but now he was reluctant to elaborate, perhaps even to acknowledge the rift that had been the last interplay between them.

'But I never expected to find her in the pool,' he said, rasping a hand over an unshaven chin. 'I didn't even look for her outside. I took my coffee out on to the patio and ... Christ ... there she was.'

Stan laid a comforting hand on his shoulder and Mark looked up at him with eyes that were full of anguish.

'If I'd come down and looked for her in the night when I found she wasn't in bed, maybe she wouldn't be dead! If I'd found her sooner, maybe I could have revived her.'

'That's nonsense, Mark,' Annabel said briskly. 'Laura came home in a taxi with me at around one. The accident must have happened a good couple of hours before you woke, so there's no point blaming yourself. If anyone's to blame it's me, for not coming in with her, making sure she was all right. But honestly she didn't seem that pissed. Just a bit unsteady. It's only with hindsight...'

'But how do you know when she went into the pool?' Mark persisted. 'Maybe she was sleepwalking. Maybe she went out there in the middle of the night, and that's what woke me. If only I'd got up then and come looking for her. She did sleepwalk, you know, sometimes, especially if she was stressed.'

'Was she wearing her nightclothes?' Annabel asked.

'No. The same outfit she had on for the party last night.'

'Well, there you are then.'

'She might have crashed out without getting undressed.' Mark seemed determined to punish himself every step of the way. 'Down here on the sofa. And then let herself out, still asleep to all intents and purposes. The patio doors were unlocked. I thought that was strange. But I blamed Darren.'

A prickle of unease skittered across my skin. 'Where is Darren now?'

Mark shrugged. 'Still in bed in the motor home, I suppose.'

'You mean he's still asleep?' I was dumbfounded. The motor home, admittedly, was parked up in the orchard, some way from the swimming pool, but all the same. 'How can he possibly still be asleep with all this going on?'

'He never surfaces till midday at the earliest.' Mark broke off, the anguished look in his eyes revealing that he had realized, too late, what an unfortunate expression he had chosen to use.

'Darren? Who's Darren?' Peter asked.

'My nephew. He's staying with us.' Mark didn't elaborate.

'Shouldn't he be told what's happened?' Peter suggested gently.

'Oh, no – please. The last thing I want is him on the scene.' Mark buried his face in his hands.

'He has *problems*,' Annabel said meaningfully. 'I don't think it would be very helpful to have him around just now.'

Peter looked doubtful, but he let it go. 'Is there anybody else who should be told, Mark? What about Laura's family?'

'Her mother and father are on a world cruise. And her sister lives in Scotland.' Mark looked very lost suddenly, very helpless.

'Well, you have to get in touch with them,' Peter said firmly. 'Do you want me to do it for you?' he asked when Mark still stared at him blankly.

'No – I should be the one to tell Lucy...'

'Come on, then, let's go and do it. Then we'll talk through what else needs to be done.' He guided Mark out of the room, heading, I suppose, for the privacy of his study, or wherever they could make the necessary phone calls undisturbed, and the rest of us looked at one another, wretched and awkward, too, at finding ourselves alone in Laura's kitchen, with Laura dead.

'Oh, I'm going to have a cigarette!' Annabel picked up her bag and headed for the door. For a reformed smoker she was certainly returning to the habit with depressing enthusiasm.

'I'll come with you,' I said.

'You want one too?'

'No, but I could do with some fresh air.'

The minute we were outside, though, I

wondered if it was such a good idea. The paved patio ran the whole length of the back of the house from the kitchen at the one end to the 'drawing room' as Laura had called it at the other and beyond the patio, at the drawing room end, was the swimming pool. It looked totally innocuous now, but my stomach turned over all the same, and I fancied I could see a large wet patch that the sun had not yet dried out on the paving stones beside it – the spot where Laura's body had lain when they'd dragged her out of the water, presumably. And just to make things worse, just a few feet away, lay the bouquet of flowers Tristan had presented her with, still in its cellophane wrapper and tied with a huge bow of yellow florist's ribbon, and under one of the patio chairs that were grouped around a dark green wrought iron table was her handbag. The contents had spilled out by the look of it, and I imagined her dumping it on the chair so carelessly that it had fallen off on to the ground.

'There's her bag,' I said, and suddenly it seemed terribly important to me that I should rescue it. It just wasn't right, Laura's most personal possessions lying in a tumbled heap like that.

I crossed to the table and crouched down, righting the bag against the leg of the chair and putting her things back inside. Her purse, cigarettes and lighter, an unopened handy-pack of tissues, a slim leather-bound diary, a half-gone tube of Polo mints, and assorted items of make-up, all loose, as if she'd thought they would take up less space than if she tried to stuff in a cosmetics bag. Lip gloss, mascara, eye-liner ... all the things she'd had to borrow from me, and which I hadn't had back. But that didn't matter now. Jenny had probably put them in *her* bag and then forgotten all about them, as I had, because we'd been distracted by Tristan's presentation.

I dropped the eyeliner pencil into Laura's bag, zipped it securely and stood up to see Annabel watching me intently.

'I have to take care of her things,' I said. 'She's not here to do it any more.'

And I burst into tears.

We cried together for a little while, Annabel and I, and she smoked another cigarette. I went to rescue Laura's bouquet, and was shocked to see that the blooms were all ruined, the heads broken off and the foliage crushed. Perhaps Mark had trodden on it in his rush to get Laura out of the pool, I thought. Whatever, it was now good for nothing but the compost heap.

Stan emerged from the house. 'We were wondering where you two had got to,' he said, pretending not to notice our tear-stained faces.

'Has Mark made his phone calls?' Annabel asked.

'Yep. He's got hold of Laura's sister, and she's going to try to reach her parents. Lucy is coming down from Scotland ASAP, so Mark is going to hold off doing anything about the funeral arrangements until she gets here. There will have to be a post-mortem, in any case, and that isn't likely to be until tomorrow or even Tuesday at the earliest, so there's no rush. It's going to be the middle of the week before her body is released.'

A post-mortem ... My stomach churned. *Before her body can be released...*

This was Laura we were talking about. Laura now lying in a hospital morgue. I couldn't bear it.

'It might be an idea to contact a funeral director, though,' Annabel was saying. 'Just to get someone on board who understands the procedures.'

'Like I said, I think Mark is going to wait until Lucy gets here,' Stan said. 'But I do think that nephew of his should be told – while we're still here, if he's as much trouble as Mark implies.'

'He is,' I said grimly.

'I'm going over to the motor home now. And he'd better not mess with me, the mood I'm in.'

Annabel and I exchanged wan smiles. I

didn't think anyone would mess with Stan, whatever his mood. He headed off in the direction of the motor home and Annabel and I waited, wondering what effect the news would have on the disturbed young man we'd confronted in the kitchen on Friday evening, and also to give Mark a little time alone with Peter. Peter was a good listener; if anyone could help Mark to come to terms with the dreadful reality of what had happened, it was Peter.

Stan was coming back – alone.

'How did he take it?' Annabel asked. 'Did he give you any trouble?'

'Hardly,' Stan said. 'He's not there.'

'Not there?' I echoed.

'Nope.'

'Where can he be then? Mark said he never wakes up till midday at the earliest. Has his bed been slept in?'

Stan snorted. 'There's no way of knowing. The place is a tip. I shouldn't think the bed is made from one week's end to the next. Anyway, the thing is, he's not there, so there's nothing we can do about it. We'll just have to wait until he turns up to break the news. Come on, let's go back in and tell Mark his lodger has gone walkabout.'

We found Mark and Peter back in the kitchen. Peter had made yet more tea and it looked as if he and Mark had been having a heart-to-heart, which I thought was a good thing.

'I'm thinking it might be a good idea to get you away from here for a bit,' Stan suggested. 'What do you say we find a quiet country pub? A change of scene might do you good. And a pint of beer or a good stiff whisky will certainly be better for you than *that...*' He nodded at the mugs of tea with a gesture of disgust.

'Nothing is going to do Mark good at the moment,' I said. 'Just because you fancy a pint, Stan, doesn't mean Mark should be dragged out in public.'

'Do you fancy a pint, mate?' Mark asked, unbelievably, in the face of all that he was going through, suddenly becoming the solicitous host. 'If you do, there are some cans in the fridge.'

'Whew, thanks, I certainly do! I've drunk enough tea this morning to rot my guts.'

'It's not up to your usual draught, but...'

'Don't worry, it'll do me fine. Do you want one, Mark? Peter?'

Peter shook his head. 'Too early in the day for me.'

'Mark? I'll get you one anyway.' He found the cans, poured two, and pushed one glass over to Mark. 'Get this down you. Now, what about you, girls?'

Annabel declined, but I succumbed. 'I'll have a glass of wine.' Early it might be, but I could do with it. As I was taking my first sip the doorbell rang.

'I'll go.' Annabel headed off into the hall. A few minutes later she was back.

'Mark – there's someone to see you.'

Something in the way she said it sent a tiny frisson of alarm tingling through my stomach. I turned to see a man in the hallway behind her, youngish – well, about our age, anyway – short brown hair, round face, wearing a brown leather jacket. I had the impression there was someone else there too but if so they were out of my line of vision. Mark got up, went towards the inner door.

'Yes? I'm Mark Calvin.'

'DS Paul Jeavons. And this is DC Paula Buchan. Do you think we could have a word in private?'

'Yes, sure. Come this way.'

The police officers disappeared from view. Stan, Peter, Annabel and I all looked at one another.

'CID?' Stan said blankly. 'Why do CID want to talk to Mark?'

'Probably just a formality,' Peter said. 'Isn't that right, Annabel?'

'Probably,' Annabel said, but she looked worried. 'I don't like this, folks.'

We were silent, each speculating but unwilling to share the thought that we must all, individually, have been thinking: why would CID get involved with an accidental death?

The minutes ticked by endlessly, then the

policewoman – Paula Buchan – came into the kitchen. She was a square-built girl in her late twenties, with shoulder-length hair tied back loosely from a rather plain face, and wearing a cropped cotton jacket over a straight, flax-coloured skirt.

'Do you think we could have some tea or coffee?' Her sharp eyes flicked over the glasses of beer and my wine. 'This may take some time.'

'What's going on?' Stan asked bluntly.

And Annabel, more tactfully: 'Is there a problem?'

'Possibly.' The policewoman looked at each of us in turn. 'We're talking to Mr Calvin now, but we shall want to speak to all of you too, so please don't leave without letting me have your names and where we can find you.'

'There *is* a problem,' Annabel said. 'Would you mind telling us exactly what it is?'

The policewoman hesitated. Again her gaze moved over each of us in turn.

'OK. The problem is that we have reason to suspect that Mrs Calvin's death might not have been an accident.'

Seven

For a moment there was complete, utter stunned silence. Then Annabel said, in a very cool, businesslike tone: 'Could you elaborate on that?'

Again the policewoman took her time about answering.

'Mrs Calvin had sustained a blow to the head,' she said at last. 'The doctor noticed it at the time he certified death, but put it down to her hitting her head on the side of the pool when she fell. On reflection, though, he decided he wasn't completely satisfied with that explanation and came back to us to report his doubts. We won't know anything for certain until the Home Office pathologist has carried out an examination, of course, but that's unlikely to be until tomorrow. In the meantime, to err on the side of caution, we are treating Mrs Calvin's death as suspicious. Which is why we'd like to talk to all of you. Now – do you think we could have that tea?'

I made it, three cups, one each for the police officers and one for Mark, but the rest

of us definitely needed something stronger.

'What on earth are they talking about?'
Stan exclaimed. 'I never heard such rubbish.'

'If there's any doubt they have to cover
their backs.' Annabel had gone into solicitor
mode. 'I think it might be an idea if I sat in
on this.' She poured herself a glass of wine,
took a big slurp, then set it down on the
counter. 'Better not take this with me. I don't
want to appear unprofessional.' She left the
kitchen.

'Bloody hell,' Peter said. It was the strongest language I'd ever heard him use. 'Surely
they can't think...?'

'It's utter rubbish,' Stan said again. 'What
else can it have been but a terrible accident?
She was pissed, fell, hit her head and drowned. What else could it be?'

'I must admit I found it pretty hard to
swallow that she just drowned,' I said doubt-
fully. 'She was a really strong swimmer.
However drunk she was, staying afloat was
second nature to her. And it's only a little
pool – what, fifteen metres or so? But I suppose if she was unconscious when she went
into the water it would go some way to
explaining it. Even so...'

I tried very hard to imagine how such a
thing could have happened and did not
succeed. Laura could have decided to go and

sit on the patio for a while before going to bed, I conceded; it had been a warm, fine night. And if she'd had more to drink and become clumsy, she could have upset her bag and maybe trampled on her flowers. But if she'd simply tripped and banged her head, how had she come to end up in the water? I simply couldn't see it. And I was thinking, too, of a very disturbed young man who might well have been high on drugs, and who had disappeared from the motor home he'd been living in.

'You don't think Mark's nephew had anything to do with this, do you?' I said.

'Mark's nephew?' Peter sounded startled. 'Why would he have anything to do with it?'

'He seemed a pretty unsavoury character to me,' I said. 'He was in the kitchen on Friday evening looking for cheese, and...'

'Perhaps he was hungry,' Peter suggested.

'Cheese? Just a lump of cheese? And Annabel said he came back later asking for whisky.' They still looked doubtful and I went on: 'You didn't see him. He was ... weird. He frightened the life out of Jenny. Look, even Mark didn't want him around this morning, and he's his uncle! And you said he wasn't in the motor home, Stan.'

'No, he's not there. But what are you saying, Hannah?'

'I don't know really. But supposing he came over last night when Laura got home.

121

Supposing he was out by the pool, out of his skull on drugs, doing something really stupid, whatever people do when they're on a trip. Laura went out to remonstrate with him and he lost it. Hit her. She fell in the pool, or he pushed her, and then, when he realized what he'd done, he made a run for it. Oh, I know it sounds like something out of a made-for-TV movie, but ... well, it makes more sense to me than that Laura just fell in the pool and drowned. She wasn't that drunk. Really she wasn't.'

'It has to be a possibility, I suppose,' Peter said slowly.

'Do you think I should go in there and tell them? Mark doesn't even know Darren is missing, does he? And even if he did, he's too shocked to be able to put two and two together.'

'I wouldn't interrupt them,' Peter said. 'We'll get our chance to speak up later. You heard that detective. They'll want to interview all of us. And they'll want to do it pretty soon, before the trail goes cold. If Laura *was* murdered...'

It was the first time that dreadful word had been used. It hung in the air, adding a new dimension of horror to the already tense atmosphere. Murdered. Laura. Bad enough that she was dead. But *murdered*...

There was movement and action out in the hall. It sounded like one person – no, two people, were going upstairs. Then the policewoman and Annabel came back into the kitchen. Both looked extremely serious.

'I'm afraid we're going to have to continue this down at the station,' the policewoman, Paula Buchan, said. 'We need to secure this house as a crime scene.'

I felt the blood draining out of my body.

'Darren,' I whispered, 'I was right then.'

Paula Buchan threw me a puzzled look. 'Darren?'

'Mark's nephew. Was he responsible?'

'That's not a name that's come up so far in our inquiries,' she said crisply. 'Perhaps you can tell us more when you're interviewed. You're all staying at The Beeches, I understand? We can probably see you there, along with anyone else who may be able to help us. But I'll take your names and addresses just in case any of you need to leave before we get around to talking to you.'

Her personal radio crackled into life. 'Excuse me...' She stepped out into the hall to answer it.

'What's going on?' I asked Annabel urgently. 'Why have they suddenly decided to secure the house as a crime scene? That detective didn't seem to have even heard of Mark's nephew.'

'No, it's Mark they're interested in.' Annabel spoke in a low whisper.

'Mark! But...'

'They've somehow learned about the row that he and Laura had – how he stormed out of the reunion. They put it to him and he admitted it. And that he had grave suspicions that Laura was having an affair – and not for the first time. It would seem things have been stormy between them for some time.'

'But they can't think that *Mark*...'

'The husband is always the prime suspect,' Annabel said. 'If Laura's death was as a result of foul play, then Mark was always going to be in the frame. And the evidence of trouble between them fuels the flames.'

'That is the most ridiculous thing I ever heard!' I exploded. 'Mark would never harm Laura! Mark would never harm anyone! He's kind and generous. He's taken in his troublesome nephew to try and set his life straight. He even gave that idiot Becky a job because he felt sorry for her.'

'And he has a violent temper,' Annabel argued. 'You saw him last night, Hannah.'

For some reason, I felt driven to defend Mark. Old habits die hard, I guess. The man I'd once been crazy about couldn't be a murderer.

'He was provoked,' I said. 'He thought Laura was carrying on with Aaron. That's why he lost it.'

'Exactly. Well, supposing when Laura came

home she provoked him again? Supposing the row continued, out on the patio, and escalated? If, for instance, she told him she was leaving him? Supposing he hit out at her...?'

'No, he wouldn't!' I interrupted vehemently. 'He wouldn't! Not in a million years!'

But I was remembering, all the same, the last conversation I'd had with Laura. She had told me herself that Mark could change in an instant; that he 'turned into an animal' when something caused him to lose his temper. That she'd thought he was going to hit Aaron last night. That he'd half-killed one of the animal rights protestors when they'd targeted his home. And that she'd warned him that if ever he raised a hand to her, she'd leave him.

What if last night when she'd come home she'd been at the end of her patience with him and told him she'd had enough? What if he'd snapped? I closed my eyes briefly and felt a shudder run through me. Then, determinedly, I pushed the thought away. Mark might have a temper, but I couldn't believe he could be responsible for Laura's death. Violence against a young thug who was damaging his property and his life, or against a man he thought was having an affair with his wife, was one thing. Violence against the wife he loved dearly was quite another.

'You've seen the state he's in, Annabel,' I

125

said. 'Devastated. You can't honestly believe that *Mark* killed Laura.'

'No, of course I don't.' She gave a quick, impatient shake of her head. 'I'm only telling you how it might look to an outsider. Mark had motive and opportunity. They're bound to treat him as a suspect.'

'But we don't even know yet that Laura's death was anything other than a terrible accident,' I argued weakly, though from the start I'd had serious doubts about that myself.

'No, but the police have to err on the side of caution,' Annabel said. 'If the post-mortem shows someone did strike her before she went into the pool, then the scene has to be secured to preserve evidence. It's important to act quickly, or vital clues could be lost for ever.'

The policewoman, Paula Buchan, came back into the kitchen and our conversation was brought to an end. As she was taking down our names and addresses, I heard Mark and DS Jeavons come back downstairs; the policeman had accompanied him to make sure he did not take the opportunity to tamper with evidence, I presumed. And almost simultaneously the two uniformed policemen we'd seen leaving when we arrived returned – to 'secure the scene' as they had described it.

Paula Buchan ushered us out of the house.

Mark, looking if possible even more stunned than he had earlier, and not a little lost, was standing on the drive, a big soft holdall, which I assumed contained all the things he would need, by his side. I went up to him and touched his arm, my heart aching for him.

'Where are you going to go, Mark?'

'At the moment – to the police station.' His voice was flat, emotionless.

'I know – but after that. Is there someone you can stay with?'

'I don't know. I'll have to think.'

'We'll sort something out.' Annabel had joined us. 'I'm going to the police station with him, Hannah. This is really not my bag, but for the moment, until we can sort him out a lawyer, it's a damn sight better than a duty solicitor who doesn't know him from Adam. Thank goodness I brought my own car. I can follow them, and be ready to see him through the formalities.'

DS Jeavons emerged from the house where one of the uniformed constables was now stationed outside the front door. 'Let's go then, sir,' he said to Mark.

DC Paula Buchan assisted Mark into the rear passenger seat of their light blue un-marked car and got in beside him. They drove off, and there was nothing left for the rest of us but to pile into Stan's 4x4 and Annabel's racy little coupe and follow them.

We drove back to The Beeches in near silence where we were able to find spaces next to one another.

'You realize we should have vacated our rooms by now?' Peter said as we piled out of our respective vehicles. 'The domestic staff will be chomping at the bit – and we'll probably be charged an extra night into the bargain.'

'Well, that's just tough,' Stan said firmly. 'We've had more important things on our minds. And to be frank, if they do charge us extra after all the money they made out of us last night, I reckon it's a pretty poor show.'

'I'm OK,' I said. 'I booked for the week. I thought it would make a nice break and I could see something of Laura and Jenny...' My voice tailed away miserably.

'Actually,' Stan went on as we walked back towards the hotel, 'I think I might try to stay on an extra night or so anyway. I reckon Mark is going to be in need of a bit of moral support. I've got some time off due to me – I could get away with a couple of days at least. Just until we know for sure what's happening, and Mark can get back home again.'

'Good plan,' Peter approved. 'I wish I could say I'd do the same, but I'm going to have to get away today. I've got cover for this weekend, but that's it. If I want more time off, I'll have to arrange a locum.'

'What about making a statement to the police?' I asked.

'They've got my home address if they don't get round to me before I have to go,' Peter said. 'I don't think there's anything I can tell them in any case apart from giving Mark a character reference.'

'Nor me really.' Stan said.

'You're the one who can tell them most, Hannah,' Peter said.

'I know.' And I didn't like it one little bit. 'They're going to ask me about the row Mark and Laura had last night, aren't they? Although they seem to know about it already. I wonder who told them? There was only Jenny there.'

I suddenly remembered. Jenny. We hadn't done anything about letting Jenny know what had happened. I'd intended to discuss with Annabel the best way to go about it, but somehow it had slipped my mind and now, with the new developments, a telephone call to her husband to ask him to break it to her seemed inappropriate.

'I think I'd better go over and see her,' I said.

'Now?'

'Yes, now. I don't want her to hear it on the local news or something before I've had the chance to speak to her.'

'Have a sandwich or something first,' Stan suggested. 'You did miss breakfast – we all did.'

'I'm not going to die of starvation,' I said grimly. 'And I don't think I could eat anyway. Let me get this over with and I'll have something later.'

'Well, if I'm not here when you get back, Hannah, you take care,' Peter said.

'I will.'

'And I'll see you soon.'

'Yes.' We both knew what he meant. Laura's funeral. My stomach clenched; tears ached in my throat. I turned away, digging in my bag for my car keys to hide the fact that I was welling up.

'Good luck with Jenny,' Stan said.

I nodded mutely, not turning round. By the time I had my car unlocked, the boys had gone. I looked at their retreating backs – big, solid Stan, neat, polite Peter, shoulder to shoulder as they had always been – and thought I had never felt more alone in my life.

Jenny lived in a modern semi-detached house in a new estate that had gone up on the outskirts of town. I'd only been there a couple of times and I had to really concentrate to find her close amongst the maze of roads, avenues and cul-de-sacs that spread out from a central green area. I made it eventually, though, and found a space at the kerb to park.

My stomach was churning and I took a minute to get myself together. I wasn't looking forward to this at all, but it had to be done. Taking a deep breath, I locked the car and started up Jenny's drive. Before I reached the point where a narrow path angled off towards the front of the house, two little boys erupted from the back door, which opened directly on to the drive in front of the gravel-washed garage; laughing and enthusiastic, they grabbed up bicycles which were abandoned haphazardly on the drive.

'Back in half an hour, do you hear?' Jenny's voice, calling after them.

'Yeah! Yeah!'

They leaped on to their bicycles and shot down the drive, narrowly avoiding me. One was Jack, Jenny's second eldest, I guessed, the other a friend. Knowing now that Jenny was in the kitchen I abandoned my intention of ringing the front doorbell and instead went straight up the drive to the back.

The door, bright with new paint, was ajar; the smell of roasting meat wafted out. I tapped on it, dreading the moment I would have to tell Jenny the terrible news. The moment she opened it, though, I knew that I would, at least, be spared that. Jenny's soft, pretty face was crumpled somehow, and her eyes were swollen.

'Oh, Hannah – it's you!' she said, and we fell into one another's arms. Hugging wasn't easy, the size Jenny was, but somehow we managed it.

'Oh, Hannah – it's just so awful!' Jenny said, turning away at last to turn down the heat under a pan that was boiling on the stove. 'I've been trying to get in touch with you and Annabel but nobody seemed to know where you were and I don't have your mobile numbers.'

'We've been to Mark's,' I said. 'We didn't mean to leave you out, Jenny, but with your family commitments...'

As if to prove a point, a smaller version of the boy I'd seen outside burst into the kitchen.

'Mummy – Mummy – Noah's got my Power Ranger laser gun and he won't give it back!'

Jenny went to the door into the hall and called up the stairs. 'Chloe! Will you come down and look after your brothers for a minute, please? I've got a visitor.' Footsteps on the stairs and a pretty girl of eleven or twelve who was the spitting image of her mother at the same age, right down to the glasses, came into the kitchen.

'Noah is teasing Daniel again. Will you please sort them out for me?' Jenny entreated her. Chloe took the little boy, ushering him out.

'Isn't Ben here with you?' I asked.

'He always takes Chloe for her riding lesson on a Sunday morning and keeps an eye on the stables for Sheila, who owns the place, while she's out with Chloe and the others in their little group. Chloe wasn't feeling well this morning, but Ben didn't want to let Sheila down, so he's gone anyway. And now ... all this. Oh, Hannah, I simply can't believe it!'

'How did you come to hear about it, Jenny?' I asked, curious.

She grimaced. 'Becky phoned.'

'Becky!' *Now why didn't that surprise me?* She hadn't been in evidence when we'd left The Beeches and we certainly hadn't told her. But I supposed either Stan or Peter might have mentioned to someone what had happened and the bush telegraph had swung into operation. It was absolutely typical of Becky that she would want to be part of the action; make herself important by being the one to tell Jenny.

'She said Laura had drowned herself in her swimming pool,' Jenny said.

'Drowned herself!' I was outraged. 'There's been no suggestion she did any such thing! Honestly, it's unbelievable the rumours people put about.'

'But she is dead?'

'Yes, I'm afraid so. And there is more. The police suspect foul play.'

133

Jenny's jaw dropped; her eyes went wide with shock.

'You mean – she was *murdered*?'

'It seems to be a possibility. And that's not the worst of it.'

I went on to tell her all that had happened; that Annabel was at the police station now with Mark, that Stan was going to stay on for a few days, and that the police were certain to want to interview her. I hated upsetting her in her condition, but I felt it was best it came from me rather than from some impersonal policeman who might just turn up on her doorstep. Or from Becky. I could well imagine her ringing Jenny with every snippet of news she got hold of, and twisting it to make it as sensational as possible, just as she'd twisted the fact that Laura had drowned. Really, she was not a nice person. In fact, I could kill her.

The thought brought me up short. Becky was very much alive, but it was beginning to look as if someone *had* killed Laura.

'I'm not looking forward to having to make a statement to the police,' I admitted. 'They're bound to want to know about the row between Laura and Mark and I don't want to say anything that might make things look worse for him.'

'You wouldn't do that. And if they knew about it already...'

I bit my lip, thinking of the things Laura

had said to me when she was upset.

'Jenny, you've seen more of Laura over the past few years than any of us. She's never said anything to you, has she, about problems at home?'

'Problems? What sort of problems?'

'Mark's temper.'

'No.' Jenny shook her head emphatically. 'She was always bright and bubbly – you know, just Laura. Why?'

'No reason.' I didn't want to repeat to anyone, not even to Jenny, what Laura had said. And I certainly didn't want to help the police build a case against Mark. It was possible, I supposed, that she'd said the same things to someone else, but they weren't going to hear it from me. Even if I was withholding evidence. If I'd believed for a moment that Mark was responsible for Laura's death, I'd have been the first in line to accuse him. But I didn't believe it. Absolutely not. Laura had been upset last night when she'd said what she said; she had probably exaggerated, but even in the state she was in she had been adamant he'd never raised a hand to her. As for the incident involving the animal rights protester, there was no doubt he'd been provoked beyond endurance. The mildest of men could be forgiven for losing it with someone who'd done the things those people had done.

A thought suddenly struck me.

'I don't suppose the animal rights activists could be involved in it?' I said, as much to myself as to Jenny.

She clapped a hand over her mouth, eyes wide above it. 'Oh, surely not? Things have quietened down on that front, as I understand it. And they'd never go so far as to kill Laura.'

'Didn't they try to kidnap her once? And what happened might not have been intentional. Supposing they'd intended to have another go at polluting the swimming pool and Laura heard them out there and went out to remonstrate with them. They might have panicked and things got out of hand.' Jenny was shaking her head. 'I know you've got some sympathy with them,' I said, 'but some of them are pretty deranged.'

'Laura was afraid of them,' Jenny argued. 'She'd never have gone out alone to confront them. She'd have woken Mark, or called the police. And there'd be evidence, surely? I can't see them stopping to clean up after themselves after they realized things had gone horribly wrong and Laura was dead.'

'No, I suppose you're right,' I admitted. 'And I found her flowers and her bag on the patio too. She wouldn't have taken them with her if she'd heard something suspicious and gone out to investigate. No, to be honest, I'm more inclined to think if there was foul play, it's Mark's nephew we should be looking to. Oh Lord! I was going to tell the police about him, and that he seems to have gone walkabout, but everything happened so fast I didn't get around to it.'

'I'm sure Mark will tell them,' Jenny consoled me.

'Mark doesn't even know he's missing.'

'But Annabel does, and she's with Mark. She's very competent, Hannah. I know she's not a criminal lawyer, but she won't let anything get past her. Stop worrying. The truth will out, whatever it is.'

'Oh, I hope you're right.' I couldn't forget the sight of Mark, shocked and grieving, being bundled into the back of the police car. 'As if it wasn't bad enough for poor Mark to lose his wife, on top of that to be suspected of her murder. It doesn't bear thinking about.'

The back door opened and the boy I'd seen earlier going off on his bicycle erupted into the kitchen.

'Dad's home. Is lunch ready? I'm starving!'

'No, it's not ready.' Jenny looked flustered now and I thought the time had probably come for me to leave.

'I'd better get back to The Beeches,' I said.

'OK. But you will keep me posted, won't you?'

'Yes, of course.'

'And if there's anything at all I can do...'

'I'll let you know.'

But Jenny had enough on her plate already. And the less stressed out she was in her condition, the better.

Ben was getting out of his car on the drive as I left, trailing clumps of dried mud from his Wellington boots on to the pristine paving slabs.

'Hannah! What a surprise!' But he didn't sound overly pleased to see me. Perhaps he didn't like being caught in his manure-stained jeans and a tee-shirt stuck with bits of straw, I thought. Or perhaps he thought I was going to delay his Sunday roast.

'I'm just leaving,' I said. And then, an understatement if ever there was one: 'Jenny's had a bit of a shock. She'll tell you all about it.' I turned away, turned back, touching his arm. 'Take care of her, Ben.'

Then I headed down the drive to my own car, mentally steeling myself to be ready to face whatever awaited me back at The Beeches.

Eight

Looking back now, I can honestly say that whole day was the longest and most horrible I have ever had the misfortune to live through. Though there were others yet to come, equally grim and even more threatening, it is the pervading feeling of living a nightmare that day that remains with me more overwhelmingly than any other.

When I arrived back at The Beeches there was a police car parked on the forecourt and a uniformed officer in the foyer talking to the receptionist and making notes. He was getting the details of all the guests who had stayed here last night, I assumed. I was half tempted to approach him there and then rather than waiting for the inevitable summons, but decided to find Stan and Peter first to try and find out if there were any further developments.

I found Stan in the bar, as I'd expected I would, but of Peter there was no sign.

'He's being interviewed now,' Stan told me. 'A couple of uniform officers arrived soon after we got back here. They've taken over the conservatory and they want to talk to anyone who was at the reunion last night.'

'We must be pretty high on their list,' I said, 'being Mark and Laura's closest friends.'

'Yes, I've already made my statement.' Stan fished some money out of his wallet. 'Can I get you a drink, Hannah?'

'Oh, yes, please.' I'd never felt more in need of a drink in my life. 'Can I have a gin and tonic?'

'You've got it.' He waved to the barman and when we'd been served, suggested we move to one of the tables – 'Less bloody conspicuous', as he put it. I couldn't have agreed more. The police activity had fuelled a lot of interest and as characters fairly central to the drama we were attracting a fair amount of attention.

We chose a corner from where we could see without being too readily seen.

'So what did they want to know?' I asked when we'd settled ourselves.

Stan shrugged, attacking his fresh pint of beer. 'Oh, just the kind of things you'd expect – how well did I know Mark and Laura? Whether I'd seen anything of the row they had last night? What time they left? – there wasn't much I could tell them really. Oh – and they wanted to know *my* movements.'

'*Your* movements?'

'I guess if there's a suggestion that Laura

had a lover, he has to be in the frame. And at the moment they either don't know, or aren't saying, who that is.'

'I thought it was Aaron,' I said. 'At least, that's who she was outside with when Mark caught her. But she's such a flirt ... *was* such a flirt ... I suppose there could have been someone else too.'

'Well, it sure as heck wasn't me.' Stan took another long pull of his beer. 'I told them that a few of us had a nightcap in the bar after the party broke up, and after that I was tucked up in bed and snoring. Not that I can prove it, of course, any more than any of the rest of us can – unless old passions were re-ignited and a bit of bed-hopping went on.'

'As far as I'm concerned there's only one serious suspect,' I said. 'If anyone was responsible for Laura's death, I'd put money on it being Darren.'

'I did mention it to the police,' Stan said. 'Not that I've met him myself, of course, but since you and Annabel seemed to think he was a dodgy character, I just said that Mark had a nephew living in his motor home and that there was no sign of him this morning, and left them to draw their own conclusions.'

'Well, I shall certainly tell them about him,' I said. 'They should never have had him there. It was asking for trouble.'

'It's Mark all over though, isn't it? Trying to do a good turn. Anyway, I have to say I got

141

the impression they already knew about Darren.'

'They knew!' I set my G and T down on the table with a thud. 'So, why aren't they out looking for him instead of harassing poor Mark? And how did they know anyway? Oh – don't tell me – Becky again, I expect. She was there on Friday when we found him in the kitchen looking for cheese, and I expect she was one of the first to present herself for interview. Do you know, she'd actually rung Jenny and told her about Laura before I got there? She is the limit, really she is!'

'I thought you felt sorry for her,' Stan said.

'I did. I do! But I'm also remembering exactly why I disliked her so much at school. It's less than twenty-four hours since I saw her again and already I'm hoping I won't see her for another twenty years – or longer. Any time at all would be too soon.'

'I'd keep your voice down then, if I was you,' Stan said mildly. 'She's over by the bar.'

'No!'

'She's looking round ... oh, too late. She's seen us.'

'Oh, hell!'

'Hannah – Stan. Isn't this just too awful?' Becky's face was carefully arranged into a sombre expression, but there was an under-lying eagerness in her voice that told me she was enjoying this.

'It's terrible, yes,' I said, praying she would

not sit down and muscle in. I couldn't bear her near me just now and I didn't trust myself not to say things I'd later regret.

'Look, I've come to say goodbye really,' Becky said. 'I was only booked in for the two nights and I have to be going. But you have my address and phone number, don't you, Hannah?'

'Actually no,' I said flatly.

'Oh, I'll write them down for you.' She tore a page out of her diary, scribbled for a moment and handed it to me. 'Would you let me know the funeral arrangements? I could ring Mark, of course, but I don't want to pester him at a time like this.'

'Did you know that Mark is at the police station being questioned about Laura's death?'

I don't know why I said it; certainly not because I wanted to share information with her. Perhaps it was a childish desire to tell her, for once, something she didn't already know; perhaps I just wanted to wipe that look of sanctimonious tragedy off her face. If so, I certainly succeeded.

'You mean they think *Mark* had something to do with it?' she asked in a shocked whisper.

'There's a suggestion someone else was involved, yes. Laura has an unexplained wound to her head and it seems possible that she was unconscious when she went into the pool,' I said.

'Someone *attacked* her?' Becky said, incredulous. 'Oh my God, that's terrible! But Mark! That's crazy! No one in their right mind could think that *Mark...*!'

She was beside herself now – and I remembered just how besotted she was with him. But I was beyond feeling any sympathy for her; if anything I wanted her to hurt as much as I was hurting.

'The husband is always the prime suspect,' I said. 'He was on the spot, he found the body, and there was the row last night. I suppose it was you who told the police about that.'

'No!' Becky's retort was explosive.

'Oh, really? You're very fond of imparting information.'

'I didn't know about any row!' Becky protested. 'And if I had, I'd have kept quiet about it. I'd never do anything to hurt Mark. Never!'

Strangely enough, I believed her. No, I didn't think she would do anything that she thought might harm Mark.

'Do they have any other evidence?' Becky asked.

'I haven't a clue. As far as I know, they're waiting on the result of the post-mortem as to whether the wound could have been caused by falling on the edge of the pool. But they're covering all options in case it wasn't.

The house has been secured as a crime scene, and it's the reason why they want to talk to anyone who might know anything at all.'

'Perhaps I should wait then,' Becky said. 'Especially as I used to work for Mark. I can tell them what a wonderful man he is. That he would never … never…'

'I wouldn't hang around if I were you,' Stan interrupted – anxious to get rid of her, no doubt. 'You live locally, after all. They're going to want to talk first to people who have to get away.'

'That's true.' Becky looked undecided, and I backed Stan up.

'They can see you any time they want to.'

'I suppose you're right. But you will tell them, won't you, that I want to have my say? And let me know if there are any developments?'

We promised we would – anything to get rid of her! – and she left.

'Bloody woman!' Stan exploded. 'A character reference from her could be the kiss of death. Oh my God – there's Tristan heading this way now. How the hell did we manage to get lumbered with so many idiots in our year?'

'I expect every class has them,' I said. 'And we had some pretty good friends too.'

Tristan had barely joined us, expressing the same shock everyone else was feeling, when

I saw Becky coming back in.

'I was just thinking—' her piggy little face was furrowed, as if the effort had imprinted itself on to her features – 'if Laura was attacked, there are at least two people who could have been responsible. There's that nephew of Mark's...'

'Yes, we've thought of him,' I interrupted her. 'Who else?'

Becky's lips pursed. 'Martin Golding.'

'Mr Golding!' I was totally astounded.

'Yes, I'm thinking of this business about his improper behaviour. Laura had really got the bit between her teeth about it. And Martin Golding has a lot to lose if she decided to kick up a stink.'

'What's this?' Stan looked puzzled.

'Annabel said something on Friday evening about Martin Golding taking a little too much interest in her in the days when he used to coach our swimming team,' I explained. 'Laura got very upset about it. She was goading him yesterday, more or less intimating that she was going to spill the beans.'

'After all this time?' Stan sounded sceptical. 'Surely, if it was Annabel he got fruity with, and she's kept quiet all these years, it's hardly for Laura to stir up trouble now.'

'But I think something had happened between him and Laura too,' I said. 'Very likely she thought she was the only one – that

146

she was special. Then she found out he'd tried it on with Annabel too. That's why she was so upset.'

'Her nose was put out of joint, you mean?' Stan said.

'Well, yes. And I think she felt, too, that if he was prone to that sort of behaviour, then he shouldn't still be working with young girls.'

'Which, of course, is true,' Tristan put in.

'He was very young then – by the time we were in the sixth form I suppose there wasn't a lot of difference in age between him and us. He's older now, married with children. I can't see him risking his career by messing about with pupils young enough to be his daughter. And I have to say he was never anything but kind to me, and perfectly properly behaved.'

'It's still not right, even then,' Stan said.

'And it gives him a motive, doesn't it?' Becky argued, clearly keen to try to shift the onus of suspicion from Mark. 'If Laura dredged up some explosive stuff, it would be the end of him as a teacher.'

'He could even go to prison if she went to the police,' Tristan added.

I felt as if I'd been hit over the head with a hammer all over again.

'I don't think he tried anything when we were younger though,' I said. 'I'm sure if anything happened at all it was much later, when we were seventeen or eighteen. And I still think Mark's nephew is the most likely suspect. I can't see Mr Golding turning violent. But a lad out of his skull on drugs, well, that's a very different matter.'

'I think,' Stan said, level and sensible as ever, 'that we should stop speculating and leave it to the police to do their job.'

I nodded, agreeing wholeheartedly with him. I'd heard before that in cases like this, the murdered person was only one of the victims. That speculation, spreading like the ripples from a pebble tossed into a pond, could have all kinds of repercussions not only for the major players but for anyone with any connection, however slight, to the crime. That lives could be changed for ever as stones were overturned and the nasty secrets lurking beneath them were revealed. I was now seeing it in action, and I didn't like it one little bit.

Heaven only knew what else might come out before this was over. But it was almost inevitable. None of us was going to escape from this unscathed. That was a cross we were going to have to bear on top of the tragedy of losing Laura.

As Stan had suggested, the police seemed to be concentrating their efforts on the people who needed to leave for home before the end of the day, Tristan among them. He was next to be called to the conservatory when they had finished interviewing Peter.

'There's really nothing I can tell them,' he said, gathering up his belongings.

'A handbag!' Stan said in disgust after he had left. 'Did you see? He's got a bloody handbag!'

'I don't think he'd call it that,' I said, but to be honest, I was much less concerned about Tristan's accoutrements than I was about what he might say when interviewed. I very much hoped he wouldn't repeat the story about Martin Golding. Much as I wanted to see Mark off the hook, I didn't think it was fair that Martin should be offered up as an alternative sacrifice.

Becky finally left and Peter too. I forced down a cheese roll at Stan's insistence and we'd gone outside for a breath of fresh air when the policeman came looking for me. They seemed to be getting through witnesses at a fairly rapid pace; they were getting tired of taking almost identical statements from one after another, I guessed.

Working on that assumption, I answered their questions as honestly as I could, though I played down the row. I told them about Darren, Mark's nephew, but I did not go so far as to voice my suspicions. After all, we didn't yet know for certain whether Laura had been involved in an altercation with anyone; her death could yet prove to be a tragic accident, though somehow I doubted that. And I made no mention either of the conversation regarding Martin Golding, or the things Laura had said to me about Mark's temper. I felt a little guilty, it's true, when they asked me if there was anything I could add that might be useful, and I shook my head, but as far as Mark was concerned, I didn't want to say anything that might make things worse for him, and I didn't want to be the one to open the can of worms about Martin Golding either. If Becky told them about it – and I had no doubt she would – then I'd have to confirm her story, and explain myself for not having mentioned it earlier. I'd deal with that if, and when, it arose. For the moment I simply couldn't see the point of dragging his name through the mire to no purpose.

When I returned to the bar, which seemed to have become our meeting place, I was surprised to see Annabel sitting with Stan at the same table we had occupied earlier. She looked as drained as I felt – the long hours nursing Mark through his interview had taken its toll, I guessed.

'What's happened?' I asked anxiously.

'They arrested Mark.' Stan answered for her.

'Arrested him! Oh my God, you mean ... Laura *was* murdered?'

Annabel shook her head. 'There's nothing

definite yet. There won't be until after the post-mortem, you know that. And I didn't say Mark was *arrested*, Stan. I said they took his statement under caution.'

'Isn't that the same thing?' Stan muttered.

'No, it's not. An arrest involves fingerprints and photographs and DNA – all the formalities. A statement under caution is just a precaution, so that if they do want to use it in evidence, their backs are covered.'

'Where is he now? They haven't locked him in a cell, have they? Oh, poor Mark!'

'No, as I already said, he hasn't been arrested.' Annabel sounded tired and irritable. 'We've booked him in here, at The Beeches. He's in his room now, freshening up and having a rest.'

'On his own. He shouldn't be on his own.'

'I think that's what he wanted, Hannah. Some privacy to try to come to terms with what's happened. He certainly wouldn't want to come in here and be stared at by all and sundry, would he?'

'No, but...' My heart was bleeding for Mark, not only bereaved but also suspected of causing Laura's death, and I wished desperately there was something I could do to help make things easier for him. But Annabel was right, of course. What he needed most just now was privacy to grieve. He knew we were here for him when he needed us.

We sat there glumly discussing the situation.

'I haven't seen Aaron all day, have you?' I said suddenly.

'No, I haven't either.' Stan was finishing yet another pint, evidence of his capacity to down enough to sink a battleship and yet remain stone cold sober. 'Maybe he left early this morning, before the news broke.'

'Maybe. But it's rather ironic, considering...'

Considering he was the one who had been the catalyst for the whole terrible chain of events. The one whom Mark had suspected of having a fling with Laura.

'Do you think there was anything going on between them?' Annabel asked, taking me by surprise. Annabel was not a one for idle gossip.

'She was flirting with him,' I said, feeling guilty at participating in this conversation. To talk about Laura in such a way when she was so recently dead seemed disrespectful somehow. 'And they did go outside, and somehow I can't see Mark going ballistic the way he did if they were only talking. But I can't imagine there's any more to it than that.'

'Maybe not.' Annabel was still looking thoughtful, worried almost. 'It's just that ... well, she was very cagey about him, wasn't she? We were all under the impression she

152

hadn't been able to locate him. Then she said she'd told us he was coming. But she hadn't.'

'What are you saying? That she was having a full blown affair with him?'

'I don't know what I'm saying really, except that Laura could be quite devious.'

'Well, it hardly matters now.' Stan was clearly uncomfortable with the conversation.

'It might.' Annabel was silent for a moment and seemed disconcerted. I wondered just what she was thinking. Was she suggesting Aaron had something to do with Laura's death? Then she changed tack completely, once more becoming the legal professional.

'I think I'll stay on for another day, until we can sort out a decent solicitor for Mark,' she said. 'I'll make some phone calls in the morning, take some soundings from my old firm as to who's best suited to deal with criminal charges.'

'It's lucky for Mark that he's got you,' I said.

'We're all lucky to have each other,' Annabel replied.

And that, I knew, was the truth. Though we'd seen little of one another over the years, the bonds formed in our youth were as strong as ever they had been. But the circle was incomplete now. Laura was gone. Nothing could ever be the same again.

We ordered bar snacks – curry for Stan,

lasagne for Annabel and me – and ate it because we were hungry though, to me at least, it tasted like sawdust. Mark would need something too, we decided, whether he wanted it or not. We asked for soup and toasted sandwiches to be sent to his room and Stan went up so as to be there with Mark when it arrived. Annabel and I sat talking for a little while longer until she decided it was time she left.

'I really need an early night so I have a clear head tomorrow,' she said. 'Say good-night to Stan for me, will you?'

I understood, but I didn't want her to go all the same. I felt very conspicuous, sitting alone in the bar, though I didn't suppose any of the other people drinking there had the faintest idea who I was and that I had any connection to Laura, even if they knew what had happened. And since most of our party had left now there was little danger I'd have to talk to anyone about it either.

It was a very long time before Stan came back, and I was on the verge of deciding to go to bed myself when he lumbered in. 'God, I need a drink!'

'Don't you think you've had enough?' I said sternly.

'Whatever, I still need another. Poor old Mark. He is in one hell of a state.' He went to the bar, and came back with what looked like a double whisky for himself instead of his usual beer, and a gin and tonic for me. I didn't really want it; I had the beginnings of a headache and I thought I was in danger of turning into an alcoholic myself, but it had been a dreadful day and anything that eased the pain had to be more or less excusable.

'I asked him if he thought that nephew of his could have had anything to do with it,' Stan said, sipping his whisky.

'And?'

'He won't have it. Says he's harmless. But then, he's in denial about everything. It did emerge, though, that Laura was less than happy about having Darren there. It was Mark's idea, it seems, and Laura wanted rid.'

'I'm not surprised,' I said. 'But it makes him even more of a suspect, doesn't it? If he was drugged up to the eyeballs last night and made a nuisance of himself, and Laura told him he was no longer welcome ... well, he might very well have turned nasty.'

'And all Mark is worried about is that Darren is going to come back, find police at the door and have nowhere to sleep.' Stan shook his head in bewilderment. 'I told him – forget the little bugger, mate. You've got more to worry about than him. It's mid-summer, it's not cold, it won't hurt him to kip under a hedge. Might bring him to his senses.'

'I doubt it,' I said. 'It doesn't work like that, I'm afraid.' I frowned. 'I wonder where he's getting his supplies? There must be a local dealer. Well...' I laughed shortly at myself. 'Of course there's a local dealer. Or three. And their hangers-on. All he'd have to do would be to go into a pub and ask around. It's hard to imagine though, isn't it, here in Mowbury? I mean in cities, yes, you kind of expect it, but your own home town.'

Stan sighed. 'Yep, I don't know what the world's coming to, Hannah.'

Any time now we were going to get maudlin, I knew.

'We're beginning to sound like our parents,' I said. 'Can you imagine what we'd have said last time we were together if somebody had told us we'd begin to sound like our parents before we were even forty?'

'Times have changed since then, Hannah.'

'Tell me about it.' I finished my drink. 'Stan, I've had enough. I'm going to bed. I'll see you in the morning.'

'OK. Breakfast at ... what? Say eight.'

I nodded. 'Yes. Oh, Stan – what a day.'

'Wouldn't want too many like it.'

'You can say that again.'

But even as I said it I was wondering what tomorrow would bring. This was far from over yet. In fact, I had the most awful premonition that it was only just beginning.

Nine

The first bombshell hit as we were finishing breakfast – just me and Stan. Mark was still having meals delivered to his room; Stan had been in to see him, though, and reported that he looked terrible.

'I don't think he's had any sleep at all. He's like a zombie. I even had to chivvy him to have a wash and shave.'

It was a depressing indication of Mark's state of mind; normally he was immaculately turned out. But all the same...

'I'm not surprised he couldn't sleep,' I said. 'I had a pretty bad night myself.'

Stan helped himself to more toast and marmalade; his appetite, at least, seemed to have returned and he was making up for having eaten very little yesterday. My mouth was like the bottom of a parrot's cage, though, and nothing tasted as it should. But I was going for the coffee in a big way; we were already on our second pot when Stan's mobile rang.

He answered it. 'Hi, babe.' Zoe, his wife, I presumed. Then I saw his face change.

'When? Is she all right? Oh, bloody hell. OK, love. I'll get back as soon as I can. About an hour, say? Hour and a half tops.'

He switched off his mobile, already pushing back his chair. 'Hannah, I'm sorry, but I'm going to have to go home. Alice has fallen off the trampoline. Zoe thinks she's broken her arm. They're on their way to the hospital now. A neighbour is minding the other two, but I'm going to have to get back pronto. I'm sorry,' he said again.

My heart had sunk like a stone. Dear God, what timing! But I tried to hide my dismay.

'Of course you've got to go, Stan. Your family must come first.'

'Bloody trampoline! I knew it was a mistake. But the girls kept on and on. Will you be OK, Hannah? Can you cope here?'

'Yes, of course. I'll be fine.'

'You'll have to nursemaid Mark.'

'I know. Stop worrying, Stan. Just go.'

He went.

When I'd finished the coffee I went back to my room and called Annabel.

'Oh, shit,' she said bluntly when I told her what had happened. 'We were relying on Stan to look after Mark, weren't we? You're there, I know, but it's not the same as having another man, is it?'

'Are you coming over?'

'Not for a while. I've got a few phone calls

158

to make and I have to prepare a file – thank heavens I brought my laptop with me! Then I need to see whoever is taking on Mark's case to hand it all over and talk them through what happened yesterday.'

'Yes, of course.'

I could see that she was going to be busy and understood the importance of what she was doing, but I felt bleak and isolated all the same, especially when she added: 'I'm going to have to leave late afternoon – early evening, anyway. I've got a hearing in the family court tomorrow, and there's no way I can miss that.'

It looked, I thought, as though it was going to be down to me from now on. And I wasn't looking forward to it one little bit.

There was nothing for it, I'd have to go up and see Mark. It might be, of course, that he'd prefer to be left alone and if so, though it doesn't make me proud to admit it, I thought that would be quite a relief. Steeling myself, I went up the carpeted staircase and tapped on his door.

'Mark? It's me – Hannah.'

After a few moments that felt like a lifetime the door opened.

'Hannah. Come in.'

As Stan had said, Mark looked terrible; pale and drawn, he seemed to have aged ten years.

'Stan's had to go home then,' he said. 'Poor kid, breaking her arm. That's really bad luck. How the hell do you cope with a five-year-old with her arm in plaster? And Stan worships those girls, too. He must be in one hell of a state.'

'Never mind about Stan and Alice,' I said. 'How are you?'

'Oh ... you know.'

'Have you had any breakfast?' My answer lay in the tray set down on the counter – a plate of bacon and tomatoes virtually untouched. 'You must eat, Mark.'

'I'll have something when I feel like it.'

'I've spoken to Annabel,' I said. 'She's beavering away on your behalf and she'll be over later to let you know what arrangements she's made.'

'She's been great,' Mark said dully. 'You all have.'

'That's what friends are for.' I was silent, at a loss to know what else to say. The hotel room, though bright and comfortably furnished, seemed to be closing in around me, claustrophobic as a prison cell. It couldn't be good for Mark, I thought, cooped up here alone.

'Do you feel like going for a walk?' I suggested. 'It's a beautiful day and we're not likely to bump into anyone you know. They all left yesterday. I really think some fresh air would do you good.'

160

'Whatever.' Mark was listless, robotic almost. 'Just as long as I don't have to talk to anyone.'

'Come on then. Don't forget your room key.'

We went downstairs and into the grounds. As I'd predicted, we saw nobody except a maid vacuuming the corridor, and she didn't so much as glance at us as we passed her.

'I'd better not go too far away,' Mark said. 'The police may want to speak to me again.'

'They'll find you easily enough.' But it occurred to me that the solicitor Annabel was briefing would very likely want to see Mark as soon as possible to talk things through. 'Look – there's a bench over on the far side of the lawn. That's far enough away from curious eyes, but we can see the entrance to the drive.'

I checked that my mobile was switched on in case Annabel wanted to make contact and we set out on a circular route around the flowerbeds.

'I can't believe Laura's gone,' Mark said, and nodded in the direction of the car park. 'Look – there's her car still there. I keep expecting to see her get out of it...' His voice tailed away.

'I know,' I said. 'This is so terrible for you, Mark.'

'I don't know what the hell I'm going to do without her.' He was silent for a moment, then went on reflectively, almost. 'Oh, I know we had our ups and downs. Things weren't always perfect. But what in life is? Laura was a free spirit. She wasn't a home bird like Jenny, but life was never dull with her around. Bit of a roller coaster really. She liked a good time, and I couldn't always keep up with her. I was too busy with the business, too damned tired. But I loved her, Hannah. How could anyone think I'd ever harm her?'

'No one who knows you does think that, Mark,' I said.

'The police seem to. I suppose I'm the obvious suspect, really, and having that damned row with her at the reunion didn't help. I am so sorry about that. Sorry you had to witness it.'

'You don't have to apologize to me,' I put in.

'I shall never forgive myself, you know,' Mark went on. 'The last words I spoke to her were in anger. That's what I can't get out of my head.' His voice cracked, he turned his head away from me and I knew he was fighting a battle not to break down.

I covered his hand with mine. 'Don't torture yourself, Mark.'

'Why not? If I hadn't lost my temper, gone off and left her there, this wouldn't have happened. We'd have gone home together, left one of the cars here, probably, and come back for it next day. We'd have had a night-cap and gone to bed, and Laura would still be alive.' He was silent for a moment, then he punched the bench with his fist. 'That bloody Aaron! He always was trouble. He'd been seeing her, you know. It started when she contacted him about the reunion. They'd been e-mailing and phoning one another, and meeting up. Becky saw them in town together and mentioned it to me. I don't suppose she thought anything of it, but I knew straight away there was something going on.'

'Becky?' I repeated, startled. 'But we were all under the impression Laura hadn't been able to contact Aaron...' I broke off, re-membering how sure Becky had been that it was Aaron we'd passed in the drive when we were leaving for Laura's on Friday evening, and how she'd started to tell Annabel she was wrong about Laura's failure to contact Aaron. At the time we'd ignored her as we so often did, putting it down to her trying to be the important one, the one in the know. Perhaps this time she really had been. But for some reason she hadn't wanted Laura to know that she knew and that was why she'd said no more about it when Laura had come back with the jug of fruit punch. She'd simply hugged her little bombshell to her-self. It was her all over – knowledge to her was power. Whilst she was keeper of the

secret she felt in control. How much to let out. To whom. When. And she'd chosen to set the cat among the pigeons by telling Mark.

If it was true.

'Are you sure she wasn't making it up just to cause trouble?' I asked. 'She's got rather a thing about you, you know. And you know what she's like.'

'Oh, yes, I know Becky. But I also know Laura,' Mark said. He sounded more sad than angry now. 'I'm afraid that given her track record I find it all too easy to believe that she was having an affair. It wouldn't be the first time. She's had a few flings over the years. But if I had any doubts at all, they vanished when I saw her with Aaron. It was as plain as the nose on your face what was going on. And when they went outside, well … I just saw red, I'm afraid.'

I didn't know what to say. I felt awkward, embarrassed and tongue-tied. I remembered what Laura had said to me on Saturday evening about Mark's jealous nature. She'd claimed his suspicion of her was unfounded, but on balance, although she had been my friend, I was inclined to believe Mark's side of the story. It wasn't hard to imagine that Laura had been unfaithful. She had been a butterfly – no, a firefly, bright, skittering, elusive, or even a moth, flying dangerously close to the flame. And with my own eyes I'd seen the way she was flirting with Aaron.

No, it wouldn't surprise me if Laura had been having a fling with him. He was undoubtedly a very attractive man, and she had certainly kept very quiet about having been in contact with him.

What *was* puzzling me, though, was why Becky had kept quiet about it in the light of what had happened. But then, I supposed she must have realized, as I was now realizing, that it could only make things worse for Mark if the truth came out. Bad enough that he should have had a public row with Laura on the night of her death – and I'd still very much like to know who had told the police about that, since it clearly hadn't been Becky – but if it came to light that she had been having an affair and Mark knew about it, it only made it the more feasible that they had continued arguing when she had arrived home and things had got out of hand.

I didn't believe it for a moment, of course, but that was neither here nor there. It was how things would look to the police that mattered. That – and any evidence they might have. But what evidence could there be? I'd been at the house that morning and I'd seen nothing untoward at all. Nothing but a trodden-on bouquet of flowers and a handbag spilling its contents on to the patio.

And an abandoned motor home.

I wasn't at all sure this was the right moment to raise the subject of Mark's nephew again, but the thought of him was still nagging at me. I pictured him as I'd seen him in the kitchen, spaced out and scary, and thought that if anyone was responsible for Laura's death, he was by far and away the most likely suspect.

'Stan said you were worried about Darren,' I said cautiously.

'Of course I'm worried about him!' Mark retorted sharply. 'God knows what he'll do if he comes back and finds the place all sealed off. I don't want him finishing up back with his friends in some smack house or squat. That's exactly what I've been trying to keep him away from.'

'And you've been doing a great job,' I soothed.

'Have I? I'm not so sure. I thought if we got him away from Bristol we stood a chance of getting him to clean up his act, but I'm not so sure we've succeeded. There are drugs everywhere these days. Dealers on street corners – outside schools even. And where was he on Saturday night, I'd like to know? Why didn't he come home?'

I said nothing. I didn't have the courage to tell Mark what was on my mind – that his nephew had gone on the run because he was responsible for Laura's death. It would only cause him more anguish and give him yet another reason to blame himself, and more anguish and extra guilt were the last things Mark needed at the moment.

'What a bloody awful mess, Hannah,' Mark said. 'What a homecoming for you.'

Something contracted deep inside me, the stirring of a long-forgotten emotion tugging at me.

'You have to stop worrying about other people, Mark,' I said. 'We'll be OK. Our lives are still out there, waiting for us. You're the one who matters in all this. You have to think about yourself.'

Even as I said it, it occurred to me that perhaps it was how Mark was coping, a concern for other people diverting his attention from his own unbearable grief and guilt. But that was Mark all over. He'd always been affected by the problems of those around him, doing his best to put things right. If it hadn't been for that trait he'd never have given Becky a job as his PA, I felt sure, inventing a job so as to help her out of a hole. He'd never have taken in his wayward nephew and all the problems he'd brought along with him. And Laura would still be alive, bubbly and irrepressible, high herself, no doubt, on the success of the reunion she'd organized instead of lying dead on a mortuary slab, all dignity lost along with her life. Tears pricked at my eyes. I fumbled in my bag for a tissue.

'Oh God,' Mark said. His tone was still flat, yet at the same time full of dread.

I looked up and saw a car turning in through the gates. Though it was unmarked, I recognized it instantly as the one the two detectives had been driving – the one in which Mark had been taken to the police station. Mark was very still, the apprehension I'd heard in his voice mirrored in the tautness of his face, the rigidity of every muscle. Then he seemed to summon up reserves of strength, inhaling deeply and getting up.

'I'd better see what they want,' he said, very matter-of-factly. And without a backward glance set off like a radio-controlled robot across the lawn.

For a few moments I hung back, then, somewhat hesitantly, I followed. I'd like to think it was to give Mark moral support and I'm sure that was my main motive, but I have to admit an overwhelming need to know what was going on came into it too. The post-mortem had probably been completed by now and very likely the police would inform Mark of the result. Really it was none of my business. But at the same time it was. I'd been drawn into this whole dreadful affair and I needed to know the worst. Though I think I knew already. Had done from the moment I'd learned that Laura had drowned. Something had happened to her before she went into the water. Given her ability to swim like a fish it was the only thing that made any sense.

The same two detectives who had come to the house yesterday had got out of the car now and approached Mark. The man – DS Jeavons – was talking to him, the girl, Paula Buchan, standing watchfully at his elbow. I was still too far away to hear what was being said but there was a purposefulness in the sergeant's body language that did not bode well. Mark's head slumped forward on to his chest for a moment, though by the time I reached them he was looking straight at DS Jeavons once more, his jaw clenched and the muscles in his neck taut and corded.

'What's happened?' I asked – though I already knew.

DS Jeavons ignored me, concentrating on Mark.

'You do not have to say anything but it may harm your defence...' I caught the words of the formal caution, then the policeman touched Mark's arm. 'Let's go.'

My knees went weak. Mark was being arrested.

'No!' My voice seemed not to belong to me. 'You can't! Where are you taking him?'

DS Jeavons' hand was on Mark's head, guiding him into the rear of the car. He slammed the door, walked around the car and got in beside Mark.

'What's happening?' I screamed. It was insane, really; I knew very well. But I was so distraught these idiotic questions went on tumbling out of my mouth.

DC Paula Buchan's eyes were cold as chips of steel, her mouth set in a tight line. 'Mr Calvin is coming to the station with us to help us with our inquiries.' Her voice was cold, too, and hard.

'But ... you've arrested him!'

'The post-mortem has shown that Mrs Calvin's death was not accidental. We're looking at murder here. Now, if you don't mind, we have a job to do.' She turned briskly, walking round the car and getting into the driver's seat. The engine sparked into life.

Mark turned his head, looking at me. His expression was stunned, his eyes dead. For the moment, I guessed, he was numb, paralysed almost. But inside he must be silently screaming for help. Without thinking what I was doing I ran around the front of the car.

'You can't do this!' I cried desperately through the open window. 'You've got it all wrong! Mark didn't kill Laura! It's his nephew you should be arresting! He's the one – you've got to find him!'

'Madam,' Paula Buchan said harshly, 'will you please get out of the way?'

She gunned the engine, tyres scrunched

on gravel. There was nothing more I could do.

I was beside myself. I'd left my bag on the seat where Mark and I had been sitting. I ran back across the grass, rescued it, pulled out my mobile and scrolled down the phone book for Annabel's mobile number. It rang endlessly, then the mechanical voice of her server was grating in my ear, asking if I would like to leave a message.

I wouldn't. But I had no option. Annabel would get back to me as soon as she picked up my message, I consoled myself. And now that Mark had been formally arrested they couldn't interview him without a solicitor present if he requested one – could they? But it didn't help much. My nerves were jangling, my stomach churning. I wanted to speak to Annabel *now*.

I started back towards the hotel, mobile still in my hand, willing it to ring. And as I crossed the forecourt, who should I run straight into but Tristan. I was surprised – I'd thought he was leaving yesterday. But here he was, large as life, smiling his sickly smile.

'Hannah! We really must stop meeting like this.'

'Tristan. I thought you'd gone home.' I sounded as impatient as I felt.

'No, I decided to stay on for a few days –

make the break worthwhile.' His eyes narrowed. 'Are you all right?'

'Not really, no. Mark has been arrested.'

'Ah.' The sickly smile faded, replaced by a look of concern that seemed curiously overdone – theatrical, almost – and oddly false. 'When was this?'

'Just now. Apparently the post-mortem on Laura confirmed the doctor's suspicions. The policewoman said they're looking at murder. They've arrested Mark and taken him away, and I can't get hold of Annabel. It's just her messaging service.'

'I'm sure she'll call you back very soon,' Tristan said soothingly.

'I certainly hope so! I can't bear to think of Mark...' Tears sprang to my eyes as I pictured him all alone at the police station. Being fingerprinted. Having one of those horrible triptych-style photographs taken holding up a number. Giving DNA swabs. The cell door clanging shut behind him. Waiting ... waiting for his legal representative to arrive. Sick. Hurting. Dazed. He didn't deserve this! He'd done nothing wrong, I felt sure. And he'd just lost his wife in the most tragic of circumstances.

'Come on, Hannah.' Tristan touched my arm. 'Let's go and have a coffee.'

'I can't sit and drink coffee while Mark is being grilled for something any sane person knows he didn't do.'

'There's nothing you can do at the moment,' Tristan said sensibly. 'Come on, coffee. I insist.'

I went with him. I wasn't up to arguing. And though Tristan was not my favourite person, not the one I'd have chosen to share my anguish with, it really was a case of any port in a storm.

And I have to admit he was very good, very solicitous and discreet. He installed me at one of the wicker tables in the conservatory, which at this time on a Monday morning was empty of other guests, and went off to order the coffee.

'This must be very hard for you, Hannah,' he said, coming back and sliding into a chair beside mine. 'You and Laura were always very close. Well, all of you, really. Such a tight-knit group. You've no idea how I used to envy you.'

I glanced up at him, surprised. 'You envied us?'

He smiled faintly. 'Oh, yes. I'd have given anything to be part of your gang. To me, the eight of you exuded glamour. You were all confident, nice looking, good at sport – it seemed to me you had everything. Not to mention each other. The perfect unit. Where-as I...'

'You were very clever. Top in practically every subject, as I remember it.'

'The class swot, you mean.'

'No!'

'Yes. I had to shine at something, and there wasn't much to distract me. But I promise you, I'd have traded all my good grades in an instant if I could have had just a little of the aura that surrounded your circle. And you all gelled so effortlessly, whereas I always found it difficult to make friends. And impossible to communicate as I wanted to. I always felt like a bit of a freak.'

My mind was wandering; I really wasn't finding it easy to concentrate on what he was saying.

'You're all right now though,' I said, rather inanely.

That faint smile again, a pale shadow of its usual self. 'Oh, life has treated me pretty well. Good job. Nice lifestyle. But I'm still on the outside looking in. And still wishing...'

My phone started ringing. I jammed it to my ear. 'Annabel?'

'Yes. What's wrong?' I told her. 'OK, leave it with me,' she said. 'I'll get straight on to Ken Taylor – he's the solicitor I've lined up for Mark. He'll take it from here. And I'll be right over. I need to talk to you, Hannah.' And she was gone.

The coffee had arrived; Tristan was pouring it.

'Annabel's coming over,' I said. 'She's arranged for a solicitor who specializes in criminal law to take over Mark's case. I only

hope he's as good as she thinks he is. Someone has to make the police see that Mark
could never have done something like this.
It's just awful that they should suspect him
on top of everything else.'

'You're very worried about Mark, aren't
you?' Tristan said reflectively.

'Yes, I am!' I was still seeing him as he'd
looked as he'd been driven away in the police
car, defeated, broken, as unlike the Mark I
knew as was possible to imagine. And I was
still charged with a sense of urgency that
prickled on my skin and in my blood like a
fever. 'I'd do anything to spare him all this!'
I said.

Tristan was looking at me oddly. 'You
really are very involved, aren't you, Hannah?'

And suddenly it was as if he was holding up
a mirror to me and I was seeing in it something I really didn't care for at all. Was it
possible that the anguish I was feeling on
Mark's behalf went far deeper than natural
concern for an old friend? I'd thought I'd got
over my 'crush' on Mark years ago, and the
feelings I'd once had for him had faded along
with the rosy flush of youth. Now it occurred
to me that, just to complicate matters, I
might not have got over him at all. That the
old feelings were still there beneath the
layers of convention, a little dusty and rusty,
but for all that as potent as ever they had

been. That, most certainly, was a distraction I could do without.

When Annabel arrived, Tristan left. He guessed, I suppose, that we wanted to talk in private, and unlike Becky he had more tact and good manners than to force his company on us.

'It's a good thing I didn't waste any time before sorting out a good solicitor for Mark,' Annabel said when we were alone. 'I'm assured Ken Taylor is the best man for the job, and knows all the best briefs.'

'A barrister, you mean? But surely Mark will only need a barrister if it comes to court. And it won't, will it? They'll realize they've made a bad mistake when they find that nephew of his.'

'That's one of the things I wanted to talk to you about.' Annabel's expression was grim. 'The nephew, I'm afraid, is out of the frame.'

'Out of the frame?' I repeated stupidly. 'But surely he's the obvious suspect. How can he be out of the frame?'

Annabel ran her fingers through her short, sharply styled hair. 'Apparently he turned up back at the house last night,' she said. 'The uniformed officer on duty apprehended him. He was taken in for questioning, and it turns out he has a cast-iron alibi.'

'But he's got to be the one responsible!' I whispered desperately. 'What alibi could he possibly have?'

'The best possible,' Annabel said grimly. 'He was in police custody.'

'What!'

'He went to Bristol on Saturday, it seems, unbeknown to Laura and Mark, who were too tied up with the reunion to keep an eye on him. He got into some kind of trouble and spent the night in the cells.'

'What kind of trouble?'

'What do you think? Drugs. I don't know the details, and it scarcely matters. Darren had a small amount in his possession, it seems, though I think some of his pals are in deeper trouble. Dealing was mentioned. Presumably he was released and made his way back to Mowbury. But the important point is he couldn't possibly have been involved in Laura's death.'

My heart had dropped like a stone. If Darren's whereabouts could be vouched for by Bristol's finest, it explained why the local police had arrested Mark and taken him in for further questioning.

Once again he was firmly in the frame.

Ten

I pushed the cup of coffee Tristan had poured away from me – the very thought of drinking it now made me feel nauseous – and wrapped my arms around myself as if I could somehow ward off all the blows that fate seemed to be firing.

'So what happens now?'

'The police have thirty-six hours to question Mark,' Annabel explained. 'Then, unless the magistrates grant them an extension, they either have to charge him or let him go. It all depends whether they think they've got enough to make it stick.'

'Thirty-six hours!' I repeated, horrified. 'That takes us up to tomorrow night! They can't keep poor Mark at the police station all that time!'

'I'm afraid they can,' Annabel said grimly. 'Especially if they should come up with any extra evidence.'

I shook my head, bewildered. 'What extra evidence could there be?'

Annabel was silent for a moment. Then she crossed one neatly trousered ankle over the other and leaned forward, elbows resting on the table. 'You remember you found Laura's bag on the patio?'

'Yes. Everything had been tipped out of it.'

'And you put it back in.' I nodded. 'Do you remember if her mobile phone was amongst it?'

'Her mobile phone?' I screwed up my face, trying to do a mental inventory – purse, cigarettes, lighter, diary, Polo mints, make-up. 'No, I don't think so. Why?'

'As I thought,' Annabel said. 'I don't re-member seeing it either. But she definitely had it with her when we were in the taxi. It rang and she answered it. We were going through a black spot at the time – dodgy reception – and she lost the signal. Then it rang again just as she got out of the taxi. The last I saw of her she was walking up the drive with the phone to her ear. It's worrying me, Hannah. Who would ring her at that time of night? We're not really into girlie chats in the wee small hours at our age, are we? At least, I know I'm not. To be honest, I can only think of one person it could have been. Mark. And if it was – well, you realize, don't you, what that means? Mark wasn't in bed and asleep when she got home as he says he was.'

'Annabel!' I said, horrified. 'You're not turning against Mark too, are you?'

She didn't answer my question. 'I asked

him if he'd phoned Laura and he denied it. But I just can't imagine who else but Mark would have rung her on her mobile at that time of night,' she said instead.

My thoughts were whirling. It was true that the most likely person to call Laura would have been Mark, worrying about her, perhaps, wondering how she was going to get home. But as Annabel had pointed out, if it had been Mark, then it also meant he had lied about being asleep.

'Look,' Annabel said, 'I'm doing my level best for Mark, OK? I haven't mentioned this before because I knew it would look bad for him and I didn't want to stir up trouble if it wasn't necessary. But this is a murder inquiry now. I don't think I have any choice but to say something. I can't withhold evidence. I'm a solicitor, for God's sake. I know how serious something like that is.'

I closed my eyes briefly, thinking of the possible evidence I was withholding and knowing that even now I couldn't bring myself to say anything that might count against Mark. Not as long as I was convinced of his innocence. And I was.

'What I'm wondering is where is Laura's phone now?' Annabel went on. 'I'd have thought she'd have put it back in her bag. But it wasn't there. You've just confirmed that.'

'Perhaps it had rolled away. Fallen into the

pool even,' I said. I had a horrible feeling I knew where Annabel was going with this. 'Or perhaps she put it down in the house.'

'And perhaps whoever killed her took it to make it appear she didn't have it with her. Perhaps they didn't want anyone checking it to see if she made or received any calls that evening.'

'But surely the police could get that information from the phone company even if her mobile is missing?' I said.

'Yes, they could. My point is that if it was thought she didn't have a phone with her, they might not even check. Or maybe, if someone did phone, they didn't realize the calls could be checked even without the phone. Either way, she definitely had it with her when she left me, and it seems to be missing now. The police can't have it – they hadn't begun investigating and taking away evidence when we found Laura's things scattered on the patio. So unless she did leave it in the house, I think it's a pretty fair bet that the person who called her and her killer are one and the same. And like it or not, that keeps bringing me back to Mark.'

I shivered violently, then shook my head.

'I don't believe it, Annabel, and I can't believe you do either.'

'I don't want to, that's for sure.'

'You don't know there's any connection,' I argued desperately. 'And you don't even know for certain it was Mark who called her. She didn't call him by name, did she?'

'No,' Annabel admitted.

'So it could have been anyone.'

'Like who?'

'I don't know...' I searched wildly for a feasible alternative. 'One of her boyfriends, perhaps. Mark told me she's had a few over the years.'

'She didn't actually sound very pleased to hear from whoever it was,' Annabel said.

'So, what did she say?'

'Hardly anything. I told you, the signal broke up more or less straight away, and in any case, I wasn't really listening. But her tone of voice wasn't exactly enthusiastic. It was just like: "Oh, hi." Very cool. Cold, almost. Very flat. That's another reason I thought it might be Mark.'

'Surely after the situation between them when he left she'd have been more likely to tell him to go and take a running jump?'

'You don't know how they behave after they've had a row,' Annabel pointed out.

That was true. Obviously there had been rows in the past, pretty violent ones, given Mark's temper, and just as obviously they had buried the hatchet afterwards. A cool "Oh, hi," could have been the first step towards doing just that again.

But if it had been Mark phoning Laura, then he had been awake when she got home, not asleep as he had claimed, and it was unlikely anyone else had been in the house that night. If the number was checked and it turned out to be his, either his mobile or their home land line, things would look very bad for him.

Equally, if it had not been him, the person who had called had been the last person to speak to Laura before she died, apart from her killer, and it could be they were one and the same.

'Suppose whoever called did so to ask Laura if they could come over and see her?' I suggested urgently. Annabel gave me a straight stare, waiting for me to elaborate. I didn't think she wanted it to be Mark any more than I did. 'Who might have done that?' I went on. 'What about Aaron?'

'Do you really think he would have risked coming to the house with Mark there after what happened?' Annabel chewed on her lip. 'And as I already said, it didn't sound like a lover she was talking to.'

'But if she was tired and fed up, perhaps she just couldn't be bothered to be nice to them.' I was clutching at straws.

'But why would Aaron kill her? It doesn't make any sense. He has no motive that I can see.'

'Unless she told him it was over and he lost it.'

'Mark is the one with the temper,' Annabel

pointed out. 'For all his faults, I can't imagine Aaron flying into a murderous rage. He's too laid back.'

In spite of myself, I was forced to agree. And unless there had been a violent argument, it was true that Aaron had no motive whatever – that I knew of, anyway.

But there was someone who did.

'Martin Golding,' I said.

'Martin!'

'He's the one with the strongest motive of all,' I went on. 'Becky mentioned it and we dismissed it as we dismiss pretty well everything she says. But actually she is absolutely right. Laura threatened him more or less straight out that she was going to report him for improper behaviour. If she'd done that, all hell would have broken loose. His career would be over, his marriage would be bound to suffer, he might even go to prison. He'd have been desperate to stop her from saying anything that would ruin his life.'

'Hannah – you are talking premeditated murder here.'

'I know.'

'Does that sound like Martin Golding to you?'

'Well, no,' I admitted. 'But if he was desperate, who knows what he might be capable of?'

'And do you really think Laura would have agreed to meet him in the middle of the night? She could barely bring herself to speak to him at the reunion.' She gave a quick, impatient shake of her head. 'I wish to goodness I'd never opened that particular can of worms. I should have left the past where it belonged.'

'What did happen?' I asked.

'Nothing really. He gave me a lift home a few times when we were in the sixth form. He always seemed to be driving the way I was walking though he lived in the opposite direction, and one day he pulled into a lay-by and I thought he was going to try something. I let him know in no uncertain terms that I wasn't interested and that was the end of it.'

'Laura got so upset though.'

'She *did* have a fling with him, it seems. Pretty high voltage stuff as far as she was concerned. She told me all about it after the rest of you had left on Friday evening. The great forbidden love. Secret meetings, clandestine gropes in empty classrooms, and things that went a good deal further in field gateways in dark lanes. Not to mention plans to elope. Which, of course, never came to anything. Whatever, Laura remembered it as being the romance of the century, the tragic passion that could never be. She had no idea he'd tried it on with me first – and she was very hurt. Well, her pride was, anyway. You know what Laura was like.'

I half-smiled, ruefully. 'I guess I should be the one who's hurt. He never tried it with me at all.'

'You had your fair share of admirers!' Annabel countered. 'Aaron...'

'No!'

'Oh, I think so. Tristan...'

'Tristan!'

'He was pie-eyed about you. Still is, if you ask me. Mark...'

'For about three weeks.' Funny I could still remember so clearly after all these years how heartbroken I'd been when Mark had ditched me. Funny how I still cared so desperately about him and what was happening to him.

'To get back to Martin Golding,' I said. 'He must have been worried sick to think Laura might bring up his dalliances with pupils.'

Annabel nodded. 'I'm sure he was. But to be honest, I don't think she would actually have done anything about it after all these years. When she thought about it, I'm pretty sure she'd have decided to let sleeping dogs lie.'

'He wasn't to know that, though, was he?' I argued.

'I still can't see her agreeing to meet him in the middle of the night. And I can't see him hitting her over the head and drowning her in the swimming pool, can you?'

To be honest, I couldn't. We were going round and round in circles.

'What was she hit with?' I asked reflectively.

Annabel shook her head. 'At the moment, the police aren't saying. But you can bet your bottom dollar they know what kind of thing they're looking for. Heavy glass ashtray, bronze ornament, silver candlestick, rubber cosh – the forensic report will have given them a pretty good idea of what it was – or wasn't. And when they find it they'll be able to nail the killer.'

'If they find it. If it wasn't taken along with her phone.'

We were getting nowhere fast. I couldn't believe any of the people we'd tried to fit in the frame had killed Laura any more than I believed Mark had done so. But someone had.

Annabel was deep in thought. She was chewing on her lip, eyes narrowed, brows furrowed. 'I just thought of something,' she said.

'What?'

'No. No, that can't be, surely...'

'*What?*'

She shook her head. 'No, I've got to think this through. I can't just make wild accusations and I'm probably totally wrong.' She pushed back her chair. 'Look, Hannah, I am going to have to go. There's some work I absolutely have to do in preparation for my case tomorrow, and with all this going on, I just haven't had the chance to get down to it.'

'OK.' My heart had sunk, but at the same time I realized that being alone would give me the opportunity to do some serious thinking and perhaps conduct a little investigation of my own. Talking was getting us nowhere. Action was needed. And if at the moment I had not the first idea what that might be, I was fired up enough to be determined to think of something.

I had to get out of the hotel. I was beginning to feel as if I'd been here for ever. I could walk, or I could drive. I decided to drive.

I got into my car without any clear idea of where I was going. I could go and see Jenny, but if I did it would only be more of the same, going over and over what had happened, what might have happened, what was going to happen. And all, probably, punctuated by constant interruptions from her children. I liked children – goodness, I hoped to have some of my own before it was too late – but right now I could do without them. I needed a breathing space before the onslaught started all over again.

I drove without really thinking; my car seemed to have a mind of its own, and it was almost with a start that I realized I was very close to the turning to Laura's home. Drawn like a steel filing to a magnet, I turned into the lane. I honestly don't know what I expected to find, or intended to do. For all I knew, the house was still sealed as a crime scene with a uniformed officer outside the door. But there was no policeman in evidence, and I supposed the forensics department had already completed their search.

I parked on the turnaround and sat for a moment looking at the house that had been my friend's home. Sunlight glinted on firmly closed windows, a honeysuckle was in full bloom beside the door. It looked like the perfect example of a perfect family home; impossible, almost to believe the tragedy that had so recently played out here.

My throat closed. I got out of the car and walked around the side of the house, my feet crunching on the pristine gravel. This was a mistake, I knew, but somehow I couldn't stop myself. The narrow path led me under an archway, heavy with yet more honeysuckle, where bumblebees droned busily, before opening out on to the patio at the rear of the house. And there, right in front of me, was the swimming pool.

Again that nerve jumped in my throat as I imagined Laura's body floating, face down in the azure water. But there was no water in the pool now, it had been drained, presumably, to facilitate the search for evidence, but there was a single pink carnation head lying on the bottom. The empty pool, the dead flower and the carelessly scattered poolside furniture gave the whole area a look of desolation. I glanced at the spot where Laura's handbag had been. It had gone now, of course, collected and bagged up as evidence, I supposed, and I knew that if there had been anything else to find that I'd missed it would no longer be here, but in the possession of the police.

I looked then in the direction of the motor home, nervous suddenly that Darren might suddenly appear. Mark had said he never surfaced before midday, and I didn't know if he'd been allowed to take up residence again or not, but in any case, the motor home looked shut up, the door firmly closed and the curtains drawn at the windows. I breathed a sigh of relief. I couldn't imagine that Darren would be there, with no one in the house to provide him with food or even water, or that he'd want to be, given that the pool where his aunt had so recently died was within clear view of his window. And even if he was, I knew now that he was not dangerous in the way I'd feared he was. But I didn't fancy bumping into him all the same. Everything about him was just too disconcerting.

My eye ran along the back of the house from the kitchen door and window to the French doors that Laura had had put into the room she'd called the 'drawing room' so as to let in extra light and give direct access to the patio, and suddenly I was frowning. The floor-length curtain at one of them was stirring slightly as if in a draught. But that couldn't be – or shouldn't be. Unless the window wasn't properly closed.

That bloody boy! I exploded. I'd just been thinking he wouldn't fancy living in the motor home with no access to the house; now my immediate reasoning was that he had taken advantage of the fact that the house was empty and either let himself in with a spare key or even broken in, and was indulging himself in luxury.

My blood boiled with rage – on the edge of my nerves, it was, I suppose an understandable reaction, if a little extreme. Darren might be Mark's nephew, but I was absolutely positive that Laura wouldn't want him swanning around her unoccupied home – and it was still her house, even if she was dead. She wouldn't want it, and I was going to do something about it. Anger had completely erased my natural nervousness of Darren and blown caution to the winds. I yanked on the handle of the French door, it swung open, and I stormed into the house.

The drawing room was empty, cool, still and untouched. I marched through to the hall, yelled up the stairs. Nothing. I checked the kitchen and dining room. Equally deserted. And then for good measure, I checked upstairs too. My confidence was waning now as empty room succeeded empty room, and by the time I pushed open the door of the master bedroom I was beginning to feel not only a little foolish but also awkward and guilty. The sight of the king size bed, unmade presumably since Mark had climbed out of it on Sunday morning, champagne coloured pillows rumpled on one side only, chocolate brown duvet and champagne throw tossed to one side, intensified my sudden horrible awareness of what I had done. Darren wasn't here, and even if he had been, it was none of my business. I was the intruder, the one who had no right to be here. And I had better get out – fast.

I went back downstairs, through the house that echoed with silence, and back into the 'drawing room'. My sense of guilt wound down a notch – this was less personal territory – and I lingered for a moment, looking around and remembering the pleasant time we'd spent here all together on Friday evening. I glanced at the champagne flutes we'd drunk from, washed up now and replaced on a silver tray, and the picture of the four of us, Martin's Mermaids, proudly clutching our medals. Then I stopped, and frowned. There had been *two* pictures on Friday, one at each end of the bookcase, with the jug of silk lilies in between – the one with our medals, the other with the trophy we'd won at that same successful gala. Now that one was gone and there was nothing but an empty space that upset the symmetry of the arrangement to show that it had ever been there.

How very odd! I was sure it hadn't been amongst the memorabilia Laura had brought to the reunion; that had all been cuttings and photographs in cardboard folders not in frames, as this one had been. So why wasn't it here now? I couldn't imagine a single reason why Mark should have moved it, unless it was a favourite of his and he'd wanted to take it with him when the police moved him out of the house as a reminder of Laura. But there were far better photographs of her on display, portraits of the lovely, laughing girl she had been, and the beautiful bride. Surely he'd have chosen one of those, not a picture of four girls with their hair still damp and flattened from being squashed into a swimming cap.

Well, not for me to reason why.

About to leave the way I had come in, I realized that I was going to be unable to secure the French door from the outside. That worried me. Anyone could get into the empty house just as I had done. Burglars – Darren – even the animal rights activists, should they come calling. I wondered if I should ring the police and tell them about the unlocked window. But heaven only knew how long I'd have to wait here for them to arrive, and in any case they'd be bound to ask what I was doing here. The last thing I felt like doing was answering their questions, especially as I didn't really know myself.

And then an idea occurred to me. If the back door had been locked from the inside and the key was still there, it give me another option. I went back to the kitchen and checked. Yes, the key was there. I retraced my steps to the drawing room, secured the French windows and left the house by the back door, locking it after me. I'd either post the key through the letterbox or return it to Mark later.

The key still in my hand, I tested the door, a habit of mine, to make sure it was properly locked.

And almost jumped out of my skin as a man's voice behind me demanded: 'What the hell do you think you're doing?'

Eleven

I spun round. To my complete surprise, I found myself face to face with Aaron.

'Hannah!' He sounded almost as startled as I was. 'What are you doing here?'

Guilty, and at a loss to know what to say, I countered: 'I could ask you the same question. You frightened me half to death.'

'Sorry about that. I thought you were a newspaper reporter or something, snooping around.'

My cheeks flamed. *What was I doing if not snooping around?* 'I'm not a newspaper reporter.'

'No, I can see that now,' Aaron said dryly. 'In answer to your question, I came to see Mark, but it didn't look as if anyone was at home and when I saw a strange car on the drive I jumped to the wrong conclusion.'

That surprised me too. Given what had happened, I'd have thought Aaron would steer well clear of Mark. Perhaps he'd felt obliged to offer his condolences, but they'd never really been that close.

'Do you know where he is?' Aaron asked.

'Or how long he's likely to be?'

My breath came out on a humourless chortle. 'A very long time, I should think. Thanks to you.'

Aaron frowned. 'What do you mean?'

I could feel that edge-of-my-nerves anger bubbling again. 'Mark has been arrested. He's at the police station, being questioned about Laura's death. Mainly because of the row they had over her affair with you.'

'Affair?' Aaron looked utterly gobsmacked. 'I didn't have an affair with Laura.'

'Mark seems to think you did,' I said.

'Well, he's got hold of the wrong end of the stick,' Aaron said, matter-of-factly. He glanced at his watch. 'I think you and I should have a talk, Hannah. How about coming for a pie and a pint?'

'Oh, I don't think so, thank you.' But my curiosity was stirred, all the same, and when Aaron persisted: 'Come on. I don't take "no" for an answer. We'll go to the Hope and Anchor,' I changed my mind.

'OK. I'll drive myself, though. See you there.'

As we walked back to our cars I realized I still had Mark's back door key. Well, I wasn't going to push it through the letter-box in front of Aaron, which would be tantamount to admitting I had no right to it. Instead, I slipped it into the pocket of my trousers. I'd just have to return it to Mark when – if – he was released.

'You're not going to do a runner on me, are you?' Aaron asked as I unlocked my car. He was looking at me with that wicked half-smile of his that I had always found so disconcertingly attractive.

'Now, why would I do that?'

He shrugged, raised an eyebrow at me, but said nothing.

The Hope and Anchor was a typical country pub in a village about two miles outside Mowbury. I followed Aaron along the narrow winding lane at a speed that I was less than comfortable with, but couldn't avoid doing if I wanted to keep up with him. We pulled into a parking area on the opposite side of the road and I sat down at one of the small umbrella-shaded tables outside, while Aaron went in to get drinks and the bar menu.

'So,' he said when we'd ordered – a steak and ale pie for him, as he'd threatened, a tuna pasta bake for me – 'you never did tell me what you were doing at Laura's.'

Since I had no reasonable explanation to offer I went on to the offensive.

'I really don't think that's any concern of yours. And you haven't explained why you were there either.'

'I told you. I went to see Mark.'

'To apologize for having an affair with Laura.'

He raised his eyes heavenward. 'I did not have an affair with Laura.'

'You went outside with her at the reunion. Mark caught you.'

'Mark overreacted. We had things to talk about, that's all.'

'Really? And you were seen in town with her.'

Aaron's eyes narrowed. 'Seen? By whom?'

'Becky Westbrook. And being Becky, naturally she couldn't wait to tell Mark.' I looked at Aaron under my eyelashes. 'I suppose you had things to talk about then, too.'

'Actually, yes, I did.' Aaron swivelled his glass between his hands, leaving a circle of condensation on the Formica-topped table. 'Look, I'm going to come clean with you, Hannah. I think I can trust you to be discreet.'

My mouth tightened a shade. 'Really, Aaron, I don't want to know the gory details. It's none of my business.'

'Hannah, just shut up and listen. This wasn't about Laura. It was about Darren – Mark's nephew. He was the reason I was at the Old Vicarage today. I was aware that Mark was in custody and wouldn't be there. But I thought Darren might very well be.'

A flash of something I took to be understanding shot through my brain like a white hot bolt of lightening. Aaron, always the rebel. Aaron, who Stan had joked was always bound to end up in jail. Aaron, who had managed to avoid telling us what he did for a living, but who was driving a flashy car and didn't seem to be short of a penny or two.

'Drugs.' I said. 'This is about drugs, isn't it? Mark thought that he could get Darren off them by getting him away from the city, but he hadn't succeeded, had he? Drugs were found in his possession when he was arrested, but that was on Saturday, and without a doubt he was high when I saw him at Laura's the previous evening and he hadn't yet been to Bristol then. But he'd got them from somewhere.'

'Very good, Hannah.' That half-smile seemed to mock me. I didn't find it attractive now. I wanted to hit him.

'You're his supplier, I suppose,' I shot at him. To my chagrin, Aaron began to laugh. 'It's not funny,' I said between grated teeth. 'It's absolutely disgusting. People like you should be hung, drawn and quartered. But what really surprises me is that Laura should go along with it. Anything for a quiet life, I suppose. But to encourage that boy in his habit when she knew Mark was trying to wean him off it ... that is sick!'

Aaron was regarding me with an amused grin. 'Have you quite finished?' he asked mildly.

'I certainly have!' I scraped back my chair.

'Hannah.' He reached across, catching me

by the wrist. 'Is that what you think? That I'm a drug dealer?'

'Aren't you?'

'You really think I would have brought you here to tell you that?' He shook his head. 'Sit down. The food's here.'

'I don't want to eat with you, thank you very much.'

'Hannah, I am not a drug dealer. And I'm not an adulterer either, though it's quite a revelation to discover what your old classmates think you're capable of.'

He broke off. The waitress was hovering, laden with plates of steaming food, looking a little uncertain as to whether she should put them down on our table or not.

'Go ahead,' Aaron said to her. 'The pie is mine and the fish dish for the lady.'

Somewhat reluctantly I sat down again. 'OK. Explain.'

Aaron waited until the waitress was out of ear shot.

'I'm a policeman,' he said.

I nearly fell off my chair.

'Drugs squad,' he continued. 'I'm based in Bristol, but I've been assigned to an ongoing investigation in this neck of the woods since it's my home territory and I had the necessary contacts.'

'Laura,' I said flatly.

He nodded. 'Laura. I can't tell you too much, but suffice it to say that Mark's nephew, Darren, is one of those we've been keeping a close eye on. He's a user and he's been dealing himself in a small way. I was liaising with Laura in the hope that he would lead us to the chief source. All this has put the whole operation in jeopardy.'

'It hasn't done Laura much good either,' I said bitterly.

'No.' He had the good grace to look chastened. 'I really am very sorry about what has happened to Laura.'

Automatically I picked up my fork, poked at the melted cheese topping on my meal, then put the fork down again.

'That's why she was killed then, is it?' I asked. 'It wasn't Darren himself, but it was someone involved with this drugs ring.'

Aaron was cutting open his pie, sprinkling it liberally with salt. 'Could be. These people can get very nasty when they're crossed.'

'How could you let her put herself in danger like that?' I demanded.

'It was her choice. She came to us, not the other way around.'

I bowed my head. Brave Laura, trying to do what she believed was right. Or desperate Laura, wanting rid of a drug addict living in her back garden. It made no difference now. She'd schemed and plotted with the drugs squad and now she was dead.

'Why are the local police holding Mark if you know very well he had nothing to do with Laura's death?' I demanded.

'We don't know that for certain yet.' Aaron was struggling to open a plastic sachet of tomato sauce, finally resorting to tearing it with his teeth.

'But it's obvious.' I was getting wound up on Mark's behalf. 'Laura crosses the local drug barons and winds up dead in the swimming pool. I always knew Mark would never harm her.'

'Unfortunately it also gives him another motive,' Aaron said.

I frowned. 'What other motive?'

'If he thought Laura was prepared to sell his nephew down the river, helping the drugs squad behind his back, it may have made him very angry indeed. I'm not saying he meant to kill her, but the fact he has a temper is in no doubt. We all saw that on Saturday evening.'

Another flash of realization. 'It was you, wasn't it?' I said. 'I wondered who had told the police about the row they had. Now I know.'

Aaron didn't deny it. 'It has to be a possibility that someone as volatile as Mark could lose control if pushed to the limits over something he cared deeply about. He could very well have lost his rag and hit out, forgetting the torch was in his hand.'

'The torch,' I repeated. 'Laura was hit with a torch.'

'It would seem so, yes. A heavy rubber-handled one.' He grinned crookedly. 'Yes, that's right, you've got it in one. The sort policemen carry.'

'Have they found it?'

'They have. It had rolled into the swimming pool. Careless of the killer. But luckily for him the chemicals in the water have made any prints on it unidentifiable.'

'They didn't find a mobile phone in the pool as well, did they?' Aaron looked at me sharply, a forkful of steak pie poised halfway to his mouth. 'Laura's mobile,' I said. 'Somebody called her on it when she and Annabel were in the taxi on the way home, and again as she was getting out of the car. But it wasn't in her bag.'

I went on to explain how I'd rescued the spilled contents, and related the conversation Annabel and I had had about it.

'Has she told the police about it now?' Aaron asked. His voice had gone very hard, very official. I could see now what I'd been unable to see before: Aaron the policeman, and I recalled the flip side of Stan's remark about the route his life had taken. Either in jail ... or a sort of 007. He hadn't been so far short of the mark.

'I don't know,' I said, attempting to answer the question that had felt to me suspiciously like an interrogation. 'She was going to.'

'I should bloody well hope so!' Aaron said

with emphasis. 'She of all people should know better than to suppress evidence. I'll pass it on as soon as we've finished here in case she failed to mention it.' He gesticulated at my plate. 'Eat your fish pie or whatever it is. I didn't buy you lunch to see it all go back to the kitchen.'

Cheek!

'You don't have to buy it for me at all,' I said. 'I'm perfectly capable of paying for it myself.'

'I'm sure you are. But, a, I'm a gentleman, and b, I owe you.'

'What for? I haven't done anything.'

'Yet. But you're going to, aren't you?'

'Aaron, what are you talking about?'

'You are going to keep your ears and eyes open for me.'

'To try to find out who killed Laura?'

'No. Not my department, unless there is a connection. To keep me updated regarding Darren Calvin and his contacts. We've let him run free hoping he will lead us to the big cheeses operating out here in the sticks, and I don't want to lose him now.'

'Oh, great!' I said. 'You get Laura killed and then you want me to step into her shoes. Not the most tempting offer I've ever had, even if it is bated with tuna bake.'

'Hannah...'

I took a mouthful of the fish; it was actually very good.

'I don't see what I can do, anyway,' I said.

'You obviously have access to the house.' I had the grace to blush at that. 'And as a friend of Mark's, you're in a better position than most to find out who Darren's friends are, who comes calling on him, where he goes. I'm not asking you to stick your neck out, just make a note of any car number plates, descriptions of anyone you see him with, that sort of thing.'

'If you couldn't get that information from Laura, I really don't see how I can be of any help whatsoever,' I said. 'She was on the spot, I'm not. And I'm supposed to be going home at the end of the week in any case.'

Aaron grinned, that cheeky grin I had always found so attractive.

'Oh, well, it was a nice try, you must admit.'

'What are you talking about?'

'The best excuse I could think of to see you again.'

I stared at him and for no reason at all my stomach turned a somersault.

'Aaron, what are you like? First Laura...'

'For the last time, there was nothing going on with Laura.'

'Oh, come on! I saw the way she was flirting with you with my own eyes.'

He shrugged. 'Laura flirted with everybody.'

'And you encouraged her. To get her to do

what you wanted – cooperate so you could close your case.'

'Maybe just a little,' he admitted. 'But in the interests of the job, nothing more.'

'And now you're doing it again.'

'No, this time I'm using the job for *my* interests. There you are, cards on the table. Can I see you again, Hannah?'

To say I was flabbergasted would be an understatement.

'I don't know! This isn't a good time.'

'Maybe the only one we'll get.'

My pulses were racing. I was totally, utterly thrown. My head was telling me this was crazy. Just a few minutes ago I'd not only thought that Aaron had been having an affair with Laura, I'd also accused him of being a drug dealer. Now, God help me, I was actually considering going out with him myself!

Because I wanted to. Deep down I'd always wanted to. I wanted to dabble in the dark excitement that was Aaron just as I'd always wanted it. And I had an extra reason now. I needed some light relief from the nightmare that had enveloped me like a shroud. Needed to be in the company of someone who wasn't as emotionally bruised as I was by Laura's death, someone who wasn't grief stricken or needy. In a strange, inexplicable way, Aaron was a breath of fresh air, and it was very seductive.

'OK,' I said.

And my mobile phone rang.

'Sorry about this.' I dived into my bag and fished it out. I could feel his eyes on me, disconcerting me, making me act flustered and feel foolish. 'Hello?'

'Hannah?' Jenny's voice. She sounded flustered too. 'Oh, thank goodness. I was afraid I'd just get your voicemail or something.'

'No, I'm here. What's wrong?'

'I really could do with some help...' She stopped talking; I could hear what sounded like laboured breathing.

'Jenny, are you all right?' I asked, alarmed.

For a moment there was nothing but that heavy breathing. Then Jenny said: 'I think I've gone into labour.'

'You *think*?' I squeaked. 'For goodness sake, Jenny, you've had four babies already. Surely you must *know*.'

'OK, yes, I'm in labour. My waters broke ten minutes ago. And I'm here on my own with the little ones. Ben has taken the others to Wookey Hole and I can't get hold of him. He must be in the caves or something. Hannah, please, could you come over?'

'On my way.' I was already on my feet. 'But for God's sake, Jenny – call an ambulance *now*. Do you hear me? *Now!*'

'I will, I will. With Noah it was only just over two hours, start to finish.'

'*Now!*' I switched off my mobile, fished in

207

my bag for my car keys. 'I'm going to have to go,' I said to Aaron. 'Jenny's in labour.'

'So I gathered,' he said dryly. 'Want me to come with you?' I threw him a withering glance. 'I have got all my First Aid certificates,' he offered, but he was making no attempt to get up and leave the remains of his steak and ale pie, and the tone of his voice suggested he was treating this as some kind of joke. 'Must admit, though, I've never delivered a baby.'

'And you won't be now.' I'd located my keys, had them dangling between my fingers ready to press the remote control to unlock the car.

'Here.' Aaron was holding something out to me; I saw it was a business card. 'My number. Give me a call, yes?'

'OK.' I slipped the card into my bag and headed off across the road to my car without so much as a backward glance.

I drove to Jenny's house in sheer utter panic. What if I got there before the ambulance; what if the baby decided to put in an appearance before it arrived? Two hours last time, start to finish, Jenny had said. This time it could be even less; by the time you get around to having your fifth baby it was probably like shelling peas! But I didn't have the faintest idea what to do to assist with a delivery. They always boiled kettles in books and films, but I wasn't clear what it was for and I wasn't at all sure I wanted to find out. I couldn't deliver a baby, for God's sake! But Jenny would know what to do, I comforted myself. She'd had enough experience.

To my immense relief, however, when I finally turned into Jenny's close (I'd got lost several times in my haste, in all those confusing and similar looking roads, avenues and cul-de-sacs) I saw an ambulance drawn up outside Jenny's house with its back doors open ready, I presumed, for the patient to be loaded. The front door of the house was open too. I went in, calling out: 'Hello!' and a paramedic in a bright green jumpsuit overall came to the top of the stairs.

'You'll be the friend, I take it.'

'Yes. Is she...?'

'She won't be long, but I reckon we can just about make it to the hospital in time. So, we'll be on our way.'

A second paramedic in an identical uniform emerged from the bathroom at the top of the stairs. Jenny was in a sort of portable chair.

'Oh, Hannah, I am so sorry about this!' she managed between gasps as they carried her downstairs. 'Noah and Dan are in the living room watching television. Can you look after them, and get their tea? Though Ben should be home by four. You could try ringing him again. His mobile number is programmed

209

in...' She broke off as another pain caught her, doing that ridiculous breathing with her eyes closed and her mouth wide open.

'The children will be fine,' I said. 'Stop worrying and just go!'

They went, one paramedic in the back with Jenny, the other driving like hell with the twos and blues flashing and blaring.

Two small anxious faces appeared around the living-room door.

'What's happening?'

'Where's Mummy?'

'Mummy has gone to the hospital to get you a new brother or sister,' I said, marvelling at the fact that they did not seem unduly bothered that they didn't know me from Adam, and wondering how the hell I was going to cope.

'I'm going to ring your daddy,' I said soothingly, reaching for the phone, searching in the directory for Ben's mobile number and hoping against hope that by now he and the other children were out of those damned caves!

It was past seven by the time I arrived back at The Beeches, and I was exhausted. Totally, utterly, drained. I'd finally managed to get hold of Ben and he'd driven straight back. But in the meantime, Jenny had produced an eight pound eleven ounce baby girl – 'Goodness only knows what a bouncer it would have been if she'd gone full term!' Ben had commented – and he'd gone to the hospital to see Jenny and the new arrival, leaving me to look after not only the little ones but Chloe and Jack too. Chloe was actually very good, very helpful, but still the burden of responsibility weighed heavy on my shoulders as I tried to rustle up a meal that all of them would like in a kitchen where I had no idea where to find a saucepan, never mind a tablespoon. Baked beans, fish fingers and potato waffles may not sound much of a banquet, but believe me, it was the limit of my culinary achievement in someone else's kitchen.

When Ben finally returned to relieve me, he had imparted the news that Jenny wanted to name the new arrival Laura. That had made me fill up and I'd had to leave in a hurry so as not to make an exhibition of myself, but it had worried me a bit too. Lovely as Laura had been, much as it was a fitting, and touching, tribute to her, yet it seemed to me to be tempting fate to name the new baby for someone so recently murdered. But perhaps I was just tired and emotional. Seeing things in the blackest possible light.

I must go and get myself something to eat, I thought, as I drove through the gates of the hotel. Apart from breakfast and about half a bowl of tuna pasta, I'd had nothing all day. I had thought I'd finish up what Jenny's children didn't eat of the baked beans, but I should have been so lucky! They had wolfed down every last scrap. I changed out of the clothes I'd been wearing all day and which now smelled faintly of fish fingers and cooking oil, and made for the bar, expecting to be eating alone. At first I didn't see the familiar faces grouped around one of the tables that was tucked away behind a dried floral arrangement. Then I heard my name being called and turned to see Becky just a few feet behind me and waving to attract my attention. My surprise at seeing her was compounded by the fact that her squashed dumpling face was bright with excitement and triumph.

'Hannah! Come and see who's here!' She nodded towards the table she'd been occupying and my heart leapt.

Mark.

He still looked grey and spaced, a sad, dejected shadow of the man I knew. But at least he was here, not locked up for the night in a police cell. There was someone else at the table too, a young woman who I knew instantly, although I hadn't seen her since she was about twelve years old. She was so like Laura, with her honey coloured hair and heart shaped face that there could be no mistake.

'Isn't it wonderful? Mark has been released! Let me buy you a drink, Hannah, to celebrate!' Becky was positively bubbling – excessively so, I thought. Of course it was a huge relief to see Mark, but all the same, under the circumstances it was hardly the time to display quite such unbridled exuberance.

'I'll have a lemonade and lime,' I said, mindful of the fact that I'd consumed far too much alcohol over the past couple of days. 'But I need something to eat too.'

I picked up a plastic-coated bar menu and headed for the table where Mark and Laura's sister were sitting. 'Oh Mark, thank goodness, they've let you go.'

'For the time being. I'm on police bail. I don't think they've finished with me yet.' His tone was flat and heavy. 'Lucy, you remember Hannah?'

'Yes, of course I do.' Her eyes brimmed with unshed tears as the memories crowded in. Then she swallowed hard, composing herself.

'I just hope they can find out who was responsible,' she said. 'I can't imagine who would do something like that to my sister. The one thing I am sure of is that it wasn't Mark.' She touched his arm briefly in a gesture of support.

'Of course it wasn't Mark!' Becky said, coming back with my drink. 'We all know that. And all I hope is that now they'll start looking more closely at the people they *should* be looking at – Martin Golding, for one.'

Had she stuck the knife in yet? I wondered. And something else was puzzling me too – why on earth was Becky here, and how had she managed to muscle in on Mark's release and the arrival of Laura's sister?

'I have had a very busy afternoon,' I said. 'I've been at Jenny's. She had her baby this afternoon. A little girl.'

'So that's where you've been,' Mark said. 'I did wonder. When poor Lucy arrived she was out on a limb for a while.'

'Yes, I don't know what I'd have done without Becky.' Lucy smiled at Becky, a very Laura-like smile. 'No one here seemed to know where Mark was.'

'I'm very glad they didn't,' Mark interposed.

'So I got in touch with Becky,' Lucy went on. 'I had her number from when she worked for Mark. To be honest, I hadn't realized she was no longer with him. But she was so helpful, so supportive. Really, I can't thank you enough, Becky.'

Becky shrugged with false modesty, but I could see how secretly pleased she was to be praised and how she was revelling in being here with us now, a part of the action once more.

'Where are you staying?' I asked Lucy.

'I've got a room here for tonight,' Lucy said. 'But I think tomorrow I'll go to Mum and Dad's house. They'll be home in a couple of days anyway, just as soon as they can organize a flight. They were halfway across the Caribbean when I managed to contact them, but as soon as they touch land they'll be flying home.'

'What about you, Mark?'

'I'm staying here for the time being.'

'Oh – before I forget. I've got your back door key.' I explained what had happened this afternoon. 'I haven't got it on me now. It's in my room in the pocket of the trousers I was wearing, but I'll go and get it when I've had something to eat.'

'There's no rush,' Mark said heavily. 'I'm not in any hurry to go home.'

That didn't surprise me. After what had happened I couldn't imagine he would ever want to go home again.

'But Darren wasn't there, you say?' Mark was off on another tack, worried still about his wayward nephew.

'No, but I'm sure he's fine.'

In the light of what Aaron had told me, I wasn't sure about that at all, and I couldn't help but feel a little guilty at what I was keeping from him. Not only that Darren was still very involved with the drugs scene, but also that there was a very real possibility that some of his associates might have been

215

responsible for Laura's death. But I was mindful that Aaron had trusted me with what was no doubt confidential information and in any case I didn't want to say anything that would cause Mark further distress.

At the thought of Aaron, a sharp needle of dark excitement pricked deep inside me, that little edge of the forbidden which was so dangerously appealing. And for just a moment I dared to hope that perhaps we were over the worst of this. Mark had been released, hopefully the police would concentrate now on finding the real culprit and bringing them to justice. There had to be light at the end of the tunnel. Nothing would ever be the same again, of course. But...

'We'll get through this, Mark,' I promised.

He nodded, covered my hand with his. 'Thanks for being here for me, Hannah.'

I turned my hand over, palm up, squeezing his fingers with mine. 'We always will be, Mark. The old ties are the strongest. They'll still be there when all this is over. And it will be. Soon.' I hesitated. 'Jenny's new baby,' I said. 'She's thinking of calling her Laura.'

I saw the tears sparkling again then in Lucy's eyes, and Mark nodded, too choked now to speak. But what had seemed to me before to be tempting fate suddenly seemed absolutely right, absolutely fitting. It was, I thought, a first step towards closure, a nod to the future with a link to a happier past. A strange warm glow spread through me, as if I'd been drinking not lemonade and lime but vintage champagne.

And in that rosy flush of optimism I had not the slightest premonition of what was still to come; that events were about to take another downward spiral and the nightmare engulf us all over again.

Twelve

The fine spell of weather had broken. Instead of the clear blue skies and sunshine I had grown used to – come, almost, to take for granted – I woke to a day overcast with heavy leaden clouds and the spatter of rain on the window.

I had breakfast with Mark and Lucy and when we had finished Lucy went to settle her bill and collect her belongings. Mark had said he would drive her over to her parents' house – she had flown down from Scotland, apparently – and I thought they probably needed some private time together to talk about what had happened and discuss funeral arrangements. The coroner, it seemed, had given his permission for the funeral to go ahead provided it was a burial and not cremation. I understood the reasoning behind this, the possible need for a second post-mortem, but it was a grizzly thought I didn't care to dwell on.

Left to my own devices I decided I would go to see Jenny and the new baby. I phoned Ben to check on visiting times and was startled when he told me that Jenny was now back at home. He had collected her first thing this morning.

'She couldn't wait to get back to the other children,' he said. 'I'd have thought she'd be only too glad to get some rest while she could, but no. She says the maternity hospital is the noisiest place in the world.'

'You won't want me bothering you then,' I said, but Ben insisted that Jenny would like to see me, and I could hear Jenny herself agreeing in the background.

'You were a real friend yesterday,' Ben told me. 'You're welcome here any time at all.'

I had little option then but to go over. I found Jenny resting on the sofa with the baby fast asleep in a Moses basket on the floor beside her. Daniel, her youngest boy, was playing happily with a collection of Bob the Builder toys, taking an occasional interest in his new little sister, and with Ben busy doing something in the kitchen we had the chance to have a good chat.

When we'd covered the details of how she'd only just arrived at the hospital in time yesterday, I brought her up to date with what had happened, and like me she marvelled at how yet again Becky had managed to inveigle herself into the action.

'I'll bet she was cock-a-hoop to get a call from Lucy,' Jenny said. 'Couldn't wait to leap in and save the day.'

'I'd have thought she was at work on a Monday afternoon,' I mused. It hadn't occurred to me before.

'Probably downed tools and rushed over,' Jenny said grimly. 'She'd find it irresistible. And then getting to see Mark too – that would have been the icing on the cake. She's besotted with him, you know. Laura used to say the way she mooned around after him was pathetic.'

'She is pathetic, really,' I agreed. 'And I'm awfully afraid she's dragged Martin into it. She'll enjoy nothing more than telling the police about his indiscretions with Laura and Annabel.'

'Perhaps that's just as well,' Jenny ventured.

'But it could ruin his life, and I don't think he had anything to do with Laura's death,' I said. 'Far more likely it was someone connected with that awful Darren.'

'I thought he was out of the frame.' Jenny settled herself more comfortably.

'He is, but...' I went on to tell her about Aaron and the fact that he was investigating some kind of drugs ring in the area which Darren apparently had connections with. I knew I could trust her to keep it to herself.

'I'm not surprised,' Jenny said. 'It was pretty clear from the state of him the other night that he's getting supplies from some-where.'

'But here's something that will surprise you.' I hesitated, shy suddenly.

'He's asked you out.'

I stared at her, astonished. 'How do you know that?'

'Doesn't take a genius to work it out.' Jenny grinned. 'He always fancied you.'

I shook my head in disbelief. Annabel had said much the same thing. 'Well, I never knew,' I said.

'And you fancied him. You admitted it the other night.'

'Well, yes, but that was years ago.'

'And you don't fancy him any more?'

I chewed my lip, unwilling to admit that yes, actually I did still fancy him.

'You think I should go, then?' I asked instead.

'Why not?'

'He gave me his business card. Perhaps I'll give him a call sometime.'

'Don't leave it too long,' Jenny said. 'A good man is exactly what you need. And a couple of little ones.'

'Hey, whoa! Steady on!'

220

'Well, you do! You don't know what you're missing.'

Oh, I did, I did. And seeing Jenny here with her family, the picture of contentment, I was filled with envy. But somehow I couldn't see Aaron in the role of husband and father. He didn't fit that mould. Even if I wanted him to. Which I didn't. Aaron was a dark fantasy. Maybe that was exactly what I needed just at the moment. But nothing more.

'I'd better get going,' I said.

'There's no rush, is there? Stay and have some lunch.'

'No, thanks all the same. You've got enough on your plate.'

The phone was ringing. We heard Ben answer it, then he came into the living room holding it out to Jenny. 'For you.'

Ben disappeared again; to get on with the domestic chores, I assumed.

'Hello?' Jenny sang out, expecting, no doubt, to be greeted by some well-wisher offering her congratulations. Then her smile faded and her face grew serious. 'No. No, sorry. I can't help. Hold on a minute.' She covered the mouthpiece, turned to me. 'Have you heard anything from Annabel?'

I shook my head, puzzled. 'Not since yesterday morning.'

'Sorry,' Jenny said again into the phone. She rang off, went on staring at the receiver as if in a trance.

'Somebody looking for Annabel?' I asked, puzzled, and, without really knowing why, a little alarmed.

'Yes. A colleague at the firm of solicitors she works for in London.'

'She's in court today,' I said. 'She had to represent a client in some family matter.'

'That's just it,' Jenny said, looking more worried than ever. 'She hasn't turned up. That's why they're looking for her.'

I knew in that moment that something was very wrong. Already raw from what had happened to Laura, my nerves went taut as wires and the pit of my stomach seemed to fall away. That case had been very important to Annabel. She'd told me there was absolutely no way she could miss it. She wouldn't have missed it. Her job was her life; her clients' trust in her paramount.

'Call them back, Jenny,' I said. 'Tell them they've got to report her missing.'

'But we don't know that she is.'

'I do,' I said. My voice was shaking – I was shaking – with the absolute certainty of it. 'Call them back, Jenny.'

'I can't do that!'

'OK, give me the phone then. I will!'

Jenny hesitated; passed it to me. 'Oh, Hannah, I really don't think ... Aren't you over-reacting?'

'I bloody well hope I am!' I was punching

in 1471, pressing the button to return the call. And all the while hearing the words that had been practically the last that Annabel had spoken to me. 'I just thought of something...' And: 'No. No, that can't be, surely...'

'Hannah, please!' Jenny was getting agitated. 'You're frightening me.'

The phone was ringing.

'Laura is dead, Jenny,' I said, my voice low and deadly earnest. 'Annabel remembered something that might be important...'

'Hello. Thank you for calling. All our lines are busy at the moment, but if you'd like to leave your name and number...' An annoying, mechanical recorded message.

'Shit!' I disconnected, chewing on my lip.

'What are you talking about, Hannah?' Jenny asked.

I looked her straight in the eye. The last thing I wanted to do was upset her so soon after having the baby but there was no way I could keep to myself what I was thinking.

'Annabel remembered something that she thought was pertinent to Laura's death. She wouldn't tell me what it was, she said she couldn't start making wild accusations and she needed to think it through before she said any more. But supposing she went further than just thinking? Supposing she decided to talk to someone before she left Mowbury for London? Someone who could confirm or deny whatever it was that was on her mind?'

'Yes, but...'

'And supposing that person was the one who killed Laura? And they realized she was on to the truth? Oh my God, Jenny, if something has happened to Annabel too...'

Jenny had gone white. 'Hannah – you can't seriously think...?'

I shook my head, beside myself now. 'I don't know what I think, and I hope to goodness I'm wrong. But if the person who killed Laura thought Annabel knew and was going to give the police evidence that would point the finger at them, then to be honest, I think that person might very well kill again. I've got to do something, Jenny. This is Annabel we're talking about.'

'Try her firm again.'

'No, they won't know the background. It will take too long to explain, even when I manage to get to speak to the person who phoned just now.' My finger hovered over the key pad. 'Maybe it would be better if I rang the local police, the ones dealing with Laura's death.'

'Do you have their number? I think all calls are routed through a call centre nowadays.'

She was right. I would probably be pushed from pillar to post and end up explaining myself a dozen times before I got to speak to anyone remotely connected with the investigation into Laura's death.

But I knew someone who would help.

I fished in my bag for the card Aaron had given me.

'I'm going to ring Aaron,' I said.

I rang him. He answered immediately and I told him everything. He was in policeman mode, not at all the Aaron I had thought I knew, and I was glad of it. Though I was still worried sick about Annabel it was a huge relief to be able to unload my concerns on to someone trained to deal with the sort of situation that turns most of us into lumps of quivering jelly.

'And you've no idea at all what it was she had in mind?' Aaron asked.

'No. She wouldn't say. In fact, whatever it was, she seemed to find it incredible, and she needed to think about it some more. We'd been discussing the phone call to Laura's mobile. Is there any news on that, by the way?'

'As far as I understand it, the call was made from a pay-as-you-go phone, so there's no way of tracing it,' Aaron said. 'Anyway, go on.'

'Well, Annabel was adamant she hadn't been really listening and had no idea who Laura was talking to. But now I'm wondering if she remembered some apparently unconnected bit of information that gave her a clue as to who it might have been.'

'Could it have been a boyfriend, do you think?'

'I don't know. If so they weren't on very good terms. The one thing Annabel did say was that Laura was very cool with whoever was on the other end.'

'But that could have been a blind, if she thought Annabel was listening.' He was silent for a moment. 'OK, leave it with me. But if you think of anything that might be helpful – anything at all – ring me. And whatever you do, don't try doing any investigating of your own. It's beginning to look as though we might be dealing with a very dangerous character here.'

I shuddered. The fact that Aaron was taking me seriously, though a relief, was only making my fears more real.

'Take care, Hannah.' And he was gone.

'I'm sure she's fine,' Jenny said, possibly more to reassure herself than me. She didn't need this, I thought. With a baby to nurse, she needed to be calm, serene and rested.

'I expect you're right,' I said. 'She probably just got caught up in some traffic chaos. You know what London can be like.'

But I didn't believe it. Not for a moment. If she'd been stuck in a traffic jam, she'd have called somebody and said so. The dread weighed heavily in my stomach, feeding my nerves with sharp, spasmodic bolts of alarm. But I didn't want to inflict it on Jenny.

'I'm going to get off and leave you in peace,' I said.

Baby Laura was awake again, and the first soft snuffling cries had become a thin insistent wail. Jenny lifted her out of the Moses basket, her own face softening with love, and loosened the neck of her dress. In the doorway I paused and looked back at the cosy family scene, a picture of everyday domestic contentment and maternal joy.

'I'll be in touch, Jenny,' I said.

She nodded, her head bent over the precious bundle fastening hungrily on her nipple and I turned my back on normality and walked back into a world turned upside down by terrible things I couldn't believe were happening, but which were, all the same.

I went out to my car and Ben followed me.

'Have you heard anything about how the investigation is going?' he asked anxiously.

'Not really.' I didn't want to go into my concerns about Annabel just now. But it did occur to me to wonder if Ben had overheard something of what had been going on. 'Ben, I really have to go. Take care of Jenny, won't you?'

'What do you think?'

'Sorry. All this is making me jumpy to say the least of it.'

I got into my car, waved a bleak goodbye, and drove off.

Laura's car was no longer parked on the hard standing outside The Beeches. Perhaps the police had removed it for examination, though what clues it could possibly yield, I couldn't imagine. Or else Mark had arranged to have it removed. It must have been very upsetting for him, having to pass it each time he went in or out of the hotel, a constant reminder of Laura's last journey, and the pile of memorabilia lying on the back seat evidence of the hard work and enthusiasm she had invested in organizing the reunion that would lead to her death.

And perhaps Annabel's too...

I caught myself up, stopping the thought in its tracks. I wasn't helping by panicking. I was just making things worse. I unlocked my room and went in, intending to collect Mark's key and return it to him.

I'd left the trousers I'd worn on Monday hanging over the back of the chair – not the tidiest of things to do, but I just hadn't got round to hanging them up. Now I saw they had fallen down on to the floor. I picked them up and reached into the pocket for the key. It wasn't there. I tried the other pocket. Nothing. What in the world had I done with it? I couldn't have lost it, surely? But perhaps I had. With all that was going on, anything was possible.

The obvious place to look was in the

drawers of the little dressing chest. I pulled out the top drawer, where I'd deposited odd bits and pieces – a belt, a scarf, my jewellery box, sunglasses – and frowned. I could have sworn the sunglasses had been on top of the jewellery box. I'd worn them yesterday, and the jewellery box hadn't been opened since the night of the reunion. I wasn't really a great one for jewellery. Now the sunglasses were at the back of the drawer and the belt had become unravelled, snagging around them. Alarm bells rang, screaming along my already jangling nerves. Had the maid been rifling around in my things? I took out the jewellery box and opened it, concerned to check that nothing had gone missing. I'd brought the one good piece I owned – a piece of agate set in a silver choker – to wear on Saturday night. But no, the choker was there, and a few pairs of earrings, silver hoops and relatively worthless mock jet droppers, and my favourite everyday necklace, a sea shell on a leather thong. Nothing seemed to be missing. I was getting paranoid. And yet the unmistakeable feeling that someone had been rifling through my belongings remained.

And there was still the mystery of the missing key. I searched high and low, looking in every drawer and even turning out my handbag, but I couldn't find it. I must have lost it. It was the only explanation. Perhaps

I'd pulled it out with a handkerchief, though I had no recollection of using one. Or perhaps it had come out when I'd been attending to Jenny's children. If it wasn't here, it could be anywhere.

Oh, shit. When I'd locked up Mark's house I'd only been trying to help. Now his back door key was floating around goodness only knew where. The only consolation being that anyone finding it would have not the faintest idea what door it would unlock. Well, I'd just have to confess to my carelessness and it would be up to Mark what he decided to do about it.

I paid a visit to the bathroom and whilst there I checked the bathroom cabinet and my toiletries bag in the cupboard beneath the vanity unit just in case I'd somehow put the key down in a really stupid place when I was tired and fraught. It wasn't there, of course. But once again I had the strangest feeling that things were not quite as I'd left them. I couldn't quite put my finger on what was wrong; I was not a creature of habit who left moisturizer, toothpaste and floss lined up and ready to use, I was far more haphazard than that. Yet the feeling persisted.

It was ridiculous, of course, I told myself. My room had been locked and I had the key. I was getting totally paranoid. But was that any wonder? Laura was dead and Annabel missing ... what had happened to her? Why

230

hadn't she put in an appearance for her very important case in the family courts? Where *was* she? Again I stamped on the alarmist thoughts I could not escape, and headed for the door.

I opened it – and jumped a mile.

'Tristan!'

He'd been standing right outside. What was it with that man? How could anyone creep about as he did? It wasn't natural!

'Hannah.' He smiled that sickly, ingratiating smile. 'Did I startle you?'

'Yes, you did!' I snapped, nerves on edge. 'What do you want?'

'I just thought I'd see how you are.' As always he was a sight too smooth for my liking, a sight too plausible. How long had he been standing there outside my door, just waiting? Or – the crazy thought popped into my head – had he somehow got hold of another key to my room? Had he crept in before and gone through my things? It was illogical, of course, but jumpy as I was, I could almost imagine it to be true. He was slimy enough to do anything.

'I'm fine,' I said shortly, though of course I wasn't. And then, for no real reason that I could explain, I heard myself ask: 'Did you see Annabel yesterday?'

'You know I did,' he said smoothly. 'We were having coffee, you and I, when she arrived. Don't you remember?'

231

Of course I remembered. He'd gone off and left us alone. But how far had he gone? Had he simply retreated behind one of the screens of dried floral arrangements in his soft-soled suede shoes and sat there listening to our conversation? Engrossed as we had been, I'm not sure either of us would have noticed him. Was it possible he had over-heard Annabel say she'd thought of some-thing that might give a clue as to who was responsible for Laura's death?

'No, not then,' I said. 'I mean later.'

Tristan smiled thinly, looking vaguely be-wildered. 'No. Why?'

'Because,' I said, 'no one seems to know where she is.'

Tristan shrugged elegantly. 'Sorry, Han-nah. I'm afraid I'm unable to help. I didn't see Annabel again after I left the two of you to your private conversation.'

'I just wondered,' I said lamely. And won-dered why it was that I didn't entirely believe him. Wishful thinking, perhaps.

I didn't yet know for certain that anything terrible had happened to Annabel, of course, but I had that same awful sick feeling eating at my insides as I'd had when we'd been waiting to find out whether Laura's death had been accident or murder, and I didn't like it one little bit. When I had this feeling, insidious but inescapable, it was usually a very bad sign. It didn't necessarily have any foundation that I could explain, yet it was somehow more than merely the imaginative extension of anxiety. Not a premonition, exactly. More like a knowing. Accompanied by a feeling of helplessness and inevitability. Whenever I'd had that feeling, I'd been proved right. Right to be more worried than was reasonable or explicable in the circumstances of the given situation.

I'd had it once when David had been late home from playing golf. Common sense had told me that he'd stopped for a drink in the club house with friends, but no matter how I tried to persuade myself otherwise I had known, absolutely known, with that indefinable sixth sense, that something was dreadfully wrong. Something bad had happened to make him late. And I was right. I'd got a call from the hospital to say David was there. His car had been in collision with a lorry at a notorious junction not far from his golf club. He was lucky to be alive, the police had said later, let alone to have escaped with a broken leg and cracked ribs. And that was just one example; there had been others. The time my father had had a heart attack. The time our cat, Smokey, was knocked down and killed – David had tried to calm my fears by pointing out that Smokey had often gone missing for much longer, but though I knew that was true it didn't alter my certainty that this time he would not be coming home. And it had happened again with Laura. That same sixth sense had told me right from the outset that her death was more than a tragic accident.

Now it was nagging at me again, as inescapable as breathing. Something had happened to Annabel. And if I was right again – as I was wretchedly sure I was – then it would be too much of a coincidence for it not to be connected to Laura's death. Annabel had been representing Mark; she'd been privy to everything the police had asked him and to his replies. And she had thought of something that might be important and perhaps followed it up, making inquiries of her own before telling anyone what it was. It could be, of course, that she'd known about the drugs connection that Aaron had told me about, and got herself into dangerous waters. But I would have thought that even intrepid Annabel would have had more sense than to tackle dealers and their hangers-on in the murky world of drugs.

Which left, almost inevitably, people we knew. People who had, perhaps, been at the reunion.

I managed to shake Tristan off by saying I was going to look for Mark; even then he accompanied me across to the main hotel, and I was only able to unglue him from my heels by going up to Mark's room.

Mark wasn't there; he was still out with Lucy, I presumed, making whatever arrangements had to be made. With some trepidation I went back downstairs, and to my relief Tristan had disappeared.

I ordered a bar snack – a chicken salad – and ate it worrying about Annabel and wondering if it was really possible that someone we knew and trusted could be behind these terrible events. I made a mental list of anyone who could reasonably be considered a suspect and looked at each of them in turn.

Mark himself. Whether I believed it of him or not, all the arguments about motive and opportunity did hold water. But at least he had an alibi for yesterday every bit as strong as Darren's – he'd been in police custody.

Martin Golding. Another one with motive, certainly, though I had no idea what his movements had been. It was unlikely he'd have an alibi for Saturday, since he'd presumably driven himself home after the reunion and his wife was probably in bed and asleep when he got there. As for yesterday ... well, I had no idea whether he had an alibi for yesterday or not.

Aaron. He'd denied having an affair with Laura, and he was a policeman. But he was just about the only person, apart from Mark, that I could imagine Laura being on the patio with at one in the morning. And just because he was a policeman didn't necessarily mean he was not also a liar – and a murderer. That hard edge that made him so attractive also meant that he would, if necessary, be totally ruthless, I felt sure.

And Tristan. I couldn't think of a single reason why Tristan should kill Laura, unless there was something she knew about him that she had kept from the rest of us, but perhaps held over him. Some kind of fraud, perhaps. Tristan had a very high powered job. He would have a lot to lose. There were plenty of things that made me uneasy about Tristan. I didn't like the way he was forever creeping about, and he'd stayed on for no real reason that I could see though we'd all been under the impression he was leaving on Sunday. I was trying to build a case against him, I realized. If Laura's killer was to be found amongst friends and acquaintances, I very much hoped it was Tristan.

Oh, if only Annabel had told me what had been in her mind! If only I'd pressed her! But I hadn't, and now all I could do was try to work out for myself what it might have been.

I began another mental list, this time of the possibilities of what had made Annabel suspicious. Something she'd heard, perhaps. Something she'd seen. Something not quite right. She'd stayed on with Laura after the rest of us had left on Friday evening – was it possible something had happened, or Laura had told her something that hadn't seemed important at the time, but which she had suddenly realized might be significant? About the drugs connection, perhaps? Or something more personal?

They'd certainly talked about Martin Golding, but as far as I was aware, she'd said nothing that Annabel hadn't repeated to me. And what more could there be? Unless, of course, their affair had gone on long after our school days, or been reignited when she'd contacted him about the reunion. Laura had been such a dreadful flirt that was certainly not beyond the realms of possibility. And it could explain why she had taken it so badly to learn that he'd tried it on with Annabel before taking up with her all those years ago. It was stupid, irrational, but Laura had been a little vain, a little protective of her self image as a femme fatale. And the vicious remarks she'd made to Martin had been emotional given the time that had past.

Certainly if Annabel had been suspicious about Martin Golding, she wouldn't have been afraid to confront him. She'd put him in his place long ago; more than likely she'd feel confident of her ability to do so again. But perhaps she'd been wrong. Perhaps he'd been desperate enough to go to lengths she'd never imagined he would...

'Hannah?'

I looked up, startled. So lost in my thought

had I been that I hadn't noticed Aaron come into the bar. Now, as I saw him standing there, hands in the pockets of his leather jacket, watchful, unsmiling, my stomach lurched, and not, this time, because of the peculiar effect he had on me.

'What are you doing here?' I asked. But I knew. Already, I knew.

'I wanted to come and tell you myself,' he said. 'I didn't want you to hear it from the local police.' He paused; my heart seemed to have stopped beating; I felt sick.

'They've found Annabel,' he said. 'Hannah, I'm so very sorry, but I'm afraid she is dead.'

Thirteen

I'd already known it, yet every muscle in my body went weak with shock. I felt sick.

'How?' My voice was tight, flat.

'They found her car out at Hurleigh Pond with the engine switched on and a length of hose in the exhaust pipe. It looks as if she committed suicide, Hannah.'

'No.' I shook my head vigorously. 'She wouldn't do that.'

238

'Why else would she be at Hurleigh Pond?'

Hurleigh Pond. We used to go there on our bicycles in the happy, carefree days a lifetime ago. We'd sit at the edge with our feet dangling in the water; lie flat out on our backs in the soft leaf mould under the trees, looking up at the sun splintering through the branches, talking, joking, sharing secrets. A track ran from the road to a clearing where fishermen left their cars while they sat on the bank with rods and lines and striped umbrellas; it was there they'd found Annabel's car, I imagined. Quiet, secluded. It was unlikely there would be anyone fishing on a Monday afternoon, and maybe the local kids didn't go there any more. They were too engrossed in computer games these days to go off for long bicycle rides; their parents too afraid they'd be accosted by a paedophile or weirdo. Why had Annabel gone there when she'd been so anxious to get back to London to prepare for her case today? I didn't know. The one thing I was sure of was that she hadn't gone there to commit suicide.

'I think she went there to meet someone,' I said.

'And then quietly sat back and let them fix her car so that she'd be gassed by exhaust fumes?'

'Perhaps she was knocked unconscious like Laura was,' I said, wildly grasping at straws.

'There's no evidence of that.'

'She didn't kill herself,' I said with conviction. 'You can't believe that, Aaron. You know her. Annabel just wasn't the suicidal type. And it's just too much of a coincidence.'

'OK, perhaps it's not a coincidence.' Aaron pulled out a chair and sat down beside me. 'Perhaps their deaths are linked, but not in the way you think.'

I frowned. 'What are you talking about?'

He was silent for a moment. 'Suppose it was Annabel who killed Laura? She was the last person, as far as we know, to see Laura alive.'

'Oh, that is ridiculous! The most ridiculous thing I ever heard! Annabel dropped Laura off and went home in the taxi they'd shared.'

'We only have Annabel's word for that at the moment, though of course it can easily be checked. I doubt anyone from the taxi firm has been interviewed yet, it would hardly have seemed relevant, but they will be now. The driver can confirm whether he dropped one woman or two off at Laura's home. But even if it was just Laura, there wouldn't have been anything stopping Annabel from coming back in her own car. And we only have her word for it about the phone calls Laura received, too. Perhaps she did get a phone call, not in the taxi but afterwards, when she got home. From Annabel, asking to come back and talk to her. That's why she didn't mention the phone calls when she was first questioned. Then, when she realized the investigating officer would be curious as to why Laura's mobile was missing, she came up with the story she told you to explain it.'

'But it was Annabel who pointed out to me that Laura's phone was missing.'

'Covering herself, in anticipation of someone following up that line of inquiry.'

'And why the hell would Annabel murder Laura?' I asked, exasperated and furious.

'What about the Martin Golding connection?' Aaron suggested. 'We know that they'd discussed their relationship with him and Laura was pretty upset about the fact that she wasn't the only one. But perhaps Annabel was equally upset on the same score. How do we know she wasn't still carrying on with him?'

I snorted. 'That's one part of your hypothesis that can be safely discounted.' Aaron raised an eyebrow, questioning. 'Annabel was gay,' I said shortly.

'Ah.' For a moment the wind was taken out of his sails. 'A lover's tiff, then,' he went on after a moment. 'She and Laura...'

'Surely you're not suggesting Laura was gay too!' I'd never heard anything less likely in my life.

'She could have been bi.'

'I don't think so,' I snorted. 'In any case, I don't understand why you are trying to make out a case for Annabel having been the one who murdered Laura.'

'Because it could fit the facts. Annabel killed Laura in a fit of jealous rage, then, in a fit of remorse, killed herself. It could even explain why she went out of her way to help Mark. She knew he wasn't guilty. Besides being anxious to know just what evidence the investigating officers had.'

'It's the most ludicrous scenario I ever heard!' I said angrily. 'You can't seriously believe that Annabel...'

'No, actually I don't,' Aaron said. 'I'm playing devil's advocate, that's all.'

'Well, don't!' I was still furious. 'These are my friends you're talking about. My friends! They're dead, both of them. Somebody has murdered them, and you dare to sit there and suggest they were lesbian lovers and Annabel was a vicious jealous killer who ended up taking her own life.'

And I burst into tears.

'Oh, Hannah.' He didn't actually say he was sorry. Apologies weren't exactly Aaron's style. But he did offer me his handkerchief when I scrabbled futilely in my bag for a tissue. 'I'm a policeman. It's what I do. You have no idea what people can be capable of. Your ordinary average man in the street could spend his free time beating up his wife or accessing porn sites on the internet or abusing his children, and you might never

242

know it. The same goes for women. You'd be amazed at some of the things that go on behind closed doors. Everybody has their secrets and the darker the secret the better they are at hiding it. However well you might think you know someone, they can still surprise you.'

I blew my nose. 'Annabel certainly did not kill Laura. And she didn't kill herself either. She's been murdered because she knew something that could point the finger at whoever hit Laura over the head with a heavy torch and drowned her in her own swimming pool, I'm sure of it.'

'In that case,' Aaron said, 'we'd better find out who it was.' His gaze lingered for a moment on my face, eyes narrowed as if he was thinking something he wasn't saying. 'And we'd better do it quickly.'

We sat for the best part of an hour going over and over it. Aaron told me that Annabel had checked out of The Farm at around four, the last time anyone had seen her alive, and I shared with him all the thoughts I'd had about who might have been responsible for her death. I wasn't actually crying now. I'd managed to get myself together, but the tears were not that far away and I was still mangling Aaron's handkerchief between my hands like some sort of comfort blanket. We were getting a few odd looks from the bar staff though they were making a fair pretence of not taking any notice of us. I guessed they must be all agog at the way their rather genteel hotel had become the centre of so much drama.

'Do you think it might have something to do with the drugs connection?' I asked, still desperately reluctant to believe that someone I knew, and knew well, might be a double murderer.

'It's possible,' Aaron said. 'That's my excuse for being here now. This isn't my bag, you realize. I'm treading on someone else's turf.'

'But you're bound to be interested, given your connection with the area and the victims.'

'And given that I'm concerned about one of the people caught up in it.'

There was no mistaking what he meant. I felt heat rising in my cheeks; covered them with Aaron's handkerchief. This was not a conversation I wanted to have right now.

'To get back to the drugs affair,' I said hastily. 'It's possible, isn't it, that Laura may have known who was Darren's supplier, and she told Annabel?'

'If Laura knew, she didn't pass the information on to me, and I'm pretty sure she would have done,' Aaron said. 'She was being very helpful in every respect. She was anxious to put a stop to what was going on,

244

and get shot of Darren as soon as possible.'

'But if something happened on Friday night while Annabel was still there...' I was clutching at straws and I knew it, and Aaron shot my tentative suggestion straight out of the water.

'I talked to Laura on Saturday evening at the reunion, remember? The first legitimate chance I'd had to speak to her without worrying that someone might see us. Ironic, really, that Mark got hold of the wrong end of the stick, and thought there was something going on between us of a more personal nature.' He paused, thinking. 'Or perhaps he didn't think that at all. Perhaps he was more clued up on the situation as it really was than we realized, and knew that Laura was informing on Darren. He's very protective of that boy for some reason.'

'You mean he was angry because he knew she was colluding with you against Darren, not because he thought you were having a crafty smooch?' Aaron nodded. 'I don't think so,' I went on. 'From what he said to me I definitely got the impression he thought she was having an affair with you, and it wasn't the first time she had strayed.'

'Or that's what he wanted you to think.' Aaron was silent for a moment. I could almost hear his policeman's mind ticking over and it occurred to me to wonder if he was now considering the possibility that

Mark might somehow be involved with the drugs supplier Aaron was seeking to identify. Thinking along the lines that Mark was overly concerned with his nephew's welfare, doing too much for him, and might have an ulterior motive. 'Surely you don't think that Mark—' I began, but Aaron was following his own train of thought, returning to the last conversation he'd had with Laura.

'Laura told me on Saturday there had been no developments for a couple of days. No cars calling. And Darren hadn't been out. The only piece of information she was able to give me was that she thought she'd found out how Darren was managing to carry out his part of the supply chain. She thought he was concealing the drugs in the handlebars of his bicycle.'

'How did she know that?' I asked, surprised.

'She'd noticed him fiddling with them before pedalling off into Mowbury. She was right, too. Whilst forensics were going over the house and swimming pool in relation to Laura's death, we took the opportunity of having a look at the motor home and Darren's bicycle. There were no drugs there then, but we did find traces of illegal substances inside the handlebars. I think his regular supplier had been out of contact for a while. That's why he went into Bristol on Saturday – to get his hands on fresh supplies.

246

He must have been pretty desperate – it's a good hour on the bus, and the service is pretty infrequent. No, I don't think there was anything Laura could have told Annabel, and to be honest, I can't see Annabel being foolish enough to seek out a drugs dealer herself, anyway. She'd know what a dangerous world it is.'

My own sentiments exactly, but it wasn't what I wanted to hear.

'Let's go over your other suggestions again,' Aaron said.

We rolled them out, one by one, but we were getting nowhere.

'It may be,' Aaron said, 'that Annabel's car, or even Annabel herself, will yield up some evidence. And without an approximate time of death we can't know whether any of the suspects have alibis.'

The suspects. Mark. Martin Golding. Tristan. Aaron had been on my original list, but I supposed he could be discounted now. Or could he? How did I know he was on the straight and level any more than any of the others? He could be playing a clever game of double bluff.

There was a tightness constricting my chest; I felt utterly, completely trapped, unable to comprehend what was going on, unsure as to whom I could trust. These people had been my friends; I had been so sure that I'd known them through and through. But

Laura and Annabel were both dead, and I couldn't escape the sick certainty that they had known their killer. All very well to try to blame the drugs connection – the fact remained that Laura would never have agreed to see anyone other than a friend at one in the morning, and Annabel wouldn't have driven to a secluded spot like Hurleigh Pond to meet a dangerous criminal. And she certainly hadn't gone there to commit suicide. I was even more certain of that than I had been that Laura's death was no accident.

Aaron's mobile was ringing. He answered it, half turning away, so I could not see his face, and his taut, clipped side of the conversation told me nothing. Then: 'Right. I'll meet you there in about–' he checked his watch – 'say twenty minutes? OK, will do.'

He rang off, swivelled back to face me, clipping his mobile back on to his belt.

'They've completed the PM on Annabel,' he said.

'And?'

'Cause of death, (One) Carbon monoxide poisoning.'

I swallowed hard. 'What do you mean – one?'

'They also found enough drugs in her to knock out a horse.'

My stomach contracted. 'Drugs again.'

'Yep, but not the recreational variety. When I said "knock out a horse" I meant it –

literally. The drug found in Annabel's body was one used for veterinary purposes.'

'What?'

'Exactly. Annabel had no connection with stables, did she?'

'No, absolutely not. As far as I know she's never been on a horse in her life. And now she lives in London.'

'So it's pretty unlikely she'd have access to anything like that.'

'Impossible, I'd say.'

'Besides which...' He hesitated. 'I shouldn't be telling you this, Hannah, but I'm going to. The evidence suggests that it wasn't Annabel who drove her car to Hurleigh Pond.'

'I knew it! What evidence?'

'At the moment I'm as much in the dark as you are. My information didn't run to details. I'll know more later.' He shifted in his chair; got up. 'I've got to go, Hannah. But I want you to do something for me.'

'What?'

I truly thought at that moment that Aaron was going to ask me to take over information gathering for his drugs investigation. I could not have been more wrong.

'I want you to go home, Hannah. Now, this afternoon.'

'But...'

'I mean it. There's nothing more you can do here. I want to know you're safe.'

A glow like warm honey spread through

my veins. Shocked as I was, upset as I was, the fact that someone should be concerned for me touched a cord that was close to my heart. Not just someone. Aaron. But for all that...

'I can't go home,' I said.

'Why not?'

'Mark...'

A muscle tightened in Aaron's jaw, hardening his features slightly.

'Mark,' he said in a low bitter voice that surprised me. 'Always Mark.'

'Mark needs his friends,' I said defensively. 'Now more than ever.'

'I thought you said his sister-in-law had arrived.' Aaron's tone was harsh.

'She has, but...'

'And where are his own family? Friends in the locality?'

'Ian is on holiday.'

'He must have others, surely? Doesn't it strike you as slightly odd that he seemingly has to rely on someone he's scarcely seen in twenty years?'

'Oh, for goodness sake, I don't know! I don't want to argue, Aaron. I just know it would look as if I was abandoning him if I just went home now.'

'Well, it's your decision, Hannah.' That same hard tone. 'But I think you should bear in mind – there were four of you. The Inseparables. Martin's Mermaids. Whatever you liked to call yourselves. And now two of you are dead.'

A chill whispered over my skin.

'But surely – Annabel died because of something she knew and Laura ... well, we don't know why Laura was killed.'

'Exactly. It could have been connected to the drugs dealing. Or it could have been something else entirely. Something personal.'

'Or even the animal rights protesters!' I said, remembering them suddenly. 'You said Annabel was given some veterinary drug. Vets ... animals ... now there's a possible link.'

A corner of Aaron's mouth quirked up in a grin that lacked humour. He had a small scar beside it, I noticed, and remembered a long-ago incident when he'd been hit in the face by a snowball that had contained a sharp stone. A snowball! When in the last few years had we had enough snow to make a snow-ball?

'Animal rights protesters seldom have much to do with animals,' he said. 'You may well be right, of course. There may be no connection whatever between Laura's death and Annabel's except that Annabel was getting too close to the truth for the murderer's comfort. But until we know for sure, I wouldn't want to discount any possibility. Four girls, firm friends, once the glamour

251

squad of the class, together for the first time in twenty years. Laura dies, then Annabel. I wouldn't want you to be the next, Hannah.'

'Oh, that's ridiculous!' But I was remembering, all the same, how I'd thought that someone was watching me, following me, on Friday night when I'd parked my car after getting back from Laura's get-together. The horrible feeling I'd had this morning that someone had been through my things whilst I was out, even though my hotel room was locked and nothing had been taken as far as I was aware. Except that I hadn't been able to find the key that I'd been so sure had been in my pocket. And something else – something I'd thought was odd and then forgotten about. Discounted as fanciful nonsense. A photograph of the four of us showing off our medals after a swimming gala. A photograph that had been in Laura's drawing room on Friday night and was no longer there on Monday morning.

Aaron must have seen my face change. He leaned forward. 'What?'

'It's probably nothing, but...' I told him. It meant admitting to having been in Laura's home with no business to be on the day he caught me there, but I told him anyway.

'And you're sure Laura didn't take the picture to the reunion?' he asked.

'Pretty sure.' I told him about the missing key too.

'For goodness sake, Hannah, you have got to stop keeping these things to yourself!' he snapped. 'Don't you realize we're dealing with something very serious here? Look, I'll pass on what you've told me to the murder team. They can check whether or not that photograph is amongst the stuff in Laura's car, the stuff she brought to the reunion, and take it from there. And they'll probably want to talk to you again.'

'But why would anyone want to take that photograph?' I asked, still puzzled.

'Could be a trophy. If so, we are dealing with one very sick individual. Are you sure I can't persuade you to go home?'

'I can't.'

'Then for goodness sake start acting sensibly.' He still sounded cross, no sign now of the caring warmth I'd glimpsed earlier. For some reason, I felt bereft.

'I've got to go.' He got up. 'Take care, Hannah.'

Then he was gone, and I was alone.

Something was nagging at me. Something I couldn't quite grasp, and it had to do with the inexplicable certainty that someone had been in my room this morning, rifling through my things.

I ran over it all again in my mind. The missing key I could have lost. The pocket I'd put it in wasn't deep or fastened in any way.

My trousers had been on the floor instead of hanging over the back of the chair where I'd left them, but they could have slipped when the maid moved the chair to clean the room, or fallen off after she'd finished and left if she'd destabilized them somehow. And I could have rearranged the things in the drawer myself without realizing it, especially in my present distracted state.

But there was something else, something not quite right, that I'd noticed subconsciously and for the life of me I didn't know what it was. Perhaps it would come to me if I stopped trying so hard to pinpoint it. For the moment it was nothing but a darting discomfort in the pit of my stomach, a foreboding on the edges of my consciousness. Given all that had happened, that was hardly surprising. But for all that, I couldn't escape the feeling that whatever it was I was missing it was important and might just provide the key to this whole terrible business.

I spent a wretched afternoon alone in my room – I'd spotted Tristan passing through the hotel lobby and decided to escape before he could track me down. I didn't want to have to talk to anyone about Annabel at the moment, least of all Tristan, though I did ring Ben and ask him to break the news as gently as he could to Jenny. Then I moped about, making myself cups of tea and coffee from the sachets on the courtesy tray and alternating between staring miserably out of the window at the rain that had begun to fall steadily from a dull leaden sky as if it were weeping for Annabel, and lying on the bed crying tears of my own.

It seemed a supreme irony that Annabel, who I would have said was the strongest of the four of us, and the canniest of us, should have fallen victim to a murderer, and even more ironic that she should have met her death at Hurleigh Pond where we had all spent so many happy hours.

I closed my eyes, remembering how Annabel had gone skinny dipping there one warm summer evening.

We never took swimsuits with us to the Pond. We knew we were not allowed to bathe there. Strong swimmers though we were, there was always the danger of becoming entangled in weed, or hurting ourselves on some piece of scrap that had been dumped illegally and was hiding beneath the still, brackish water, or even, as my mother suggested rather implausibly, 'Catching some nasty disease.' And in any case, swimming for fun didn't figure very highly on our leisure agenda. We spent far too many hours in the pool training for the water to hold any great attraction for us.

That evening, though, Annabel decided we should go in. How it all started, I can't remember, but I think we had got hold of some cans of lager and we were all mildly intoxicated. A joke suggestion became a challenge and then a dare which somehow ended with Annabel stripping off to her bra and pants and posing on the bank. I was shocked, I recall, that she should let the boys see her underwear, which was lemon coloured and lacy, and even more shocked when I realized that her nipples and the dark cushion of her pubes were clearly visible through the thin fabric. But Annabel was quite unabashed, and seemingly unaware of the spectacle she made.

'Come on you lot, don't be party poopers!' She was cavorting, dipping her toes into the water and taking them out again, beckoning to the rest of us.

Laura was the next to get undressed. I guess she just couldn't bear that it was Annabel in the limelight and not her. But she did it a good deal more teasingly and coyly, with a wiggle of her hips and a seductive cupping of her breasts so that all you could see were chocolate brown straps crossing smooth honey coloured shoulders.

I had no intention of taking off my clothes; I'd have died first. And Jenny, always the sensible one, began to get annoyed and lecture them.

'Don't be so silly, you two. You can't go in the lake. It might be dangerous.'

'Oh, pooh, who cares about that?' And Annabel dived in, aiming for the deeper water beyond the narrow shelf that edged the bank. 'Come on, you are all scaredy-cats!' she yelled, surfacing and treading water.

That was enough for the boys. They weren't going to be outdone by a girl. They scrambled out of their shorts and tee-shirts and went in after her.

None of them stayed in very long. The water must have been very cold and probably none too clean, and after a few minutes' horseplay, with a lot of screaming and shouting and splashing, they all scrambled out again, teeth chattering. They had no towels, of course, they had to dry themselves with their clothes and I wondered what on earth Annabel's mother would say when she got home with wet hair. But then again, maybe she was so used to seeing Annabel with wet hair that she wouldn't even notice.

Now, lying on the bed in my hotel room, I closed my eyes and conjured up the image of Annabel as she had been that day. Dusk had been falling and the light filtering through the trees had a rosy tint to it, lending a light flush to Annabel's taut, glowing skin and glancing off the long, firm muscles in her back and legs. Her hair was dripping water across her shoulders; it glistened in that pearly pink light. And she was laughing with delight at her own daring, the imp of mischief sparkling in her eyes.

'You didn't think I'd do that, did you, chaps?' she had said afterwards.

'And you'd better not do it again,' Jenny had answered. 'It was really stupid, Annabel. Anything could have happened.'

'But it didn't, did it?' She'd stood there, hands on hips, brave, invincible, full of life. 'I'm still in one piece, and so are the boys. We all lived to tell the tale.'

The tears filled my eyes again now as I remembered. Nothing had happened that day. As Annabel had said, we'd lived to tell the tale – and tell it we did. The account of our exploit at the lake went around our year like wild fire and soon became legend, exaggerated way beyond what had actually happened. According to rumour we had all gone into the water stark naked and then, dripping wet, indulged in some sort of orgy under the trees – details of that varied depending on who was spreading the story. Now once again Annabel's name would be linked with Hurleigh Pond, and talked about this time by people who didn't even know her. 'The woman who was murdered.' Drugged with veterinary medication and gassed in her car. The pain of it weighed so heavily on my heart that I thought I could not bear it. Oh, Annabel. Oh, Laura. Why? Why?

It was around six o'clock and I was slumped in front of the TV, waiting to see if there

258

was any mention of Annabel's death on the local news when there was a tap on the door, and when I opened it I found Mark standing there, back from his day spent with Lucy. So I was going to have to talk about Annabel after all. And as far as I was aware, he didn't even know she'd failed to turn up for her family court hearing this morning. I stood aside for him to come in and quickly turned off the television. I didn't want him to hear the terrible news from some impersonal presenter.

His first words took me by surprise.

'Is Peter back?'

I shook my head, puzzled.

'No, why?'

'Oh, nothing. I just thought I saw him in town ... Lucy and I have been to see an undertaker to start sorting out the funeral arrangements.' His voice tone was the flat, mechanical one that seemed to have become the norm since Laura died. 'We've settled on Wednesday of next week, which should give her parents time to get home. It will have to be a burial rather than a cremation, but I think that's what Laura would have wanted anyway. She liked the idea of being at one with nature. The funeral director was very good, very helpful. I had the idea they were all sepulchral men in black ties and half-mast striped trousers, but this was a woman, and a very caring one. I think Laura would have liked that.'

'I think she would. Mark...'

'We need to decide on music for the service,' Mark went on, unaware that I was miserably trying to broach the subject of Annabel. 'Lucy thought maybe we could have something by Wham. For either going in or coming out. George Michael was Laura's hero when they were growing up. And I suggested maybe the old school hymn.'

'Mark,' I said again. 'Why don't you sit down? There's something I have to tell you.'

In the briefest of pauses the strangest expression flickered in Mark's eyes and across his face. At the time I was in no mood to try and identify it. Later, thinking about it, I realized it was fear. Then he said flatly: 'The police have been to see you again.'

'No ... yes.' I hesitated, some instinct warning me not to tell Mark that Aaron was a policeman. 'It's about Annabel. Terrible news,' I said instead. 'And I really do think that you should sit down.'

I told him. He listened without a word and when I'd finished, buried his head in his hands.

'I think she knew something,' I said. In the long, lonely hours I'd gone back to my original reasoning; it was easier to handle than Aaron's suggestion that we four, Martin's Mermaids, were being targeted for some inexplicable reason. 'She as good as said so to me before she left.'

He raised his face, grey and ravaged. 'What could she have known?'

'I don't know. She never told me. But if she went to see somebody, tackled them about whatever it was, then they might have panicked. Realized she was a danger to them.' I broke off. Administering a dose of some kind of horse dope to Annabel didn't sound like something someone would do in a panic. Not at all the sort of thing you carried round with you or kept in your kitchen cabinet along with the tea bags and instant coffee. I was talking myself out of my own theory here. Resolutely I pushed the thought aside.

'Whatever. At least you're in the clear on this one,' I said. 'You have as good an alibi for Annabel's death as Darren did for Laura's. You were in police custody.'

'What time did she die then?' Mark asked. It seemed an odd question to me.

'I don't know. Aaron ... the police,' I quickly corrected myself, but Mark didn't appear to have noticed my slip of the tongue. He was too preoccupied, I guessed, to be paying any great attention to detail. 'They said she checked out at The Farm at about four.' I frowned. 'I wonder what she was doing until then? I got the distinct impression she was anxious to get back to London as soon as possible.'

'That's it then,' Mark said flatly.

'What do you mean?'

'The police released me soon after three.'

I stared at him, uncomprehending. 'But ... when Lucy arrived she couldn't get hold of you. That's why she rang Becky. Where were you, Mark?'

His shoulders hunched; he buried his head in his hands again.

'That's just it, I scarcely know myself. When the police released me I just walked and walked around the town. The solicitor Annabel fixed me up with offered to drive me back here, but I said I'd make my own way. I just wanted to be on my own for a bit. Try to clear my head.' He looked up. The faintest ironic smile curved his lips, but his eyes were bleak.

'So you see, actually I have no alibi at all. None. If I'd wanted to murder Annabel, I was perfectly free to do so.'

Fourteen

My heart sank like a stone. I started thinking furiously, unable to accept that this whole nightmare had started all over again and Mark was back in the frame.

'There will be CCTV footage. If you were walking round town, you must have been caught on camera.'

'I wouldn't bank on it. A lot of these cameras have no film in them half the time, and they're forever being vandalized. Anyway, I told you, I can't remember where I went. I can't see the police examining every CCTV camera in Mowbury on the off-chance of proving my story. Especially since they very likely think I'm guilty. They think I killed Laura; it follows they'll think I killed Annabel too.'

'But if they think that, why did they let you go?' I argued. 'Annabel said they were within their rights to hold you for thirty-six hours.'

Mark shrugged fatalistically. 'Tactics on their part, maybe. And a good solicitor on mine.'

'What tactics?'

'To give me enough rope to hang myself, maybe.'

'Oh, for goodness sake!' My frayed nerves were making me snap and a horrible insidious thought had popped into my head. Annabel could very well have known that Mark had been released. The solicitor who'd taken over from her had quite possibly rung to tell her. Had she been anticipating it? Was that the reason she had delayed her return to London? Because there was something she wanted to check out with Mark before she left? I tried to forget that such a thing had occurred to me. 'They'd hardly have let you go wandering off if they'd thought you were likely to murder someone else,' I said shortly.

'Someone else,' Mark repeated, his voice heavy with irony. 'You think I killed Laura then, do you?'

'Oh, no, of course I don't!' I was regretting my choice of words; wishing wholeheartedly that edge of doubt regarding Mark's innocence had ever crept into my mind at all.

'Because if *you* thought I was guilty too, Hannah, I don't think I could take it.' The despair was raw in his voice; there were tears gathering in his eyes.

'I don't.' I dropped to my haunches beside him, taking his hands, equally anxious now to convince him I was telling the truth as I was to convince myself. 'Of course I think no such thing. You're just not capable of such a thing.'

His mouth twisted into a bitter line. 'Aren't you forgetting my fabled temper?'

'Annabel wasn't killed by someone in a temper. It was planned, premeditated. And you'd certainly never have harmed Laura.'

'I'm glad you've got faith in me. There were times, mind you, when I had to keep myself in check. The things she said, and did. She could be pretty provocative, you know.'

'But you wouldn't hurt her. You couldn't. It's not in your nature.'

'Thank God for you, Hannah.' He turned his hands over, gripping mine and looking at me with an intensity that made a nerve dart deep inside me. 'Sometimes,' he said, 'I think I ended up with the wrong girl.'

He leaned towards me, resting his forehead against mine, and I felt my throat close. I'd wanted to comfort him, wanted to be there for him. But this was way too intimate. As his mouth sought mine I jerked away, rocked backwards and overbalanced into an unseemly heap. Mark's face was stricken now, embarrassment mingling with all the other emotions.

'I'm sorry, Hannah, I didn't mean...' He held his hand out to help me up but I was already scrambling to my feet all by myself. I didn't want any more physical contact with him.

'Don't be silly, you don't have to apologize.' I was trying to restore some normality to this very awkward situation.

'I shouldn't have. But you and I – we go way back, don't we?'

Way back. You could say that. Three blissful weeks more than twenty years ago. A lifetime had gone by since then and it was not a country I wanted to revisit, even if Laura had not been so newly dead. I knew it from the way every inch of my body had recoiled from his touch. Somewhere deep within my psyche I still remembered and treasured the bitter-sweet emotions of my teenage self, the heady romantic aura of first love. But I'd moved on. I was a different person now and so was Mark. Battle-scarred. Wary. There was no way of recapturing the innocence and the magic. I didn't want there to be. The old closeness had engendered affection and loyalty. But that was all.

'Forget it, Mark. Let's change the subject.'

But what the hell to? Annabel's death? Laura's funeral? There was no small talk to make. We were caught in this quagmire of unreal nightmare that was nonetheless all too real.

'I think I'm going to go home tomorrow,' Mark said. 'I've got to face it sometime. It might as well be now.'

I wondered briefly if the new awkwardness between us had any bearing on his decision, then decided I was flattering myself. He'd probably thought this through whilst talking to Lucy. But it opened the door for me. I desperately needed a breathing space too. The constant pressure was wearing me down and Aaron's warnings weighed heavily on me. I was longing for my own home and some semblance of normality, and if Mark was booking out of The Beeches it presented me with a get-out too.

'I was thinking the same thing,' I said. 'I'd really like to go home for a few days at any rate, just to recharge my batteries. Lucy is here now to help you with all the arrangements and you know if you need anything you only have to give me a call.'

'Right,' Mark said tonelessly. 'Thanks.'

'And Stan said he'd be at the end of the line if you need him.' I made a mental note to phone Stan to tell him about Annabel. 'I know he's not quite as free an agent as I am, but he's there for you too. At the very least he's a willing ear if you need to talk.'

And one of your oldest friends. And a man. No risk of emotional involvement of the wrong kind. The blind alley I'd unwittingly stumbled into with the best of intentions, well-meaning but somewhat naïve, leaving my actions open to misinterpretation.

'Ian will be back in a few days, anyway,' Mark said, gathering himself together. 'It was just a snatched break. No, if you want to

267

go home, Hannah, don't stay on my account. You've already done far more than anyone could expect. For which I shall always be grateful.'

A stab of guilt. I almost changed my mind. But the urgency to escape was paramount.

'If you're sure...'

'Of course I'm sure.' Mark got up. 'I'll leave you in peace. I need to speak to Reception anyway, tell them I'm checking out. And you'll want to do your packing. I'll see you later.'

'Yes. I'm sorry, Mark.' I wasn't sure exactly what I was apologizing for. Leaving him in the lurch when he was obviously still so needy? Giving him the wrong impression about my concern for him? Being a part of this whole dreadful mess?

'Don't think twice about it, Hannah.'

I would, I knew. It wasn't in my nature to be able to simply walk away from a challenge. But I also knew that for my own sanity I had to.

'OK,' I said. 'I'll try.'

When Mark had gone I rang Stan and broke the news about Annabel. As was only to be expected, he was totally and utterly shocked.

'God, Hannah, whatever next! Look, I'll see what I can do. I'll try and get back for a couple of days, just to give Mark a bit of moral support, if nothing else. I'm just not sure if I can make it until the weekend, though. Zoe's got her hands full with Alice, and my work has been piling up.'

'Give Mark a ring, why don't you?' I suggested. 'I'm sure he'd appreciate the chance to talk.'

'Yes, I'll do that. God, I just don't believe this – first Laura, now Annabel. What the hell is going on?'

'I wish I knew.'

'Well, you take care, Hannah.'

'I will.'

His words made me think of Aaron again and when I'd finished talking to Stan I got out his card and dialled the number of his mobile, hoping that this wasn't an inconvenient moment and I would be interrupting something important. But I very much wanted to speak to him so I overcame my misgivings and took the risk.

Aaron answered straight away.

'It's me,' I said. 'Hannah.'

'Hannah. Are you OK?' I could hear the concern in his voice and it warmed me through.

'Not really, but there you go. I just wanted to let you know I've decided to take your advice and go home.'

'I'm glad to hear you've seen sense! When are you leaving? Today?'

'Tomorrow. Straight after breakfast, I should think. Then I'll be home in good time to get to the supermarket for essential supplies and generally sort myself out.'

'So, how about letting me take you out for a meal tonight?'

'Aren't you back in Bristol?'

'No, still in Mowbury.'

I thought about it, but not for very long. I wanted to get out of The Beeches. I'd prefer not to be alone in Mark's company and I sure as hell didn't want to get lumbered with Tristan. That was a point – *he* was still here. He'd probably be only too happy to give Mark some moral support. And I wanted to see Aaron. Simple as that.

'OK.'

'Good. I'll pick you up. About half past seven?'

'I'll be looking out for you.'

I put the phone down and realized that in spite of all the terrible things that had happened, a small, hidden part of me was actually happy.

I spoke to Reception, and told them I was checking out tomorrow.

'You were booked in until Friday,' the receptionist said, censorious and a little intimidating.

'I know. And if you want to charge me for the whole week I shall quite understand. But I would be grateful if you'd sort out my bill so that I can leave first thing in the morning.'

I wasn't the least concerned about having to pay for time I wouldn't be spending at The Beeches. In fact, at that moment, I think I'd have paid extra just to get away!

I decided on a natural coloured linen shirt dress and sandals to wear this evening. It would go anywhere, I thought, posh or relaxed. Then I packed the rest of my clothes into my holdall with a feeling of immense relief, but also sadness. I'd been so looking forward to this week, and instead it had turned into a nightmare with two of my oldest friends dead.

I packed my toiletries next, leaving out just the things I'd need tonight and tomorrow morning, and moved to the dressing table drawer. Jewellery. Again, I'd just keep out what I was going to wear tonight and pack the rest. I opened my little jewellery box, considering. The silver choker wouldn't be right with the linen dress, much too formal. The shell on a leather thong would be much better. I fished it out and managed to spill several earrings that were tangled in it.

It was as I was replacing them that the thought occurred to me. I froze for a second, as if I'd been struck by a bolt of lightening, then tipped everything out on to the polished wood surface of the dressing table, separating it out, checking and double-checking with fingers gone clumsy with urgency and sudden chill fear.

I knew what it was that I'd realized subconsciously earlier and not been able to identify, the feeling that I was missing something that was proof that someone had been through my things. There was something that should have been in my jewellery box and wasn't.

My swimming medal. The one we'd won in the team event, the very same one that had been captured for posterity in the photographs Laura had had on display in her drawing room. I'd brought that medal with me, I was sure I had, not because I had intended to wear it, but just as a memento, a link with old times.

And now it was missing.

Never in the whole of my life have I been so pleased to see anyone as I was to see Aaron. The discovery of my missing medal had shaken me badly, even though I was questioning whether in fact my jangling nerves were playing tricks on me and I'd dreamed up the whole thing. I'd intended to bring the medal with me, but perhaps in the end I'd never put it in my jewellery box at all, and when I got home I'd find it on my dressing table, large as life. But however hard I tried to convince myself that the answer was that simple and not in the least threatening, I remained unconvinced. If it had been only the medal that was missing, then I might have believed it, but the key had gone too. I still couldn't see how I could have lost it and the two things put together seemed to back up that instinct that had told me someone had been in my room, going through my things.

But who? And why? It made no sense at all. And I couldn't see how anyone could have got in anyway. My room had been locked, the windows closed, and they were all in full view of the car park in any case. The little bathroom didn't even have a window; it was served by a ventilation system that started up when the light was switched on. As for Hotel Reception, they certainly wouldn't hand out room keys willy-nilly. The only person who could possibly have had access to my room was the maid, and she was a cheerful Eastern European girl who spoke barely a word of English. She had no reason at all to take Mark's house key and I couldn't see that she would have stolen the medal either. It had no value whatsoever beyond the sentimental and I couldn't imagine her risking her job for what was basically nothing more than a disc made of tin on a length of ribbon.

I told myself I was going crazy, but it didn't help much. The sick certainty that I was right refused to go away and the feeling that I was trapped in a nightmare was so strong I felt I was suffocating.

The phone beside the bed rang once, and I rushed out of the shower to answer it, dripping water all over the carpet. But it was only Mark, calling on the internal line to tell me he had been invited to Jenny's for supper.

I was surprised by that; I'd have thought Jenny had more than enough on her plate without entertaining visitors. But I supposed looking after new babies was second nature to her now, and with Ben at home to help her out, she had felt she wanted to do her bit in supporting Mark. The old network had survived pretty well and seemed only to have been strengthened by recent events. It was almost as if the rest of us had drawn tighter together to fill the gaps left by Laura and Annabel.

'Jenny suggested you should come too,' Mark said.

'Oh, that's kind of her, but no, I won't.'

'Are you sure? I don't like to think of you eating on your own on your last night,' Mark said, and though I hadn't wanted to mention it, I was left with very little option but to tell him that I was, in fact, meeting Aaron.

'Aaron!' He sounded surprised and a little hurt. 'Oh, well, enjoy your evening.'

'I will. I'll see you in the morning, I expect, before we both leave.'

I finished my shower and then thought I really should ring Jenny to thank her for the invitation and to tell her I was going home tomorrow. She seemed faintly distracted – I could hear the baby crying in the background – and I thought I'd keep it fairly short and sweet.

'Sorry I can't make dinner this evening. It was really nice of you to ask us both, though.'

'Actually I didn't,' Jenny said. 'Mark rang and invited himself. I wasn't really best pleased, but in his situation ... well, what else could I do except say: "Sure, come on over"? But to be honest, I'm not looking forward to it. I won't know what on earth to say to him and Ben scarcely knows him at all, which is why I suggested you come too. Are you sure you can't make it?'

'Sorry. Actually...' I laughed, a little self deprecatingly. 'I've got a date.'

'A date! Who with?' We might have been fifteen years old again.

'Aaron. Well, not really a date. But he's taking me out to dinner.'

'Sounds exactly like a date to me!' The baby's wailing was becoming more insistent. 'Hannah, I am going to have to go. This little one needs feeding.'

'Just very quickly, Jenny, I've decided to go home tomorrow.'

'I can't say I blame you. I'm surprised you've stayed this long. Look – call round and see me before you leave, why don't you? Don't just disappear again without saying goodbye.' Her voice cracked suddenly and there was a lump in my throat too. We were both thinking, I knew, of Laura and Annabel, taken so suddenly, so shockingly, with no warning whatsoever. 'Take care, Hannah,' she finished. 'And see you tomorrow, yes? Then you can tell me all about how you got on.'

'Got on?' My mind had wandered.

'With Aaron. On your date.'

'Oh, yes, will do. Bye, Jenny.'

And then there was nothing left for me to do but get myself ready and kill a couple of hours until seven thirty.

Aaron arrived on the dot, well, a few minutes early actually, and sat in his car waiting. I knew because I had been watching for him from the window and for some reason it amused me that Aaron should be such a stickler for punctuality. As with so many other things, it wasn't a quality I'd have associated with him and I'd have been quite wrong. He really was a man of mystery, totally unpredictable.

And very dishy, I thought, as I watched him get out of his car and lock it. Tall, dark and handsome: a cliché that could have been invented to describe him. And there was an air of panache about him that was very appealing too. Along with that ever-present edge of something that fell midway between mystery and danger.

I moved away from the window, checking my hair in the mirror and adding a quick coat of lip gloss. I didn't want Aaron to know

I'd been watching out for him.

A few minutes later he was ringing my bell. I hadn't even realized the room had one, but Aaron had found it. It buzzed loudly. I waited a moment, then went to answer it.

'Hi. All ready then?'

'Just about.'

'Shall we go?'

For a blissful moment I thought I'd returned to the normality I craved.

'I hope you like Italian food,' Aaron said as we drove out of The Beeches.

'Love it.'

'Good. I've booked a table at a bistro in town. I've heard very good reports of it, though I must admit I've never been there myself.'

'I'm sure it will be fine. At the moment just the thought of another bar snack makes me feel quite ill. It's a bit like airline food on long haul. The first one is quite nice, the second is OK, by the time you get to your destination you never want to see another plastic knife and fork and foil tray as long as you live.'

'Have you done much long haul flying then?'

This *was* normality. A conversation about something other than the awful events of the last few days.

'I used to.' David had been fond of travel;

in our years together we'd done the Far East, Mexico, a safari. Since we'd split up I hadn't had the spare cash or, to be honest, the inclination to go so far afield. The last couple of years I'd stuck to Europe – a skiing holiday in the French Alps, a couple of weeks soaking up the sun in Spain. 'Have you?' I asked.

'Not so as you'd notice. I fancy New Zealand. Or taking a Harley down the west coast of America.'

I smiled. Yes, I could imagine Aaron on a Harley. Or driving a motor home round New Zealand or Australia. David had favoured five-star hotels or luxury resorts. I didn't imagine they would be Aaron's style at all.

'Have you ever been married?' I asked.

'Not me. I'm wedded to the job.' He cast me a sideways glance. 'Or maybe I've just never yet met the right girl.'

My cheeks went hot. How the hell could Aaron do this to me, make me feel and react as if I was a teenager again?

We were in town now and Aaron was looking for a place to park. It provided a welcome diversion. As we drove along the narrow one-way street, I suddenly did a double take. Turning into one of the little lanes that forked off it was a man who, from behind at least, looked exactly like Peter. Same hair, same conservative style of dress, same build, same walk.

'Was that *Peter*?' I asked incredulously.

'Didn't see.' Aaron had eyes only for a possible parking space.

'Well, it certainly looked like him. And Mark thought he saw him the other day too. But it can't be him, surely. Why would he be back in Mowbury? And if he was, he'd have been in touch, wouldn't he? He must have a double.'

Aaron had spotted a space by the kerb and wasn't really listening.

'Hang on, I could get in there if only I didn't have white van man up my backside...'

By the time he'd completed the parking manoeuvre and we were walking back along the street to the bistro I'd forgotten about the man who looked like Peter. Instead I was swamped by memories. The Bistro itself, for starters.

'I remember when this was an ironmonger's shop!' I said. 'They had watering cans and saucepans hanging on hooks and stands of drawers where they kept nails and screws and washers. A bit like that Ronnie Barker sketch, do you remember?'

'The four candles – fork handles one, you mean.'

'Yes.' I was foolishly delighted that he knew it too, though I could scarcely imagine there was anyone in the country who didn't.

The place had certainly changed since its incarnation as an ironmonger's. The poky dark shop I remembered had been converted into a bar area and beyond it a softly lit dining room had been installed in what I imagined had once been the overflowing stock room into which the ironmonger in his grey overall had disappeared for items not on display. The tables were covered in bright chequered cloths, each sporting a candle in a wine bottle, and there was a delicious garlicky aroma wafting from a kitchen area where chefs were busy cooking in full view of the diners.

'What wine do you like?' Aaron asked.

'Any. I honestly don't mind.'

'OK.' Aaron studied the wine list while I perused the menu. Spoiled for choice! Eventually I settled for penne with tuna fish and olives and Aaron went for a hearty spaghetti Bolognese. Whilst we waited for it we sipped wine and nibbled on bread sticks and not a single word was spoken about Laura or Annabel. Instead, we talked about our lives since schooldays and explored our likes and dislikes as if we were any other couple on a first date, though to be honest, I think Aaron found out a great deal more about me than I did about him. Given his job, I suppose he was adept at asking the questions to draw someone out, at listening rather than talking. But his reticence was somehow part of his attraction. He was, I thought, a little like one of those little wooden Russian dolls, one nesting inside the other, and the challenge of unpicking him layer by layer was as fascinating as it was frustrating. I looked at him across the table, his face all planes and shadows in the candlelight, and that little scar where he'd been hit by the stone in the snowball standing out white and jagged, at the deep creases that had formed between nose and mouth and only added character, and the strong angular jaw and deep mysterious eyes, and thought that given the chance I would very much enjoy getting to know Aaron as he really was.

We couldn't escape the subject of the awful events of the past few days for ever, though. We were both too caught up in what had happened, each in our own way, and we both knew it was far from over yet.

'I'm glad you've decided to go home,' Aaron said.

We had finished our main courses and indulged in the most mouth-wateringly delicious zabaglione, and now we were drinking café lattes which had come accompanied by little amaretto biscuits. 'What changed your mind?'

'Basically I've simply reached the end of my tether,' I said. 'Lucy is here now with Mark, and he's decided to move back home.' I wasn't going to tell him, of course, that Mark had misinterpreted my reasons for supporting him; that was an embarrassing situation best forgotten. 'And actually, I am getting a bit spooked,' I added.

Aaron's eyes narrowed; he sat back in his chair regarding me steadily. 'Why?'

I told him, about the missing key and the medal I'd been sure I'd brought with me, but which was no longer in my jewellery case.

'It's probably just my imagination running away with me,' I finished. 'I can't think why anyone would want a worthless bit of tin on a string and I can't see how they can have got into my room in any case. But as I say, it's spooked me. And if I'm beginning to be paranoid enough to dream up something like that, I think it's time I went home.'

'And not before time.' Aaron was silent for a moment. 'Hannah, I'm not happy about this at all. I'm not actually happy about you even staying overnight at The Beeches.'

The seriousness with which he was taking this chilled me.

'What are you saying?'

'We've been looking at this whole thing from the point of view of motive. The motivation of a sane person. Now I'm beginning to wonder. First you say the photograph of the four of you was missing from Laura's house. That rang alarm bells with me. Someone killing her for a specific reason wouldn't stop to take a trophy; wouldn't want one. If the killer was someone connected to the drugs case, for instance, that photograph would mean nothing to them. Now you tell me your medal has gone missing.'

'I *think* it's missing.'

'Yes. Well, if it is, then there's a pattern emerging here. And we're no longer looking for a sane individual who murdered for a specific reason, or simply lost control and panicked, we are talking about someone who is deranged. Someone with an obsession. And the link is the four of you. Laura and Annabel and Jenny and you.'

I shook my head in bewilderment; my thoughts were racing, my nerves taut as bow strings. The nightmare had begun all over again.

'But who?'

Aaron raised a speculative eyebrow. 'Frankly, it could be anyone.'

'Tristan,' I said. 'There is something very odd about Tristan. He gives me the creeps. He pops up from nowhere. He's stayed on when we thought he was leaving. And he admitted to me that he envied our little gang.'

'It need not necessarily be someone you think of as odd,' Aaron warned. 'People who suffer this kind of mental sickness – and that's what it is, a sickness – can be very good at hiding it. To all intents and purposes they can appear perfectly normal. And I mean truly normal, not strange or threatening in any way.'

I closed my eyes, digesting what he had said, frightened and confused. But I could see where he was coming from. Paedophiles and rapists didn't always walk around in dirty macs, they were often ordinary, outwardly respectable, some with families. Wife and child beaters weren't always ugly brutes, but the man next door. Burglars didn't wear stripey jumpers and carry a sack marked 'swag'. And murderers weren't obviously armed with guns and knives and garrottes. You could pass any of them in the street and never give them a second glance. You could talk to them, drink with them, share a meal, and never know.

'You mean it really could be anyone at all,' I said.

'That's exactly what I mean, Hannah. It could, as you say, be Tristan. He could have a history of feeling rejected, going back to early childhood. Then at school he felt left out, slighted. Maybe he lusted after you four girls and you all turned your backs on him, or sniggered at him behind your hands, whispered together that if he was the last boy on earth you'd never go out with him. That sort of thing could well light a slow burning fuse in a certain type of personality. But Tristan is not the only possibility. It could be there's someone who was obsessed by you and you never realized it. And they still are.

Seeing you all together again has triggered an old ardour or a desire to take revenge. Who knows what goes on in a twisted mind? I don't. But it's why I am seriously concerned for your safety.'

'But ... I'll be OK at The Beeches,' I said, as much to reassure myself as to convince Aaron.

'I suppose so.' He didn't sound confident enough for my liking. 'To be honest, I'd rather you were well out of the way. If someone did get into your room...'

'I can double-lock the door.'

'Make sure that you do.' He was silent for a moment. 'I could stay with you.'

'Oh, there's no need for that. I'll be fine, really.'

But I was thinking of Laura, dead in her swimming pool, and Annabel, doped with some sort of veterinary drug and poisoned with carbon monoxide. I was not a happy bunny.

'I don't mean to frighten you, Hannah.' Aaron finished his coffee. 'I'm only trying to make you see that you really must not trust anyone.'

I smiled slightly. 'Even you.'

Yesterday I wouldn't have said that. Yesterday I'd even wondered if Aaron might not be what he seemed. I didn't think that any more; I wouldn't be sitting here with him now if I did. But for all that I couldn't escape the thought that if it was Aaron who was emotionally and mentally sick and hiding it as he'd explained that such a person could be very clever at doing, I was taking a huge risk.

Aaron was not offended by my weak attempt at humour but he didn't seem to find it remotely funny either.

'Even me. You were wise to refuse my offer to stay with you, Hannah. Your room is not even in the main hotel. It's pretty isolated, particularly if they're not busy and not needing to put guests in the stable block. No one would ever know what went on behind closed doors.'

'You'll have me calling a taxi next rather than getting in the car with you,' I said, and heard the little tremble in my own voice.

'I hope not.' He grinned. 'I promise you, Hannah, I'm perfectly harmless. Well, that's not entirely true actually. I have all kinds of designs on you, but murder isn't one of them.'

Something in the way he was looking at me struck a chord deep inside me. Perhaps fear had heightened my awareness, galvanized emotional reactions that were never far from the surface where Aaron was concerned.

'I think,' I said, 'that it's time we were going.' But there was a mischief in my tone that I could hardly believe, given the circumstances, and a lightness in my heart which was totally at odds with all the other emotions that were churning inside me.

'You're the boss, ma'am,' Aaron said, and grinned wickedly.

In spite of those treacherous prickles of excitement and the glow in my veins that told tales about the way Aaron made me feel, I had not the slightest intention of doing anything about it. We were in the middle of a nightmare, for goodness sake. This was not the time for a romantic interlude, let alone an emotional entanglement. But that was before we drew up outside my room. Before he kissed me.

The moment I felt his fingers firm on my jaw, turning my head towards his, I was lost. Perhaps after all I needed this. Needed something to make me forget the black chamber of horrors I was drowning in. I needed to trust someone, even though he had warned me I should not. I found myself looking directly into his eyes, felt his hand slide around to the nape of my neck, and felt no fear, nothing but a stillness in which I could hear the beat of my own heart, and an ache of longing. They were hypnotizing me, those eyes, and I wanted to be hypnotized. Then his face was out of focus and I felt first his breath on my cheek, then his mouth. He smelled faintly of wine and coffee and musk, not as potent as an aftershave or cologne, but more subtle, shaving soap perhaps. He kissed me carefully at first and then as I kissed him back, more deeply. And I thought, in some corner of my brain that was still functioning, that at least some good had come out of this whole dreadful business.

He drew away. 'Thanks for a great evening, Hannah. Take care. And let me know when you're safely home, won't you?'

And suddenly I didn't want him to go; didn't want to be alone with the grief and the fear and the endless churning turmoil of trying to make sense of all that had happened and wondering what the hell was going to happen next.

'Is that offer still open?' I asked.

'What offer?'

A nerve tightened in my throat. Perhaps he hadn't been serious. Oh, well, go for broke.

'To stay with me tonight.'

'You want me to?'

'Yes.' It came out sounding husky, uncertain. 'Yes,' I said more emphatically. 'If it's all the same to you, I really would like you to stay.'

Fifteen

I have never been one for casual encounters and one-night stands. All my sexual experiences have been in the context of a stable, loving relationship, even before I met David, and for the past two years since we split up I had lived the life of a nun. It hadn't been difficult. I was too bruised and raw from the breakdown of our marriage to want to put myself in the firing line for any more emotional upheaval. It wasn't that I'd turned against men, but I suppose at some deep level my ability to trust had been undermined, not so much my ability to trust a man as my ability to trust my own judgement. I didn't want to make another mistake. Better by far to be independent, to avoid the complications a relationship brings. I'd resisted all the efforts of well-meaning friends to set me up or pair me off and I'd run a mile at the first suggestion that anyone was showing a little too much interest in me for my liking.

But with Aaron it was different. It felt right, so right that I didn't really need to give it any thought. And it didn't feel like a one-night stand either. It felt like the beginning of something that was going to go on for a very long time.

The shadow of all that had happened hung over us, of course. There was no way of escaping it. But it also lent a sense of urgency, an edge of poignant awareness. And a realization that life can be short and is always uncertain, that we should make the most of it and take what is offered here, now. Tomorrow may be too late.

It was a welcome and wonderful hiatus, that night with Aaron. I was awake when the sky began to lighten for dawn, drowsy, replete, listening to his deep even breathing, feeling the warmth and slight stickiness of his skin next to mine and the weight of his arm across my breasts, breathing in the scent of him and wishing that this night could last forever. There was a soft luminescence about the room, pearly grey dawn slowly taking on tinges of salmon pink. *Red sky in the morning, shepherd's warning.* As it lightened, so smoothly that the change was almost imperceptible, it was as if the very atmosphere was growing heavier, the weight of it returning to crush me. I didn't want day to break. I didn't want Aaron to go. I didn't want to return to the living nightmare of the past few days. I wanted to hold on to the serenity and the rapture and the safety and the closeness and never let them go.

But stopping the passage of the earth round the sun is as impossible as holding back the tide, as King Canute learned to his cost. Like the waves first rippling around and then breaking over his throne, the dawn brightened to full clear light. A bit grey, a bit overcast, not quite fulfilling its early promise, but the morning of a new day nonetheless. And I felt sick with apprehension as to what it would bring.

Beside me Aaron stirred, his hand moving to cup my breast, his body moving closer to fit against mine, one knee lying crooked across my thigh like an anchor. I reached across to lay my hand on his shoulder. Beneath my exploring fingers it felt hard and strong, muscle bunched over bone.

'OK?' he murmured sleepily.

'OK.'

We moved together, made love again, this time with an added edge of urgency.

'I don't want to leave you,' Aaron said when it was over and we were lying entwined.

'I don't want you to.'

'But I have to.' He shifted, checking his watch. 'I've really got to get moving, Hannah.'

'I know.'

'You promise me to take care of yourself. And ring me as soon as you're safely home.'

'I will. That'll be lunchtime-ish, I should

think. I must go and see Jenny before I leave.'

'Why?' There was the faintest note of aggression in his tone.

'I can't go without saying goodbye. And besides, she should be warned. If you think there's the slightest chance that we, as a four-some, are being targeted, then Jenny could be at risk too.'

'I'd rather you didn't. Why don't you ring her? I'd much prefer to see you safely in your car and on your way.'

'I'll be fine,' I said, bristling slightly. While it was a good feeling that he wanted to care for me, look out for me, I wasn't ready to be told what to do. Two years of being single, making decisions for myself without refer-ence to anyone else's opinions or needs had rekindled my independence without me realizing it. 'The one person we can be absolutely sure is not implicated in this is Jenny. And she has the right to know what's going on, and hear it face to face.'

Aaron couldn't argue with that. He didn't, anyway.

'Don't even think of seeing Mark, though. The further you stay away from him, the better.'

'I won't.' He was warning me, I knew, because he counted Mark amongst his list of possible suspects, and I wasn't about to enlighten him as to the real reason I in-tended to put some distance between myself and Mark.

'I've really got to get on.' He pushed aside the covers, swung out of bed. I watched him stretch. Long, lean, muscular. I wished he'd kiss me again, but he didn't. His mind was elsewhere now.

'You can have the shower first,' I said, matching his new mood of purpose, and knew that this very welcome interlude was well and truly over.

When Aaron had left and I'd showered and dressed I went over to the hotel for breakfast. I was very much hoping I wouldn't bump into Tristan; added now to my innate distaste for being in his company was the edge of suspicion Aaron had aroused in me that Tristan might, just possibly, be the one behind all the terrible things that had happened. To me, it seemed, he fitted the profile of the killer – a loner, with emotions that ran far deeper than anyone might suspect under that suave exterior. Added to that, he was on the spot, staying on longer than he'd originally intended to, and he was very much a free agent. I couldn't imagine that he had an alibi for either Laura's murder or Annabel's. And I'd thought of something else, too. Tristan worked for a drugs company. It was possible they produced medications for veterinary use as well as human, and if so, Tristan might well have access to the drug that had been used on Annabel.

No, all in all, I definitely did not want to meet Tristan and I was mightily relieved that he was nowhere to be seen. As I was eating breakfast another thought occurred to me, one that I didn't like at all. Peter. I'd thought I'd seen Peter in town, Mark thought he'd seen Peter in town. I'd dismissed it as coincidence, that he had a double. But thinking about Tristan's job connection with drugs must have triggered something subliminally, because suddenly a horrible thought flashed into my mind. Peter was a vet. He, of all people, would have access to animal drugs. Oh-my-God. Could it be Peter? Surely, surely not! Peter was the most stable person I knew. But all the same, I thought I'd mention it to Aaron. I was at the point where I could suspect almost anybody.

I finished my breakfast, demolished a pot of coffee and called at Reception to settle my bill. Then I went back to my room to finish off the last of my packing.

I had just stuffed my toiletries bag into my holdall and zipped it up when the phone rang, a loud, unexpected buzz that made me jump.

'Ah, Mrs Wilde, you are still there. I wasn't sure if you'd already left.' It was the receptionist.

'I'm still here. Is there a problem with my credit card?'

'Oh, no, nothing like that. But I have a gentleman here who was hoping to see you. I told him I rather thought he'd missed you, but it seems he's in luck after all.'

I frowned. 'A gentleman?'

'Yes. Just a moment and I'll ask his name.'

I waited, puzzled and instinctively a little alarmed. It couldn't be the police – the receptionist would surely have known if it had been. It couldn't be Mark or Stan, if he'd come back – both of them knew which room I was in and would have come straight here to find me.

'Hello, Mrs Wilde? The gentleman who'd like a word with you ... His name is Mr Golding. Martin Golding.'

Martin Golding! What the hell did he want to see me for? Had he just heard about Annabel? Did he want to be kept informed about arrangements for Laura's funeral? Or was it connected in some way to the allegations they'd made against him? The possibilities raced through my head, a string of imponderables that could only be answered by speaking to him.

I had no intention of seeing him alone, here in my room, though. I was far too jumpy and mindful of Aaron's warnings that the killer could be just about anyone for that. How could I be sure that Martin Golding had not harboured a dangerous obsession for the four of us that went right back to the days when we had been his relay team? But even leaving that new theory aside, Martin had one of the strongest motives for wanting both Laura and Annabel dead. He would also know that as one of their closest friends, I was very likely to have known about the allegations, and possibly guess at who would want Laura and Annabel out of the way.

'Tell him I'll meet him in Reception,' I said.

I shrugged a linen jacket on over my tee shirt and trousers, locked up securely and walked over to the hotel.

Martin Golding was waiting for me just inside the door. He looked anxious and much older, as if worry, or sleepless nights, or both had etched deep lines and pouches into the contours of his face, and there were dark circles under his eyes.

'Hannah,' he greeted me. 'Thanks for seeing me.'

'You very nearly missed me,' I said. 'I was just leaving.'

'I came over yesterday, actually,' he said. 'But you were out.'

Alarm bells rang in my head. He'd been here yesterday, when I suspected someone had been rifling through my things. Was it possible the receptionist or someone else had given him my room number? That he'd rung the bell at the precise time when the maid

296

had been making the bed and she'd let him in? And when she'd finished and gone he'd stayed there, poking about? He'd remember the medal all right; it would mean something to him. If he was the killer, obsessed with the past, it would be a fitting trophy. But that didn't apply to Mark's key; he wouldn't have had a clue what door it fitted and would have no earthly reason for taking it.

But perhaps there was no connection between the two items that were missing. Perhaps I'd simply lost the key as I'd thought in the first place. Oh, this was driving me insane! I just didn't know what to think any more.

'You've heard about Annabel?' I said.

Martin Golding ran a hand through his hair, leaving a bit of it sticking up at an odd angle. 'Yes, it's terrible. I just keep seeing the four of you girls as you were when you were my swimming team, and now two of you are dead.'

I swallowed hard at the knot of tears that was there suddenly in my throat.

'What can I do for you?'

He looked around, awkward, visibly nervous. 'Is there anywhere a bit more private?'

Not my room, Mr Golding. Definitely not my room.

'We could go into the conservatory,' I suggested.

The conservatory was empty but for a

middle-aged couple reading newspapers and drinking coffee. We sat down as far away from them as possible.

'OK, go ahead.'

'It's awkward.' Martin Golding was fiddling with his wedding ring, twisting it round and round on his finger. 'Embarrassing, really.'

'Let me help you,' I said. 'You had an affair with Laura.'

He pulled a face. 'I wouldn't call it an affair.'

'What, then?'

'I took her out a couple of times when you were in your final year at school. But it was all pretty innocent. I was too shit scared to let things go too far. Though there wasn't much difference in our ages, I was very aware that she was my pupil and I was stepping way out of line.'

'That's not the way Laura told it.' I was watching him closely.

A corner of his mouth quirked up in a humourless grin. 'No, I didn't think it would be.'

'And Annabel?' I said.

'Nothing ever happened with Annabel.'

'You asked her out.'

'Yes.' He chewed on his lip, sighed, looked me straight in the eye. 'Look, I'm going to come clean with you, Hannah. I was pretty smitten with Annabel. Couldn't get her out of my head. I did behave rather foolishly and I'm very ashamed now. I used to drive the way I knew she'd be walking home, stop, and offer her a lift. At first she seemed quite pleased; it was something of a cache, I suppose, riding in a teacher's car, and it saved her walking. But then she woke up to the fact that I wasn't passing her by accident. She told me to back off, in no uncertain terms. Really put me in my place. And it was then that Laura started coming on to me.'

I frowned. 'Laura came on to you?'

'Oh, yes. She was very precocious, was Laura. To begin with, I was flattered, I suppose. But she scared the hell out of me, I can tell you. Nothing untoward ever happened between us, I swear, but it certainly would have done if I'd taken advantage of what was on offer. I only took her out a couple of times because I realized I was in dangerous waters. By necessity we had to go to out of the way places where we weren't likely to be spotted. I could have had an affair with Laura. The opportunity was there all right. But I didn't. Things never went beyond a few kisses. And that is God's honest truth.'

Strangely enough, I believed him. Or almost believed him, anyway; there was still just a nagging sliver of doubt in my mind. But his account had the ring of truth about it. Laura had been precocious; she'd been the first of us to lose her virginity, and very smug she'd been about it, too. She had always been a dreadful flirt, and enjoyed leading boys on. She loved nothing better than being the centre of attention, and being seen as something of a femme fatale. If she'd suspected Martin Golding fancied Annabel it would almost certainly have been enough to make her come on to him. She wouldn't have been able to bear it that Annabel was getting more attention than her, and especially the attention of our hero. I could well imagine how she'd reeled him in with pert glances and provocative, not-quite-accidental touches, with subtle flattery and unspoken, but very clear, promises that she may, or may not, keep. I'd seen her technique at close quarters during our growing-up years, and I'd seen it again on the night of the reunion.

And I could well imagine, too, the tender trap Martin Golding had found himself in. A young man with the testosterone running high, confronted with a pretty, tantalizing girl, who happened to also be his pupil. It all added together to make a pretty convincing picture, even down to the fact that Laura had made a play for him when she had realized it was Annabel and not her that Martin Golding had fancied. It was exactly the sort of thing Laura might easily have done.

The one thing I didn't understand was why Laura had become so upset by Annabel's admission if she'd known about it all these years. Why it should have suddenly become such a big deal that she'd threatened to go public with her own story. Unless, of course, it had been the rather inflammatory way Annabel had described his interest in her that had upset Laura. Annabel had called him a pervert, as far as I could remember. Maybe from that Laura had inferred that there had been more to it than she'd ever thought there had been; that he'd been more involved with Annabel than her. If she thought he had pursued an intimate relationship with Annabel yet rejected her own advances and unceremoniously dumped her, her fierce pride would be badly dented. So badly dented that she had wanted to hit out at him; punish him. If I was totally honest, that was in character too.

'Why are you telling me this?' I asked.

Martin was sweating. I could see the sheen of moisture on his skin around his hairline and at the open neck of his polo shirt and he shifted uncomfortably in his seat.

'I guessed you knew about it from Laura and Annabel, and I know how prone Laura was to exaggeration. I wanted to tell you my side in the hope that ... well, I'm asking you to keep it to yourself, Hannah. If it gets out, especially Laura's version, I could lose my job. I know it's a hell of a long time ago, but an investigation would totally undermine my position at the school. It makes too good a story. "Teacher seduced pupils in his care". That's the line the papers would take. Even if nothing could be proved, people would still say that there is no smoke without fire.'

'But nothing could be proved now, could it?' I said, staring hard at him. 'Laura and Annabel are both dead.'

For a moment he looked shocked, then horrified by my implicit accusation.

'For God's sake, Hannah ... you can't think that I...'

'The police might though, mightn't they? The two girls you were involved with, both murdered? Just when they were threatening to spill the beans? It's a pretty strong motive.'

'Well, I can assure you...' Martin's shock was giving way to angry indignation; his voice rose so that the couple at the far end of the conservatory lowered their newspapers, staring at us disapprovingly. 'I can assure you,' he went on in a quieter tone, but none the less emphatic, 'that however anxious I might be that they shouldn't stir up trouble for me with the authorities, I would never do them any harm. And if you think that I could ... well, I'm speechless, Hannah.'

'This whole thing is just getting to me. My friends are dead. Someone has murdered them both. I don't know who, or why. And I'm terrified that I might be next. Or Jenny. But no, I don't think you killed them, of course I don't. If I did, I'd have told the police what I know.'

He leaned forward. I could smell the fresh sweat on him now; clearly he was going out of his mind with worry – or guilt – or both.

'You didn't tell them?'

'No. And I won't. But there's someone else who knows about what happened all those years ago. And she might very well say something.'

Martin Golding's eyes narrowed. 'Who are you talking about?'

I hesitated, wondering that if Martin was the killer I might be signing Becky's death warrant by mentioning her name.

'If I tell you that, and anything happens to her...'

His lips twisted bitterly. 'So you still think I might have had something to do with it? I reiterate – I did not. But I have to talk to anyone who knows about me and Laura, tell them the truth about what happened and try to persuade them to keep it to themselves. My career depends on it. Everything I've worked for. I've got a wife, three children, a mortgage. It's vital to me that nothing of what happened twenty years ago gets out.'

I did believe him. He was a desperate man, haunted by the indiscretions of his youth, but no way was he a murderer.

A memory came to me. Once, in a gala, Jenny, swimming breaststroke, had started taking in water. Once you start swallowing water when you're swimming breaststroke, you've had it unless you stop and get your breath. But Jenny, desperate not to let the team down, had carried right on. From my position at the end of the pool, waiting to swim the freestyle leg, I'd seen her getting lower and lower in the water, and vaguely wondered what was wrong. But with the adrenalin running high all that I was really concerned about was for her to reach the end of the pool and touch so that Annabel could take over, hand over to me and I could go-go-go! Mr Golding saw though, and realized she was in trouble. He sprinted down the side of the pool, kicked off his flip-flops and went in after her, still wearing his tee shirt and training trousers. He fished her out, coughing and spluttering and struggling to breathe and sat her on the side and looked after her until she was all right again. It was the end of our race, of course, not one of our finest moments, but at least it wasn't the end of Jenny.

No, there was no way the man who had dived in to rescue Jenny was going to kill any of us. I didn't know how I could have thought for a moment that he was capable of such a thing, however distraught he might be.

'It's Becky,' I said.

'Becky Westbrook!' He looked startled. 'I

didn't think you four were that close to Becky.'

'She was at Laura's house on Friday night when they were talking about it. Look, I'm really sorry, but she did say she thought she should tell the police. I'm honestly surprised that she didn't mention it when they interviewed her. But she can't have done, I suppose. If she had they'd have come knocking on your door by now.'

Martin was silent for a moment, twisting his wedding ring again as he seemed to do when he was agitated, to remind him of his happy marriage, perhaps, an anchor in this turbulent sea we'd all found ourselves adrift in.

'It could be she thinks she owes me one,' he said at last. 'Or is afraid that if she starts making allegations against me she just might open a whole can of worms.'

Suddenly I was very alert. 'What can of worms?'

'Well...' He hesitated, obviously reluctant to say aloud what was on his mind. 'I know something about Becky. Something she really wouldn't want me to repeat. Even after all these years. Becky was going through a very difficult and upsetting time. She confided in me, and I decided it was in everybody's best interests to keep her secret.'

I waited. I was curious, of course I was, but I thought that if I pressed him he might retreat back into the shell of silence he'd maintained for twenty years, and in any case I was very aware that it was none of my business. But I once read somewhere that waiting can be an important trigger in getting more information; that the person under fire feels an irrepressible urge to fill the silence. I didn't do it deliberately; I'm not that clever. But I waited, and I got my answer.

'Do you remember Becky lost her mother?' Martin Golding said at last.

'Yes. She was drunk and fell down the stairs. Becky found her when she got home from school.'

'Right on two counts, wrong on one. Yes, she was drunk and fell down the stairs. But Becky didn't find her when she got home from school. She was there when it happened.'

My eyes widened. Still I waited, wondering what was coming next.

'It seems that Becky got home that day to find her mother asleep on the sofa surrounded by empty spirit bottles. She started trying to make herself some tea. Her mother woke up, ranted at her for disturbing her, and a lot more besides. Becky went upstairs to her room to get out of her mother's way, but her mother followed her. The argument continued at the top of the stairs, with her mother hanging on to Becky's clothes, trying to pull her back. Becky lashed out. She pushed her mother. And her mother fell down the stairs and broke her neck. Understandably, Becky was in a terrible state. Her mother was dead, and rightly or wrongly she felt that it was her fault. She couldn't face telling anyone what had really happened, so she said instead that she had found her mother dead when she got home from school.'

'Oh God.' I was shocked. 'Poor Becky! No wonder she's so screwed up. But if she was so intent on keeping it secret, why did she tell you?'

'I suppose she just had to share the truth with someone,' Martin said. 'I called her in to have a chat with her – her behaviour was becoming increasingly destructive and her work was suffering. I thought if she talked about what had happened she might begin to come to terms with it and find some sort of closure. And it all came pouring out. As I say, I thought it was in her best interests to keep quiet about what she told me. Her mother was dead; nothing would bring her back, and I couldn't see that it would be to anyone's advantage, least of all Becky's, to have it all dragged up again. And it did seem that unburdening herself helped. She began to get back on track, thanks in no small measure to you four girls. You took her under your wing for a while if I remember rightly.'

'We felt sorry for her,' I said. 'She isn't the

easiest person in the world to like, but we did our best.'

'I know you did. She still regards you as her best friends, that was clear when I spoke to her at the reunion. And Mark has been kind to her, too, I understand, giving her a job when she was at rock bottom.'

'Something he came to regret, unless I'm much mistaken. Becky has always had rather a bad crush on Mark. In the end he had to let her go. She works for the council re-cycling department now, I understand, and has done for some time.'

Martin glanced at his watch. 'I'm going to have to go, Hannah. My wife has an appoint-ment at the dentist's and I promised I'd be back to relieve her on the childcare front. I'm glad I caught you, though, and got the chance to tell you my side of the story.'

I could see that he was getting uncomfor-table again; whilst we had been talking about Becky he had relaxed into the Martin I remembered.

'Look, don't worry,' I said, feeling sorry for him. 'I certainly won't say anything about what happened between you and Laura and Annabel all those years ago. And if Becky was going to, I should think she would have done it by now. I think you can safely say the past will remain where it belongs – in the past.'

'Thank you, Hannah.' He shook my hand.

'It's been good to see you again, in spite of the circumstances.'

'Yes. Good to see you too.'

But I was thinking that it would have been better if this reunion had never been arranged. Too many secrets had been revealed that would have been better left buried, and two of my best friends were dead. It was one hell of a price to pay for the dubious pleasure of renewing old acquaintances.

And though I did not know it, it was not over yet.

Sixteen

When Martin Golding had gone I went back to my room, loaded my things into the car and tried to phone Jenny to tell her I was coming over to see her. Her phone was dead, though, just the loud drone of an out-of-order signal. I tried her mobile, but that was switched off. Perhaps she was trying for a bit of peace and quiet and didn't want ringing telephones to disturb her or the baby. I left a message to say I was on my way without any great hope of her picking it up. I'd just have to hope she hadn't gone out shopping or something. If so, there was nothing I could do about it. I'd just have to ring her when I got home and apologize for not having said goodbye properly.

I walked out of my room straight into Tristan. With the easy access car park half empty, he'd left his car there, right beside mine.

'Not leaving, are you, Hannah?' he asked, looking at the open boot of my car where my holdall was clearly on display.

'I am, yes. I'm just going over to see Jenny and then I'm heading for home.'

'Oh, I'm sorry to hear that. It looks as if I'll be the only one still here at The Beeches.'

'Oh, well, you'll be leaving soon too.'

'Yes, I suppose I shall.' He looked faintly regretful. Odd, I thought, under the circumstances, and I wished I hadn't mentioned that I was going to Jenny's. The less Tristan knew about my movements, the happier I would be.

Surprisingly, the space at the kerb outside Jenny's house was taken and I wondered if she had another visitor. I hoped not; I really didn't want to have to share this last meeting with her making small talk to a stranger. It could be the health visitor, of course, and if it was, I didn't suppose she would stay for too long. And at least the up-and-over garage door was open and the garage empty, indicating that Ben was out, hopefully having taken the children with him, which would mean that Jenny and I would be relatively undisturbed.

I parked on the drive and walked over to the back door. Two pairs of muddy boots were lined up on the scraper beside it – Ben's Wellingtons and Chloe's riding boots. Perhaps Ben had taken her to the stables last night to make up for having missed her ride on Sunday, I thought. And stopped short, my whole body going very still.

Stables. Horses. The drug that had killed Annabel. The connection shot down my nerves like a bolt of high-voltage electricity. Ben had access to horses. He was often alone at the stables whilst the children were out with their riding instructor. But it made no sense. Ben was Jenny's husband, the father of her children. What possible reason could he have for wanting Laura and Annabel dead? Had he been having an affair with Laura and been afraid it would come out? Had that been what Annabel had thought of, perhaps alerted by something Laura had said after we others had left our get-together the night before she died? And if Annabel had alerted Ben to what she knew, then perhaps she had had to die too.

I could scarcely believe it, but then frankly, everything that had happened was beyond belief. Please God, don't let it be Ben! I prayed. And steeled myself to put the idea out of my head for the moment at least.

The back door was ajar. I pushed it open and called out: 'Jenny? Hello! It's me. Hannah.'

'Hannah.' To my surprise it wasn't Jenny in the kitchen, but Becky. She seemed less than pleased to see me. Certainly I was less than pleased to see her. It must have been her car parked outside, I realized. I just hadn't recognized it. But then, why would I? A perfectly ordinary middle-aged blue Ford that I'd glimpsed only briefly in the hotel car park.

'What a surprise, Becky!' I said. 'What are you doing here?'

'Same as you, I expect,' she said, rather smugly. 'Visiting Jenny.'

'Well, yes.' Obvious, really.

'Well, don't stand there on the doorstep. You'd better come in.' Becky stood aside. I went into the kitchen, which looked far more cluttered than usual, as if Jenny hadn't had time to tidy it to its usual domestic perfection. I dumped my bag on the work counter and went through to the living room, expecting to find Jenny there. She wasn't, though the baby was asleep in her Moses basket on the floor beside the sofa.

'Where's Jenny?' I asked.

Becky had followed me into the living room. 'She's upstairs, asleep. She had a really bad night with the baby and she was exhausted. Really truly knackered. Ben has

312

taken the other children out for the day, so I said I'd mind the baby for an hour so that she could get some rest.'

'Oh, right.' Perhaps that was the reason I hadn't been able to get through on the phone. She'd disconnected it so as not to be disturbed, as I'd thought. And who could blame her? If there was one thing guaranteed to wake a sleeping baby it was the piercing ring of a telephone.

'Maybe I won't stay, then. I really just popped in for a quick chat. But if she's going to be asleep for the next hour ... I'm on my way home,' I explained.

'You're going home?' Becky sounded surprised. 'I thought you were here for the rest of the week.'

'I've changed my mind. To be honest, I've had enough, and I want to be back in my own space. Will you tell Jenny I called? And that I'll ring her this evening? If her phone's back on, that is.' Becky looked at me questioningly, and I went on: 'The land line seems to be out of order. Didn't you know?'

'No.'

'Better get it reported then. It's not a good idea for Jenny to have to be dependent on her mobile if she's here alone with the baby.' Becky said nothing, and I half-smiled, anxious to extricate myself. 'Right. I'll be on my way.'

'Have a coffee first,' Becky suggested.

'Jenny could wake up at any time, and she will be so disappointed to have missed you.'

I hesitated. I had not the slightest desire to sit drinking coffee with Becky, but I did want to see Jenny, and it was true she'd be sorry to have missed me. I guess I could put up with Becky for half an hour or so, and if Jenny was still asleep by then I'd give up and go anyway.

'Just a quick one then,' I said.

'I'll make it.' Becky headed off into the kitchen and I remained in the living room, feeling, for some reason I couldn't identify, vaguely resentful. Becky wasn't a close friend of Jenny's, at least, not that I knew of. Yet she was pottering about her kitchen, making herself at home, as if she was practically family. I couldn't really understand how she came to be here in the first place, though I supposed that if she was out of a job, as Martin Golding had seemed to think, she was probably kicking her heels at a loose end, and only too glad to have something to fill her days and make her feel useful. Typical of her, insinuating herself into what was left of our tight-knit little group, I thought, and immediately felt guilty, chiding myself for not being more charitable towards a girl who had always seemed to have a tough time.

I crossed to the sofa, looking down at the baby fast asleep in her Moses basket, cheeks rosy with sleep, perfect little fingers curled into dimpled fists resting on the fluffy pink blanket and felt my stomach lurch with longing. Of all of us, just as long as Ben wasn't a killer, Jenny was the one who was truly blessed! For a moment I imagined how it would feel to have a baby as beautiful and vulnerable as little Laura nestled against me. The oneness and the fiercely protective love. The sweet warm baby scent in my nostrils, the sharp tug of a determined rosebud mouth finding my nipple and fastening on. The soft covering of silky hair against my cheek. The very heart of me was yearning for a child of my own, part ache, part sweet anticipation, and I wondered if it was the terrible events of the past days that had heightened my need. I'd lost two of my oldest friends in their prime; the close contact with death had made new life all the more vitally desirable. Essential, really. And the realization of mortality had drawn out a sense of the importance of continuity.

'Here we are. White, no sugar, right?' Becky had come back in with two mugs of coffee, which she arranged fussily on coasters on the low pine glass-topped table.

'Yes. Right. How did you know?'

'I remembered,' Becky said smugly.

She went back to the kitchen and returned with a plate of biscuits, all neatly arranged, bourbon and custard creams carefully alternated and interlaced on a white paper doily.

Bizarre! I thought. Jenny always plonked the tin down with the biscuits still inside, leaving you to forage for yourself, and I was surprised that she had ever bought such a thing as a doily. Now here was Becky, playing the perfect hostess, for all the world as if it were her house, not Jenny's at all.

'Help yourself.' She smiled, still smug. It grated on my nerves.

'So, have you heard if the police are any closer to finding out who killed Laura and Annabel?' she asked, quite conversationally, pushing one of the coffees in my direction. 'Annabel was drugged and then gassed, wasn't she?'

I frowned. How did Becky know about Annabel? There seemed to have been little mention of it on the local news, as far as I was aware. It seemed the police were playing their cards close to their chests. 'A woman's body was discovered in a car at a remote spot' was about the extent of it and there had been no mention that the circumstances were in any way suspicious. Jenny must have told Becky, I presumed, but I didn't think I'd gone into the details of what Aaron had told me. I'd tried to keep it low key so as not to upset her.

'I've not heard that there have been any developments,' I said non-committally.

'It's terrible,' Becky sighed, but I had the uncomfortable feeling she was not sympathizing but gloating. 'Annabel was so successful. Too successful for her own good, really.'

I bridled. 'What on earth do you mean?'

Becky sipped her coffee reflectively. 'She'd got above herself really, hadn't she? She thought she was so clever, the big city solicitor, with her dyed hair and her flashy car and expensive clothes. Well, she wasn't as clever as she thought she was.'

'That is an awful thing to say!' I was outraged.

'And we shouldn't speak ill of the dead,' Becky said, rather sarcastically.

'No, we shouldn't.'

'It was the same with my mother,' Becky went on as if I had not spoken. 'She was a terrible woman, you know. I had one hell of a life with her. Most of the time she was drunk, and when she wasn't she was foul tempered and evil. Except when she got fits of remorse, and then she'd smother me with love and kisses, hug me so tight I couldn't breathe. Until the next time. And there always was a next time. She used to beat me, you know, when I was little, with an old cricket bat. And she would lock me in my room while she went off to the pub or made noisy love with one of the boyfriends daft enough, or desperate enough, to come home with her. I'd wake up frightened, and scream and cry, but she never came, unless it was to threaten me with another beating.

'When I was older, she'd throw things at me. She came at me once with the carving knife. Yet when she was dead, I was supposed to mourn her. "She was your mother and she loved you," the social worker used to say to me. "She was a very unhappy woman who couldn't help what she did. It was an illness, just like chicken pox, and you couldn't help getting chicken pox, could you? If you learn to forgive her, forget the bad times and just remember the good, you will feel much better." As if! I don't remember any good times. And I was glad she was dead. Glad!'

I was speechless, unable to think of a single word to say in reply to her tirade of hate about her terrible childhood. But I was thinking, all the same, of what Martin Golding had told me about how Becky's mother had died. He had said she was full of remorse, torn apart by guilt at having been responsible for her mother's fatal fall. It didn't sound to me as if she'd suffered a second's regret over what had happened. But who could tell? Perhaps she had hit out that day because her mother had been attacking her yet again, and then she had been afraid someone would learn the truth of what had happened. She had prepared a defence for herself by confessing to Martin so that one person, at least, would speak up for her. Or perhaps she had felt remorse at the time, only that had faded with the years to be replaced by all-consuming hatred and resentment. Perhaps that was her way of living with what she had done. I didn't know and I wasn't sure I wanted to. I'd been subjected to enough angst and anguish over the past days. I didn't want to be burdened with Becky's as well.

I took a good gulp of my coffee, wishing heartily I'd left the minute Becky had told me Jenny was asleep. It tasted horrible, bitter and powdery, and I wondered if Becky had let the kettle boil properly before making it.

'Laura and Annabel were great girls,' I said, steering the subject away from Becky's mother. 'Neither of them deserved to die. Especially the awful way they did.'

Becky snorted. 'You would say that. You were as thick as thieves with them. But Annabel was a stuck-up dyke and Laura was a whore.'

I was totally shocked. 'Becky, for goodness sake!' Her ugly, hate-filled words hung heavy in the room, echoing and re-echoing in my ears. 'What on earth has got into you?'

'I'm only telling the truth! Laura was a whore, well, no better than one, anyway. Any man she came across she had to have. She was always the same; you'd have thought, wouldn't you, that being lucky enough to have a husband like Mark she'd count her blessings and be satisfied? But, no, she was still always sniffing around the next conquest like a bitch on heat. And he still adored her. Made excuses for her. She had such a hold over him he just wouldn't admit she was a disaster and he should move on. Why couldn't he see it? I told him to leave her. I told him that I would never treat him like that, never! I told him he'd be better off with me and he would have been, but as long as she was there, mesmerizing him, he just couldn't see it.'

I stared at Becky, horrified by the stream of venom that was bursting from her mouth, too stunned almost to pay attention to the worm of unease that was crawling in my stomach, and somehow feeling distinctly odd.

'Well, she's dead now. Perhaps he'll see sense now that she's out of the way.' Becky glanced at the Moses basket, where baby Laura was stirring slightly, thrusting one small thumb hungrily into her puckered little mouth. 'Do you know Laura couldn't even give him a child? Or wouldn't. Afraid of spoiling her figure, I wouldn't be surprised. Well, I will! We'll have three or four. A proper family. And we shall be so happy. So very happy!'

She leaned forward over the Moses basket, the hatred on her podgy face replaced by a sort of faux tenderness which might have been touching was I not rapidly realizing that

Becky was utterly, terrifyingly crazy. As she did so the neckline of her top gaped open – and I saw it.

My swimming medal. It swung forward on its red ribbon, gleaming dully.

Horror washed over me in a flood tide, first scaldingly hot, then icy cold. Becky was the one who had been in my room. She was the one who had taken the medal, and, very likely, Mark's key too. She had been there, I remembered, when I'd told him that I had it and where it was. And she'd wanted it, an entrée to his house and his life. But stealing my medal was somehow even more sick. The worm of unease inside me was a great slithering snake now, a jellyfish sending flickering tendrils into my veins and tightening around my lungs and my heart.

'That's my medal!' I said before I could stop myself. 'How did you get my medal?' There was a little slur in my voice, and the thought that it wasn't really a very wise thing to say followed a heartbeat later, like a video film that is not running quite up to speed.

Becky jerked upright, her hand flying to it, a momentary look of dismay etched on her piggy face. Then she smiled smugly.

'It was easy. I just walked straight up to Reception and asked for your room key. I had a story ready, that you were feeling unwell and couldn't find yours, and you needed to lie down. But I didn't need it. The prat of a girl didn't raise a single objection. She just handed me a spare. Just like that! Really they should sack her. I wouldn't want to stay there again with security so lax. But I wasn't going to complain. It was the key to Mark's house I wanted really, of course. But when I saw the medal ... I always wished I had one. And I could have had one, too, if only Mr Golding had given me a chance. But it was you four, always you four. Smug and self-satisfied and always showing off. Nobody else got a look in.'

The creeping unease had escalated now into full blown alarm, and I knew. Incredible though it seemed, I knew.

It was Becky who had phoned Laura and asked to come over and see her on the night of the reunion, then removed Laura's mobile from her bag and disposed of it so as to conceal the evidence. It was Becky who had taken the photograph from Laura's drawing room as some kind of bizarre trophy. It was Becky who had somehow managed to dope Annabel with a veterinary drug and then left her to die in her fume-filled car.

It was Becky, who was obsessed with Laura's husband. Becky, who had apparently been jealous to the point of madness of all of us. Becky, who had killed her own mother, either accidentally or on purpose.

Becky, who was here with me now whilst Jenny slept upstairs...

The cold shot of fear was like a knife thrust to my heart.

'Becky,' I said, and was shocked again by the way my words were slurring. 'What have you done to Jenny?'

Her eyes opened wide, surprised innocence. 'She's having a little rest. I told you.'

'I'm going to see.' *And get my mobile out of my bag which was in the kitchen and dial 999 – why the hell had I left it in the kitchen? Or run out into the street and yell that there was a double murderer in Jenny's house...*

I tried to get to my feet; my legs felt heavy and useless. And my thoughts were becoming thick, too, as if my brain was nothing but soggy cotton wool. And my eyelids dropped...

Becky leaned forward and prodded me in the chest. My heavy wobbly legs gave way and I pitched back into the chair. Becky laughed unpleasantly.

'Oh, no, Hannah, I don't think you are going anywhere.'

'Becky, don't be silly...' Still slurred, it was an effort to form the words.

Becky's lip curled. 'That's what you think of me, isn't it – silly? Well, I'm not as silly as you think. I am really very clever. I killed my mother – the bitch – and got away with it. I've killed Laura and Annabel and no one suspects a thing. And it was so easy! Laura never guessed for a moment I meant her any

323

harm when I rang and asked if I could come over. She wasn't very nice to me, mind you. She was pretty snotty actually. It was sort of: "What do you want *now*, Becky?" Cow. Snotty, conceited cow, who treated Mark like he was something nasty she'd picked up on her shoe. I enjoyed hitting her over the head with my torch and pushing her into the pool. Enjoyed it! Poetic justice really. Laura, the star of the swimming team, drowning! And Annabel, well, she started asking awkward questions. Are you still awake? Can you hear me?'

Oh, I could hear her all right, though I was struggling to remain conscious. She had put something in my coffee, I realized. Thank God I hadn't drunk all of it. But what I'd had was enough. I was virtually helpless.

'The trouble was, she and Laura were in a taxi together when I phoned Laura,' Becky went on. 'I wasn't to know that, of course. The last I saw of Laura, she was driving off in her own car, and pretty drunk at that. She could very well have killed herself and saved me the trouble. But she'd come back and got a lift in Annabel's taxi. And it seems she made some comment that put it in Annabel's head that I was the one who phoned her. At the time Annabel didn't realize the significance of it. She thought Laura was just talking about me, slagging me off as usual, I expect. But when she got to thinking about it she put two and two together. The stupid girl thought she could pump me without me realizing what she was getting at, but I could see right through her. I knew she knew. Well, I couldn't have that, could I? Annabel going round raising suspicions about me. So I'm afraid I had to think quickly. I had a shot of horse dope that I'd saved from when I was working with the recycling department. I thought it might come in useful one day – and it did! Annabel was right out of it once I got that into her. She'd probably be dead even if I hadn't rigged up the exhaust to gas her. But I thought it was a nice touch, making it look like suicide. And driving her car out to Hurleigh Pond bought me some time.' She sniggered. 'She didn't look so bloody immaculate by the time I'd manhandled her from the driving seat to the passenger seat and back again. Her precious hair was all messed up and her skirt got yanked up nearly to her ass. She'd have had a fit if she'd thought anyone would see her looking like that. Oh, yes, I'm glad I killed her too. She asked for it.'

'But why Jenny?' I managed. 'Why me?'

'Jenny was worming her way in with Mark too. She had him here for dinner last night, did you know that? And you have been doing a pretty good job of hanging around him too. I suppose you both thought you could get in there, take Laura's place. Well, you were wrong. Mark is mine. Mine, do you hear?'

'We don't want Mark.' I struggled to make my thick tongue work, keep my eyes open. 'Jenny is happily married and I ... well I have no interest in him at all. He's yours if you want him so much. Just stop this now and leave us alone.'

For a long moment Becky seemed to be considering, then she shook her head.

'I can't trust you, either of you. You're Martin's Mermaids. The Inseparables.' She sniggered. 'Inseparable in life – and in death. Sorry, Hannah, I just don't trust you. You know far too much. Well, you do now, anyway. I really don't have any choice.'

'Becky, please, stop this now!' Again I struggled to get to my feet, again she pushed me, clearly enjoying her dominance, so that I fell back into the chair.

'Make this easy on yourself, Hannah. There's nothing you can do.' She smiled at me, almost beatifically, and, to my amazement disappeared into the kitchen. The moment she was out of sight I made another desperate attempt to get up. This time I managed it, supporting myself on the arms of the chair. I was halfway across the living room when she came back carrying something that I recognized with a wash of horror as a red plastic petrol can.

'Lucky I had this in my car, isn't it?' Becky said, almost conversationally. 'I fetched it when Jenny felt poorly and went upstairs.' She swivelled off the cap and began sloshing petrol on to the sofa.

'For God's sake, Becky! What do you think you're doing?' Momentarily fear made my stomach clench and my already unsteady legs go weak. Then a rush of adrenalin sang in my veins, and miraculously cleared my fuzzy brain. 'This is crazy! You can't...'

'I can do anything I like,' she crowed. She poured more petrol on to the hearthrug and began backing towards the door, sprinkling a trail of petrol as she went.

The baby, disturbed by our raised voices, stirred, whimpering.

'What about the baby?' I grated out. 'She hasn't done anything! You can't mean to harm the baby!'

Becky's mouth twisted, turning her face into an ugly mask of hatred.

'She's *Laura*. Jenny has called her *Laura*.' Furiously, she sloshed a pool of petrol dangerously close to the Moses basket.

The baby was crying in earnest now, a thin piercing wail. My every instinct was to pick her up, hold her tight to me and try to protect her from this madness. But I knew that with a baby in my arms I would have no hope whatever of preventing Becky from doing what she was clearly intent on doing – setting fire to the house. My mind was racing now, oddly clear. I glanced around at the windows, wondering if we could escape that way. I couldn't see any window locks, but it was always possible Jenny had them secured in some way that was not immediately obvious for the safety of the children. And in any case, Jenny was still upstairs and probably unconscious from the same drug Becky had administered to me. The best option was to try and stop Becky from doing this terrible thing. But I was very afraid she was beyond reasoning, and she was in the doorway now, blocking my way of escape.

And she had pulled a box of matches out of her pocket.

'You'll never get away with this.' Her sense of self-preservation was the only weapon I had left. 'They'll know it was you, Becky.'

She extracted a match from the box. 'I don't think so.'

'Your car's outside. Someone will have noticed it. This house isn't isolated like Laura's. Or Hurleigh Pond. There are plenty of neighbours who look out for each other. And nosy ones, who just like to know who's come calling.'

Becky hesitated, the match poised over the striking pad. Then she shook her head. 'They don't even know me. And nobody knows that car is mine.'

'It shouldn't be too difficult to find out who it belongs to, though. A blue Ford, owned by someone connected to all of us. The

328

police aren't stupid. Think about it, Becky.'

She seemed to be. I held my breath and wondered if I dared risk rushing her and trying to grab the matches. Under normal circumstances I would have stood a good chance; I was fitter and faster than she was, and, although she was bigger built that I was, I thought I was probably stronger too. But these weren't normal circumstances. I was slow and heavy from the effect of the drugs; she'd pushed me back into the chair twice with no effort at all. And the room was soaked with petrol. All it would take was for her to strike that match and drop it and the whole place would go up in a fireball.

'I'll have to take that chance, I'm afraid. You know too much, Hannah.' She went to strike the match.

'No!' I screamed. And saw the match break in two as it rasped on the striking pad.

'Damn!' Becky dropped the splintered ends of wood, went to open the box again.

In that moment I knew there was nothing I could do to stop her. With my remaining strength I somehow managed to snatch up the screaming baby from the Moses basket and dived towards the window. *Please, God, don't let it have safety locks! Please, God!*

The window opened. Behind me, the room erupted with a blinding flash, catapulting me forward. I dropped the baby into the soft flowerbed beneath, rolled out myself. I hit the ground with my shoulder and my chin simultaneously and the shock waves reverberated through me, jarring every bone and muscle. My face was pressed into soft earth, I spat it out, twisting to reach the baby and trying to scramble to my feet. Through the open window I heard the roar of flames. Half-crawling, half-stumbling, I staggered across the lawn.

Someone was running into the drive. From behind the red mist that was blurring my vision I saw who it was with a sense of disbelief.

'Tristan!' I sobbed. 'Tristan – Jenny's in there! She's upstairs! Help her – please!'

And then there was a kind of blackness closing in from the edges of my consciousness, encroaching on the red mist, and everything was fading like a photograph left out in the sun. I felt my legs begin to buckle, and cushioning the baby in my arms I folded up and in on myself, sinking gently until I felt the grass against the back of my legs and against my neck, without any real idea how I came to be there. The world was spinning, and with the stress and the enormous physical effort I'd put into escaping taking its toll, the drug that Becky had administered to me crept through me like an insidious cancer and I lapsed into unconsciousness.

Seventeen

I opened my eyes to find myself in a soft green forest. My head was throbbing dully and the light stung my eyes. I closed them again, screwing up my face against the sharp pain. For a while I drifted some more, aware only of a dull ache in my shoulder and the throb of my head, which invaded my rambling dreams. Then a sense of urgency crept in, prickling in my veins. I couldn't identify it, but it scared me fully conscious once more and I opened my eyes again.

I was still surrounded by the forest, but now I could see that the thick mass of leaves was not real and living but the pattern printed on floor length curtain that hung from a tubular rail which surrounded me on three sides. From beyond them came the clanking of a trolley and a woman's voice, with a thick foreign accent, asking: 'Tea, dearie? Two sugars? I'll put it here for you now.'

Hospital. I was in hospital. I had no recollection of how I came to be here but what had happened earlier was there all right, crystal clear – too clear for comfort. Becky drugging me. Threatening to set fire to the house. Dowsing it with petrol. Striking a match. My desperate dive through the window which I had been so afraid might be locked. The wall of flame behind me, roaring in my ears. Tristan. Tristan? What had Tristan been doing at Jenny's house? Screaming at him with the remains of my breath tearing at my lungs and the blackness closing in. 'Jenny's upstairs!' Jenny! Oh my God, Jenny. Was she all right? Had she even still been alive when Becky started the fire? Had she survived it?

'Nurse!' I called weakly. No one heard me. Or at least, no one came. I heaved myself into a sitting position, and realized there was a bell within easy reach. I rang it.

The curtains around my bed parted and a cheerful black face appeared, followed by a comfortably plump body over which a brown checked uniform overall strained at the buttons and seams.

'You're awake then! How you feeling?'

'I don't know.' I couldn't even begin to think about how I felt. All I could think about was Jenny.

'My friend,' I said. I was almost afraid to ask. I didn't suppose this cheery, friendly nurse would tell me if Jenny was dead. For starters, she probably wouldn't even know who it was I was talking about, and if she did know, it wouldn't be her place. But a blank look or an evasive one would give me my answer. That Becky had succeeded in killing yet another of Martin's Mermaids. That five children, including a tiny baby, were motherless.

'My friend Jenny Hansford,' I said. 'Is she...?'

It can only have been seconds before the nurse answered me, but those seconds stretched into eternity. An eternity when I seemed to be suspended in a vacuum, steeling myself for the worst.

'Ah, Jenny!' The plump black cheeks bunched up into a broad smile, the dark eyes danced. 'She's asleep too. I don't know what you two was up to, but whatever it was, it surely took some sleeping off!'

The relief was like a hammer blow in my stomach, making me weak, bringing tears to my eyes.

'Oh, thank God! Where is she? Do you know?'

'Why, she's right here.'

'Where?' I was afraid to believe it suddenly, afraid this kindly nurse was simply saying what I wanted to hear so as not to upset me. 'Where is she? Are you sure she's all right?'

'See for you'self.' She pulled one of the curtains aside so that the leafy womb opened out to double its size and within yet another drape of green fabric I could see the bed next door to mine. And in it, Jenny. She lay unmoving, eyes closed, and her cheeks lacked their usual rosy colour. But she was alive.

'She'll wake up soon now, I expect.' The nurse jerked the curtain back into place, restoring Jenny's privacy. 'And 'bout time too! Now, you stay right where you are. I'm gonna go get Staff to come and see you. And there's somebody waitin' too. He been here most ever since you was brought in, drinking that coffee machine out in the relative's room dry. I'll tell him he can come in now you're awake. If you feel up to seeing him, that is.'

My heart skipped a beat. 'Who is it?'

'He's called Aaron. You wanna see him?'

I nodded. My eyes were heavy; I was a little drowsy again. But there was no doubt in my mind. I'd stay awake somehow. With every fibre of my body I wanted to see Aaron.

'It was just terrible,' I said.

Aaron was sitting on the edge of my bed, holding my hand. I thought he would probably be told to move when the staff nurse or sister found him there, informed that sitting on a patient's bed was strictly forbidden in the interests of hygiene, and scolded like a schoolboy. But that wouldn't bother him. Aaron had never been one to abide by the rules.

He raised an eyebrow at me now. 'I did

334

warn you to be careful. Told you not to trust anybody.'

'I know. And I'd got to the point where I was suspicious of everybody. Peter for starters. Do you remember I thought I saw him in town? No, you probably don't. But next day I suddenly remembered that he's a vet, and would have the easiest access of anyone to animal drugs. And Ben. Dear God, when it clicked that Ben had access to a riding stable, I even thought that *Ben* might have been the one. But *Becky*...! I just can't believe it. How could she do it? How could she have so much hatred stored up inside her that she could try to kill all four of us?'

Aaron shook his head. 'Who knows what goes on in a sick mind?'

'She was obsessed with Mark, of course,' I said. 'She seemed to think that if Laura was out of the way the coast would be clear for her to get together with him. It would never have happened in a million years, of course, but she couldn't see that. All she could see was Laura, standing between her and the man she worshipped. And Annabel ... well, it seems Annabel had got too close to the truth. Laura had made some derogatory comment about Becky that night in the taxi that at the time Annabel just thought referred to the way Becky always seemed to be worming her way in and making a nuisance of herself, but later she realized it had come

335

immediately after that telephone call to Laura's mobile, and wondered if that might be what had triggered Laura's outburst. I don't think she really believed it, though. If she had she would never have been so rash as to put herself in a position where Becky could do what she did. But then, I wouldn't have believed it either. I'd never have gone out of my way to avoid Becky because I thought she might be a danger to me.'

'And look where it got you.'

'I know. But if I hadn't gone to Jenny's, then Jenny would almost certainly be dead, and perhaps the baby too. I suppose alarm bells should have rung as soon as I found her there, making herself at home, and Jenny nowhere in evidence, but I still didn't think … I mean, I knew I didn't like her, but to think she could try to kill me and that innocent little baby. Really it never entered my head.'

'Exactly. That's why I warned you about trusting anyone. Someone like that can be so dangerous and hide it so well.'

'But why? Why did she want Jenny and me dead too?'

'I guess she resented you both,' Aaron said. 'You were a threat to her on some level, and that was enough. I'm afraid her logic wouldn't be yours or mine.'

'She killed her mother for much the same reason,' I said. Aaron looked at me sharply, and I explained, giving both Martin Golding's take on it and what Becky herself had admitted to me – no, not admitted – boasted about.

Aaron listened in silence, then nodded. 'So even back then she saw killing as a way of getting rid of someone she didn't want around any more. Though I suppose it could be a chicken and egg situation.'

'What do you mean?'

'It's possible her mother's fall *was* an accident. Then afterwards it suited her ego to put a different slant on it. She convinced herself that she had found a very clever way of dealing with the problem of a drunken, abusive mother. Congratulated herself on having got away with it. And next time someone stood in the way of what she wanted, she thought all she had to do was repeat the exercise. Wave her magic wand and everything would turn out the way she wanted it to. And then she got carried away. She was high, I expect on the absolute power of being able to take the life of another human being so easily. So although there was no need for her to get rid of you and Jenny, she actually wanted to. Even if it meant killing the baby too. That would scarcely matter to her.'

'She hated the baby because Jenny was calling her Laura,' I said.

'So how's that for twisted logic?' Aaron grimaced. 'Oh, the psychologists would have had a field day with Becky.'

My eyes narrowed. I shivered involuntarily. *'Would have?'*

His fingers tightened around mine, his eyes were steady on my face.

'She didn't survive the fire, Hannah. I'm not sure whether she even tried to escape. She was found in the living room.'

My breath came out on a soft sob. Wicked as Becky had been, I still couldn't bear to think of her dying such a terrible death.

'She was sloshing petrol everywhere,' I said. 'Maybe she spilled some on herself.' I shuddered, not wanting to think that particular thought through any further.

'The place was an inferno in seconds,' Aaron said. 'If it hadn't been for Tristan, there's no doubt Jenny would have died too. Fortunately the door to the hall and stairs was closed. The fire spread to the kitchen almost immediately, but Tristan was able to get in the front door, up the stairs, and carry Jenny to safety. He's a hero, Hannah.'

'Yes, he is. To go into a blazing house like that with no thought for your own safety takes a very special person.' I was silent for a moment, regretting all the uncharitable thoughts I'd harboured for Tristan. He must have gone rushing straight into the house when I'd screamed that Jenny was in there, and found her unconscious. 'Becky must have drugged Jenny with the same stuff she gave to me, I suppose,' I went on after a moment. 'She's in the next cubicle, you know, still sleeping it off. Luckily for me, I only drank a few mouthfuls of the coffee she made me, and it made me pretty woozy. No wonder Jenny was right out of it if she drank a whole cup. But how on earth did Becky get hold of drugs used for horses?'

But even as I said it, I answered my own question. 'Of course! When she first went to work for the recycling department they were using horses. She told me so herself.'

Aaron raised an eyebrow. 'Maybe Becky pinched some of the stuff then. She fancied having it by her in case she ever had need of it. Or perhaps the staff still visit the horses in their retirement home. Whichever, it will be up to the investigating officers to find out.'

My head was spinning, but I made a huge effort to get my thoughts together.

'Going back to Tristan, hero though he is, I don't understand what he was doing at Jenny's house in the middle of the morning. Or any time at all, come to that.'

Aaron's fingers relaxed on mine, but I could still feel the warmth of them, spreading comfort through my veins.

'Apparently Tristan saw Becky go into your room the other day, using a hotel key. He knew she had no business being there and wondered what was going on. She was in your room for about twenty minutes, he said;

he sat in his car and watched. What he should have done, of course, is reported it straight away, but for some reason he didn't. He didn't want to get involved, I suppose, and at that stage it never occurred to him that Becky might be the killer. He just thought she was being nosy.'

As he is … I was instantly ashamed of the thought that flew into my mind unprompted.

'It was on his mind, though,' Aaron went on, stroking my fingers with his. 'After you left this morning he thought about it and decided you should know. You had told him you were going to Jenny's, so he tried to telephone her and, like you, found the number out of order. We suspect Becky had cut the telephone line, but until the Scenes of Crime Officers can do a thorough investigation it can only be supposition, and it's possible the fire will have destroyed the evidence in any case. If she cut it on the outside of the house, then we'll find it, but if it was in the living room, then we may never know for sure. Anyway, Tristan didn't have Jenny's mobile number and even if he had, as we know, it was switched off. So he decided to drive over to Jenny's house and try to catch you there. The rest you know.'

'Thank goodness he did. Another few minutes and there would have been no way anyone could reach Jenny in time,' I whispered. 'It's funny, isn't it? I was so resentful of the way Tristan was always creeping about and popping up unexpectedly. But in the end, it saved Jenny's life.'

'Yep. And you saved the baby.'

'Well, I wasn't going to leave her there, was I?'

'No, not you, Hannah. Some people would have thought only of saving their own skin, but not you. You're a heroine too.'

'Rubbish! No one would leave a baby to die like that,' I said. 'I certainly didn't do anything special. I'm just angry with myself for being stupid enough to let Becky drug me. Forget the heroine stuff, I was just a naive fool.'

Aaron smiled. 'Let's not argue about it, Hannah. Let's just say I like you just the way you are and leave it at that.'

I was beginning to feel sleepy again. 'I'll settle for that,' I said. And closed my eyes. I could feel Aaron's fingers still caressing mine. It was a good feeling. Content in his presence, I drifted off once more.

We were at Hurleigh Pond. We four girls, Martin's Mermaids, and the boys. Aaron was there too. I don't think he ever came to Hurleigh Pond with us in real life, but in my dream he was there. We were lying on our backs, looking up at the twilight sky through the tracery of green, and the last pinkish rays

341

of the setting sun were splintering through the branches. Aaron was holding my hand, his fingers light but firm on mine. I could hear Annabel and Laura laughing and I squinted up to see what was going on. Annabel was taking off her tee-shirt, she was wearing that lacy yellow bra and I knew that at any moment she was going to take off her shorts too.

I rolled over, pressing my face into Aaron's neck and he kissed me, a warm, sweet, chaste kiss that set my skin prickling with awareness and started a well of joy in my heart.

'Come on in!' Annabel shouted. 'The water's lovely!'

'No way,' I murmured. And snuggled up to Aaron some more.

And then I realized Annabel and Laura were no longer there. They'd gone, and I didn't know where they were. My happiness started to splinter. Tears were running down my cheeks.

'Annabel, Laura, come back!' I sobbed. And a voice in my head that might have been Aaron's and then again might not have been said: 'They're only just around the corner. Just out of sight. They can see you even if you can't see them. And they are having a ball! Just like they always did.'

The dream faded, I woke to find my cheeks wet with tears. Aaron was no longer there, and I guessed he must have crept away to let

342

me sleep in peace. Perhaps he had gone back to work, after all, he had a job to do. He couldn't sit here beside my bed for ever. Though I wished he had stayed I didn't feel bereft as I might have done. I knew without even thinking about it that he would be back.

I closed my eyes again for a moment and replayed the dream. It felt very real, as if I had somehow recaptured the careless joy of our youth. Friendship and hopes and dreams in a world where we were all immortal and the future stretched to the distant horizons of forever, rosy as that late sun that infused the soft light with a pinkish hue. I could still see Annabel in her yellow underwear looking like a Baywatch beach babe and Laura cavorting and tantalizing and laughing, lovely, funny, great-fun Laura who would never now grow old. It was, I knew, an image that would always remain with me.

I thought of it again at Laura's funeral. I stood at her graveside holding on to Aaron's arm and saw sunlight splinter through the branches of a magnolia on to the light oak of her coffin just as it had splintered through the tracery of branches at Hurleigh Pond. It looked impossibly tiny, that coffin, now that the spray of red roses had been removed and lay at the graveside, and I told myself that Laura was not there at all, but hiding somewhere, just around the corner as the voice in my dream had said. She'd be smiling, amused by the tears of the mourners, gratified at the number of people who had turned up to say their last goodbyes, revelling in being the centre of attention.

Mark looked utterly bereft. He took a single red rose from the memorial spray and tossed it down on the coffin when it had come to rest in the grave beneath the magnolia tree. But Lucy was beside him, so very like Laura, her hand comfortingly on his arm though the tears were streaming down her own cheeks. Perhaps, I thought, they would continue to console one another in the days ahead. It was too soon of course to be thinking that there might be something between them, but Mark was one of those people who seemed to need a relationship. In our youth he'd moved seamlessly from one girlfriend to the next, and I thought it was possible that nothing had changed.

The rest of us stood in a tight knot, our little citadel. Stan, Peter, Ian and his wife, Aaron and myself, Jenny and Tristan, who had stayed on especially for the funeral. This time he was not excluded; we owed him too much. Ben had stayed at home to look after the children and Jenny, still looking rather frail, was holding on to Tristan's arm. He had saved her life; now he was supporting her as she wept quietly and swayed a little on legs still unsteady from her recent ordeal. I wasn't sure she should even be here, but it would have taken wild horses to keep her away.

Also there, but standing a little apart, since she had not been an intimate member of our group, was a girl from our year named Lisa Penney who had, to my surprise, arrived with Peter. As a result of the reunion, it seemed, they had begun a relationship which Peter had kept quiet about until he saw where it was going. It had been him we'd seen in Mowbury; he'd been here meeting Lisa. I felt dreadfully guilty that I'd suspected him even for a moment, just as I felt guilty about my suspicion of Ben. But at least they didn't know what had gone through my mind, thank goodness, and I hoped they never would. When Laura's parents and Lucy had also tossed roses down on to the coffin, Jenny and I stepped forward. Jenny's children had been cultivating sunflowers in their garden, each competing for the best display, and Jenny had begged their permission to cut two perfect blooms, one for each of us. Sunflowers somehow seemed right for Laura, epitomized her, she had said, and I agreed. They were bold and bright, just like Laura; they represented her exuberance and optimism and flamboyance perfectly. They were happy flowers, too, not funereal in any way.

'God bless, Laura,' I whispered, and as the

sunflower came to rest on the brass plate bearing her name it seemed to me that Laura was smiling.

We would have to go through all this again next week, of course, for Annabel, though I knew her funeral would be very different. Annabel wouldn't have a church service and a grave beneath a magnolia tree. She was to be cremated, but there would be no less love and respect and raw grief in the crematorium chapel than there was here. Annabel, too, had been a very special person.

As we turned to make our way back to the path that wound between expanses of newly mown grass and centuries old lichened gravestones, I noticed a figure standing alone, a little removed, as if he felt he had no business being here but had wanted to come and pay his respects anyway.

Martin Golding.

'I must go and speak to him,' I said to Aaron.

Jenny heard me. 'Me too.'

We trekked across the grass towards him. None of us, I think, really knew what to say, me especially, since I still felt a little awkward that I had practically accused him of murdering Laura and Annabel. Under the circumstances though, I didn't feel guilty.

'Mark will be really glad that you came,' I said. 'You were such an important part of our lives when we were at school.'

And in that moment I realized it was no more than the truth. Perhaps things had got complicated later between him and Annabel and Laura. Perhaps lines had been crossed. But it was as our dedicated swimming coach that I would remember him. On poolside in jogging bottoms and Speedo flip flops, stopwatch in hand, encouraging us to strive for more, always more. Buying us bacon butties at the Greasy Spoon trailer in the lay-by. Beaming with pride when we stood on the rostrum, arms round each other, medals round our necks, challenge cup held aloft.

'We all have so much to thank you for,' I said; tears were thick in my throat again and the ache bittersweet in my heart.

The end of an era. Two lives cut short.

But nothing could ever take away my precious memories.

We were all together again six months later – this time for a happy occasion, the christening of baby Laura. She was now officially Annabel Laura Jane, because according to Jenny that was the order of names that sounded best, but she was still to be known as Laura.

It had been an eventful six months as far as I was concerned. As the emerald green and sapphire blue of summer had ripened to the russet hues of autumn, the relationship between me and Aaron had grown and deepened. By the time November came in, misty, murky, smelling of bonfire smoke and riven with the bangs and crashes of exploding fireworks, Aaron had given up his flat in a big old house in St Andrews, Bristol, and moved in with me. With his roving brief, he had said, it didn't really matter that he was fifteen miles from his Bristol base, and the arrangement was fine with me. I didn't have to think about finding a new job or selling my cottage again, and I was with Aaron. The best of all possible worlds. We were incredibly, foolishly happy together, making up for all the lost years, and I didn't even mind the irregular hours his job called for. It gave me the space and independence I had become used to and still desperately needed.

Aaron had at last wrapped up the Mowbury drugs investigation. The dealer had been traced – a slick ne'er-do-well lad who had been in and out of trouble with the police for one thing and another for years, and had even done time for a spate of local burglaries. Much to Mark's relief, Darren had not been implicated in the wider picture, though I believe that Aaron had a few choice words to say to him about what would happen if he came under suspicion again and we all sincerely hoped that would not happen. Certainly I thought he might well have been put off involving himself in dealing, though his own habit would be harder to kick. But Mark was doing his level best for him, and had managed to get him on to a rehabilitation programme.

As we all gathered for baby Laura's christening, it was hard to believe that the awful events of six months ago had ever happened. Hard to believe that a girl we had known from childhood days could have been capable of the things Becky had done, harder still to accept that we would never see Laura or Annabel again. And yet, if it had not been for the reunion, maybe none of us would have regenerated the closeness we had once taken for granted. Certainly the bonds between those of us that were left were now stronger than ever. And I would never have found Aaron. Perhaps it was the way things were meant to be

Laura and Annabel, forever golden girls, dancing with the dust motes in the pale winter sunshine that streamed in through the stained glass windows of the old church. The rest of us, united by the experiences we had lived through.

Jenny had asked Tristan and me to be baby Laura's godparents, along with Laura's sister Lucy. We clustered around the font. I was holding little Laura, and I gazed down at her serene, rosy face and wondered if she would cry with indignation when the vicar gushed cold water on her dear, unprotected head. But someone had emptied a kettle of boiling water into the font; a slight haze of steam rose from it and I realized that at least she would be protected from the worst of the shock. The vicar took her from me, holding her securely, and her wide eyes gazed up at him trustingly.

'I name this child Annabel Laura Jane...'

It was a tribute to the past. And a promise for the future.